THE GOLDEN PRISON

THE GOLDEN PRISON

by Paul Alexander Sangillo

RED SKY PRESENTS • NEW YORK

CONTENTS

PROLOGUE

New Years Eve, 1998

This is the end, thought Jeff. *They're going to kill me.*

Then he saw his chance. He reached into his pocket and grabbed his lighter. All he needed was a spark. With his thumb, he spun the little wheel and threw the lighter at Vick, who was suddenly engulfed in a raging fire.

It was the most horrific sight Jeff had ever seen. Vick was thrashing and flailing his arms, trying to rip the flaming jacket from his body as his hair disintegrated from the heat. Chaos erupted as the cab driver ran for cover like a rat scurrying to find a hole. The convenience store clerk grabbed a water hose and tried to alleviate Vick's suffering. Mitch didn't seem to notice. He shoved Jeff behind the wheel of the Lincoln.

"You're driving." He aimed the gun squarely at Jeff's head as he got in on the other side. "Go now," he commanded, holding the gun against Jeff's right temple. "Drive, you son of a bitch."

Jeff started the car and peeled out onto the road, heading for the on ramp to the Interstate. "Look, man," he said. "We don't have to do this. You don't want to make it worse—"

"Shut up," Mitch interrupted. "Drive."

"Where?" Jeff asked. "What are you going to do with me?"

"Shut up—just shut the fuck up! I gotta figure this out."

"Are you going to kill me?"

"Do you know what you've done, kid?" Mitch asked impatiently. "I just needed to talk to you. You fuckin' idiot. You pussy—now I might have to erase you." He cocked the gun he was holding at Jeff's temple. "You tell me what you know—and if you told anyone else."

Cold fear inched up Jeff's spine, threatening to snake into his brain and paralyze him. He didn't know everything, but he knew more than he'd ever wanted to. He knew Mitch killed Robert, and he knew why. He would give anything, at that moment, to be as ignorant and innocent as he'd been the day he'd enrolled in law school.

CHAPTER 1

A Bright Future Ahead
Autumn, 1994

Ever since Jeff Rhodes could remember, he had wanted to become an attorney. Well, except when he was about six years old. Back then, he'd briefly toyed with the idea of becoming an astronaut. His mom had videotapes of the Apollo lunar missions, and he'd found those flickering black-and-white images exciting. But that excitement quickly wore off, and aside from his brief flirtation with the idea of blasting off in a rocket and becoming the first person to land on Mars, he had always wanted to become a lawyer. He wasn't quite sure why. Maybe it was seeing how his Uncle Murray had handled the estate after his dad died, and how much respect everybody in the family gave him, including Jeff's mom.

Calling it an estate, ten-year-old Jeff had thought at the time, was kind of a stretch since all they had was a three bedroom house in Pinehill, New Jersey, and a small life insurance policy his mom learned was just enough to cover burying his dad. She considered selling the house, but it was almost paid for. There was some business with the mortgage about the last two payments. Jeff didn't know all the details, but somehow Uncle Murray had worked it out with the bank and, as his mom said, the place was theirs now, so they had better just stay put. Uncle Murray had made that possible, and everyone always said what a genius he was, and how much they respected him. Respect became supremely important to Jeff.

The next few years were a struggle for his mom but she worked two jobs to support him and his brother and sister and keep them all together. Growing up in a working class family that was always on the edge of poverty wasn't easy but his mom kept Jeff and his siblings too busy with chores and homework to worry much about what they didn't have. "If you want better," she always told them, "you have to get an education, and then you have to work harder than everyone else." She was happy when Jeff told her he'd decided to become a lawyer. From then on, she had told him repeatedly that he was meant to be going toward greatness.

Everyone encouraged him in this pursuit—his mom, his friends, and his older brother and sister, and especially his uncle, who had urged him to be outgoing, to engage others in conversation, to debate issues, and to try to look at the world analytically. Jeff had done well. He had made good grades in school and he got a part-time job after school as soon as he was old enough to get a work permit. Allowing himself only a pittance of his earnings for fun, Jeff had saved everything he could to help put himself through college. And now, he was finally about to embark on the journey for which he had been preparing throughout most of his life.

In high school he'd been an exceptional student and a good athlete with looks girls called handsome, which made him popular. He was involved in numerous extracurricular activities, including quarterbacking for the football team, participating in the debate club and even joining the senior class thespian society. Much of this he enjoyed. However, the great motivating force behind all his efforts was his desire to get into a great college, with the dream of one day attending law school. So he did everything his teachers and counselor suggested, without question and with great enthusiasm. He graduated at the top of his class, and with two scholarships—one athletic and one academic—he was able to attend one of the top five universities in the country, the prestigious Pembroke University at North Carolina. At this Ivy League institution he excelled as well.

Initially, he didn't choose Livermore for his graduate work because he thought it was the best law school and would provide the greatest intellectual challenge. He'd visited before enrolling and found he enjoyed the comfortable, laid-back attitude that seemed to permeate the entire campus. He remembered the beautiful spring afternoon like it was yesterday. Flowers were in bloom and there wasn't a cloud in the sky. People were sunning themselves on the great lawn at the center of the campus, and on what the students called The Steps. Students tossed around Frisbees and footballs, strummed away on guitars, and chatted. It seemed no one cared about doing any work. After all, The Steps belonged to the main college library, and it didn't seem like anyone was using them for anything other than leisure. He thought it must have been the most leisurely day in the entire year. He knew once he got settled into his new post-graduate routine, there would be time for an occasional party here and there, but for the most part, he was there to do some serious work.

Gazing through the bus window, Jeff turned his attention to the multitude of people outside. Taxicabs and cars swerved in and out of traffic, motorists honked their horns at one another, and multitudes of people crisscrossed the thoroughfare leading up to the university. With so little student parking available, it didn't pay to drive his beat-up old Jeep. He hardly ever took it out from in front of his apartment building, except to move it when necessary to avoid getting a ticket. Suddenly the bus came to an abrupt halt. Jeff lurched forward then bounced back into his seat, his shoulder slightly grazing the passenger next to him. The middle-aged African American woman turned to Jeff and smiled.

"I hope this bus driver hasn't been drinking," she said under her breath and Jeff laughed. He could see through the front windshield that a cab driver had cut them off, nearly causing a collision in the middle of the busy intersection. Both the bus driver and the cab driver peered out their windows, shouted insults and waved their fists at each other before they got going again. The bus inched forward at first, then moved more rapidly into the heavy traffic. With a pleasant smile, the woman commented again on the operator's erratic driving, and added, "At least we've had some good weather over the last couple of days."   .

Jeff nodded and returned her smile, although her comments had interrupted his train of thought. He had been considering how, despite all his hard work, he would now have to become even more serious about his studies. One of the most crucial things he'd have to do was convince his longtime childhood buddies who, throughout his college years, would drive up to his dorm and barge into his room unannounced. It didn't matter whether it was the week before an exam. It didn't even matter if it was the day before an exam. They would pop in and demand that Jeff go out with them and have a good time. Their intentions were always good. They knew how much stress he was under, by his own design, and they always seemed to show up when the tension in his life was greatest, when they thought he could use a little fun and entertainment the most. One of them—Bernie Abbott, who'd been his best friend since middle school—would throw rocks at Jeff's window until he finally gave in. Bernie knew if he called first, Jeff would make up any excuse to avoid going out. But all that would have to come to an end.

The woman continued in her efforts to strike up a conversation. "You have an awful lot of reading to do tonight, don't you?" she asked as she pointed to Jeff's bag full of textbooks.

"Oh, they're just getting me started with this stuff," Jeff answered with a grin. "This was my summer reading."

She leaned back in her seat and laughed. "Summer reading? You mean you got homework over the summer? What you studying to be—a lawyer or a doctor or something?"

"Actually," responded Jeff, "I'm registering today, for law school."

"Oh, well then, congratulations," she said as she held out her hand. "I'm Anita. And who might you be?"

Shaking hands with his new friend, Jeff responded. "I'm Jeff—Jeff Rhodes."

"So where are you beginning your studies?" she questioned. "Over at Livermore?"

"Yeah, I'm starting at Livermore."

"Well, I hear it's a great school. Congratulations to you again. Now tell me something. I know you're just starting and all, but would you have any idea about . . . well, I have this friend who's having a dispute with her landlord. I'm afraid she's about to get evicted. What do you think she ought to do?"

It never fails, Jeff thought. Regardless of the topic of conversation most people, once they found out someone was studying law, practicing law or interested in the law, would inevitably have some kind of story linking them to the law, or they would have a question about a legal problem.

"I really don't know the answer to that question, Anita," said Jeff, managing what he thought was his best lawyerly look of concern. "But I'll tell you what I can do. I'm almost certain Livermore has a housing clinic where they address landlord-tenant issues. I'll see what I can find out. Tell you what—here's my phone number." He tore off a corner of a page in his spiral notebook and scribbled on it. "Give me a call in a couple of days, and maybe I'll have some information for you."

Anita seemed genuinely pleased that someone really took an interest and seemed to have an earnest desire to help. "God bless you, young man," she said, then repeated, "God bless you." The bus then came to a screeching halt about a block away from the gates of Livermore.

"This is my stop, Anita," Jeff told her. "It's so nice to meet you." She pulled out a pack of gum and offered him a stick, which he was happy to accept. He needed something to calm his nerves. "Thanks," he said.

Under her breath, Anita simply responded with, "Mm-hm, mm-hm."

Jeff stood up and squeezed past her and into the aisle. She looked up and grabbed his forearm. She had a big smile on her face. "Don't worry, Jeff," she said. "You're going to be fine."

He stepped onto the street as throngs of people poured out from the subway stop. The bus rumbled away in a puff of black smoke. Jeff turned and approached the Livermore gates.

This was a university with over two hundred years of history. Like many of the Ivy League institutions, its founders had been servants of the British crown. Following the Revolution, they renamed the school after one of its early benefactors, also a prominent figure in the war for independence. Livermore was the lifeblood of Manhattan's upper west side. The outlying area of the community was mostly working class and working poor. Virtually the entire local economy depended upon the university. There was nothing, really, about the neighborhood to distinguish it from any other urban setting. There were no fabulous museums or majestic avenues here, and no looming skyscrapers like in midtown. There were a couple of nice Italian restaurants, a few bakeries, a bagel shop, a Chinese restaurant or two, even a few Indian and Thai spots. The immediate area was a diverse mish-mash of peoples, languages, faiths, and cuisines. Interesting perhaps, but not awe-inspiring. But that was life outside the Livermore gates.

Jeff reached the entrance and he was impressed anew with what he saw. It was an oasis within a concrete jungle. Passing through the gates, he felt as though he had taken a step back in time. The street leading to the main campus was broad and made of cobblestones. There was greenery, and lots of it. A gentle breeze rustled the trees, causing flower petals to glide slowly to the ground. What immediately struck Jeff as odd were the squirrels. These were no ordinary squirrels. They were fat—so fat they needed to be put on a diet. And, not surprising, they were incredibly friendly. It was amusing to see them scamper right up to a person and lean back on their hind legs, their cute little paws extended and their snouts in the air, to beg for food.

Well, if they can get along here, I suppose I can too, Jeff thought.

Besides the squirrels, he was taken by the architect's vision for the central square of the campus. Once Jeff passed through the gates, he entered a new world separate unto itself. The sight of the main library filled him with awe. Inscribed across the top of the building were names of the greatest thinkers, writers and poets, there for all to see upon entering the campus. Three presidents, countless governors past and present, major corporate CEOs and the like, had all passed through this university and law school throughout its illustrious history.

Jeff made his way across the campus walk to the entrance of the law building. He took a deep breath and then went through the revolving doors. In the distance he could see a long line of hopeful, anxious students winding through the corridor. Jeff took his place in line and waited patiently to register and receive his schedule.

After forty-five minutes, he finally arrived at the front of the line. As identification he produced his driver's license, which got him a printout of his course load for the next five months. His classes included Legal Thinking, Introduction to Legal Writing, Torts, Civil Procedure, and Property, with a required, intensive two-week immersion in Intro to Legal Writing and Legal Thinking before he could move on to the other courses.

CHAPTER 2

Introductory But Essential

As Jeff entered the room in which he would attend his first class, he could feel the tension in the air curling around him like a thick, gathering fog. It gave him small comfort to know he wasn't the only one feeling anxious.

Lecture Hall C was a huge semi-circular room with ceilings that had to be twenty-five feet high. The stairs leading to the central podium sloped downward to a pit from which the professor would speak to students, rather than talking to them from a platform above.

Professor Giles, an accomplished patent attorney who had a PhD in physics from MIT, was Jeff's teacher for Legal Thinking. Giles was a member of the Harvard Law Review and while studying at Harvard he had clerked for Justice Weinstein of the U.S. Supreme Court. In addition to this array of achievements, he was also a poet and an avid writer, and he played the violin. As Jeff settled into his chair among the buzz of students laughing and talking around him, the professor's booming voice reverberated throughout the lecture hall. Immediately the class grew silent.

"Welcome, Class of 1994. If you haven't figured it out yet, this is Legal Thinking, one of the introductory but nonetheless essential courses at Livermore. Yes, it's one of those mundane requirement courses, but we're going to take this opportunity to immerse you in the law, to teach you to begin to think like a lawyer, and to address legal questions. Now it's my understanding you had a substantive amount of reading to do over the summer. I'm going to assume you all did it."

A few chuckles, hesitant at first, rippled through the classroom, and Giles grinned. He put his hand to his chin and threaded slender fingers through his neatly trimmed black beard, which Jeff noted was streaked lightly with gray. Giles locked his sights on a student in the front row for a moment and then swept the room. "But anyway," he continued, "lest I forget to mention, for your next class I want everyone to bring in a wallet-size photo of themselves. And please consider the seats you've taken today your permanent ones."

One student, a pert little blonde, eagerly raised her hand but Giles ignored her.

"'Why?' you might ask," he said. "Simple—I will attach said photos to my seating chart above your illustrious names, so I can recognize on sight each and every one of you. And I warn all of you. The longer you delay in bringing me this photo, the more often I'll call on you in class. That's a promise. As you may know, I use the Socratic method. For those of you who don't know, the Socratic method means I'll be asking you, at my sole discretion, to answer questions on the previous day's reading or on a general legal question or perhaps even on your philosophy of life. Is there one among you eager to face the terror of being the first person called on?"

Laughter swept through the classroom, filling it, Jeff thought, with hope as Professor Giles put his students at ease.

"Well, then," Giles went on. "I think I've loosened you guys up enough. Now, as I call on you, tell me your name so I can put it in my chart." He pointed to the blonde.

"Smith," she said with an inviting smile. "Cheryl Ann Smith."

"Well, Ms. Smith, you have the good fortune of being the first person called on this year," Giles said. "I expect you'll set a fine example for your colleagues. So tell me, Ms. Smith, in Becker v. Jameson, the court ruled in favor of the plaintiff with a two-judge dissent— on the basis of?"

CHAPTER 3

Bad Habits

As the neon light flashed in the distance, *Jack's . . . Jack's . . . Jack's,* Vick shuddered inside his heavy leather jacket, his swarthy features hidden in the shadows. "What the hell we doin' up here, Mitch?" he asked, clearly annoyed.

"For the last time, I'll tell ya when it's time to tell ya."

"It's friggin freezin up here," Vick responded.

"You got some fuckin' thin blood, my friend," Mitch said. "It's only September. Suck it up, already. We got work to do."

Vick reached into his breast pocket for a Marlboro. He took a silver-plated lighter, a gift from his first wife (he was now on his third), out of the same pocket and lit the cigarette. "I can't believe this. It's a Saturday night and I'm spending it on top of an eight-story warehouse waitin' for some banana head in the meat-packing district."

"Shut up—here he comes."

A shiny black Porsche convertible with the top down moved slowly along the cracked pothole-ridden street, its motor growling in a low hum and its headlights off. Vick leaned over the side of the building to see what Mitch was seeing. In the light from the streetlamp he could clearly make out the figure of a well-built young man in his mid-twenties driving the sports car. He stopped the car and reached above the windshield to where the convertible top would lock into place, gesturing with one hand that he was going to proceed. Then he held up two fingers, making the peace sign before he put the car in gear, splashed through a puddle and parked in the loading dock.

Up above, Mitch smoothed his neatly trimmed beard for a moment, then pulled the cigarette from Vick's fingers. He put it to his mouth and took a puff as a slow grin parted his thin lips. He returned the cigarette, now only a stub, and leaned over to whisper in his companion's ear. "I'll be back in a second. Keep an eye on that guy."

"Okay. So—who is he?"

"Connection," was Mitch's terse response.

Vick wasn't about to let it go. "To who?"

Mitch sighed. "To one of the most lucrative markets we got. Now watch him. I'll want to know if he gets out of the car."

About ten seconds passed. Down below, a tall thin man wearing a tasseled jacket stepped out of the shadows and handed the driver of the sports car a brown paper bag. He patted the driver on the shoulder, walked past the back of the car, crossed the street and disappeared into the night. Up above, Mitch returned to where Vick was keeping watch.

"What the hell you gonna do with that?" Vick asked. Mitch was cradling a cinder block in his arms. Breathing heavily, he leaned over to deposit the hunk of concrete onto the roof, relieving himself of the weight.

"Help me out with this," he commanded. Together Vick and Mitch leaned over and grabbed the cinder block. They placed it on the ledge of the building and Mitch positioned it as close as he could to the edge without dropping it over the side.

"He get out of the car?" asked Mitch.

"Nah," Vick said. "Guy came out and gave him a bag, then split."

Below them, the driver opened the rumpled paper bag and with his finger he punched a hole into the plastic that lay within. He withdrew his finger to see a sugary white substance on his fingertips. Touching this to his tongue he smiled and muttered something. His smile grew bigger as he sprinkled some of the glistening white powder onto the dashboard of the car. Next he pulled a bill out of his wallet and rolled it into a cylinder.

Up above, Mitch groaned as he again lifted the cinder block and shifted it a little. He waited for the perfect instant, and took his cue when the driver bent toward the dashboard to take a hit of the white powder. Sweat rolling down his rotund cheeks, Mitch moved his round, fat hands to get a better grip on the cinder block. Once again he leaned over the edge of the building, causing his expansive waistline to become visible, the fullness of his gut hanging over his belt. He dug his fingertips into the block, holding it steady for a moment, and waiting . . . waiting . . . before he finally launched it over the side with all his might.

The block sped toward its target, tumbling eight stories to its unsuspecting victim whose head was now thrown back against his seat, his arms outstretched, as he reveled in the glory of the white dust. There was a thunderous crash, and then silence. And then they heard an agonized scream.

"What the fuck!"

And then, the car's alarm blared stridently into the night. Again Mitch and Vick peered over the side of the building. The cinder block had crushed the dashboard and steering wheel of the Porsche. Vick couldn't tell if the driver was dead or alive.

"Come on," said Mitch. "We've gotta get the shit."

The two men scrambled across the roof of the warehouse and down to the adjoining building and Vick kicked open the metal door leading to the stairwell where they would make their escape. They rushed down the stairs, bumping into one another and off of the walls and banister as they went down. Their laughter echoed through the stairwell.

As Mitch headed for the back exit, Vick grabbed his arm and stopped him. "Hey, wait up," he said. "Stop a minute—you hear sirens?"

"No!" retorted Mitch, pulling impatiently on his beard. "We got time. Let's go!" He flipped his companion the finger and bolted for the front entrance.

"You crazy bastard!" Vick exclaimed and went after him, struggling to keep up. Almost simultaneously they crashed through the front door, leaped off of the loading platform, and arrived at the Porsche to gaze at the results of Mitch's handiwork. The sight of the smashed glass made Mitch laugh. Careful not to let his finger touch the driver, he pointed to the young man's crushed hand. "How about that—he broke the cinder block in two! What are ya, kid? Some kinda fuckin' ninja?"

"What the fuck, Mitch?" the kid repeated with an agonized groan.

Vick reached for the paper bag, which had fallen to the floor of the passenger seat in a pool of the kid's blood.

"Wait, you idiot," Mitch said, reaching into his breast pocket.

Alarmed, the young man threw up his good hand. "Come on, Mitch," he begged. "I was just having a little taste, to test it—"

"You were just helping yourself to a little off the top, like you been doing for weeks." He laughed and pulled a handkerchief out of his pocket. He tossed it to Vick. "Here—use this."

Vick caught the handkerchief and Mitch turned back to the kid. "Listen, genius. This is a warning—you hear me?"

"Yeah. Loud and clear."

"Good. My boss don't like to feel taken advantage of, especially by some snot-nosed law student who's using the stuff more than he's selling it. Next time it won't be your hand. It'll be your head."

Vick tossed the paper bag away and stuffed the plastic bag into his pocket. Then they heard the low wail of an approaching siren. He grabbed Mitch's arm. "Come on, man," he said. "We gotta go."

"Yeah—let's get the fuck out of here."

As the two men drove away, Vick asked, "So—what's next?"

"I'm hungry," Mitch said. "You know of any after-hours places around here where I can get a nice plate of pasta?"

CHAPTER 4

Bright Lights

For the next several days, Professor Giles kept all his students alert and ready for questions with plenty of assigned reading. By this time, he had completed his collection of photos and had pasted each and every one of them, arranged in the exact location of their owners, on his seating chart, a huge piece of cardboard he kept on the dais. Thus the professor committed each and every student's name and face to memory. There were over a hundred in his class, and within a week he could call every one of them by name, without hesitation.

"Ms. Robbins, would you please answer this question?"

"Mr. Markson, please tell us about your reflections on the outcome of this case."

Jeff thought this aspect of Professor Giles' teaching method was really impressive. He had excellent rapport with his students, and his enthusiasm for the law was evident in his lectures. The lecture hall was his stage, and in this arena he felt most comfortable. But on the few occasions Jeff attempted to make contact with him after class, the professor's persona changed dramatically.

It's as if he has two personalities, Jeff thought. Like he's schizophrenic or something. When Giles was on stage, he was playful, jovial and entertaining. He had a marvelous wit about him, and when the students fired challenging questions at him, he always returned a volley of quick and insightful answers which, on many occasions, were also witty and entertaining.

Jeff wondered how this person who gave the impression of being so warm and welcoming publicly could be so awkward, short and dismissive when someone approached him privately. Twice Jeff went to the esteemed professor after class to discuss case law he had just covered. A political science major in college, Jeff found the Chadha case involving the legislative veto to be particularly interesting.

He was so nervous when he approached the professor his palms were sweating. After class, students milled about discussing legal issues they'd found interesting, some hoping to catch the professor's attention for a moment and ask him a question or two, and Jeff was content to wait his turn. He practiced the question in his head over and over, in an effort to maximize both flow and substance, before he opened his mouth. Positive Giles would impart some wisdom, Jeff asked his question, integrating his own impressions on the topic—and he thought he sounded pretty damn smart. He anticipated that Giles, whether or not he had anything of importance to say on the topic, would at least try to look interested and encourage a first year student to be inquisitive, and to show enthusiasm for the law.

Instead of dissecting and analyzing Jeff's question, the professor refrained from addressing it at all. "Interesting," he'd said, and nothing more. He'd simply swept Jeff aside and moved on, which was supremely disappointing. After all, Jeff had always believed learning doesn't take place in a vacuum. He thought ideas were meant to be exchanged, and when someone was discouraged from asking questions and volunteering impressions, something was seriously lost from the educational process.

Well, I guess that's just a lesson I have to learn, Jeff thought. *Maybe I'm not as insightful as some of the other students. Maybe I should keep quiet until I'm sure I have something compelling to say.*

That day, class ended a little earlier than usual. Professor Giles had to hurry out to catch a plane for Tokyo. "I'll be away for the next couple of days, lecturing on the American legal system," he'd announced as he'd folded the cardboard photo chart and tucked it under his arm. "In the meantime, I encourage all of you to take a moment and sit in on the moot court competition taking place in the Roosevelt Room. It would be nice for you to stop by to lend support to the Livermore upperclassmen representing us, and to see some real stars in action." With that he had stepped away from the dais and bounded out of the lecture hall to exit through the side door.

The Roosevelt Room was a large, imposing auditorium with a mock courtroom set up on the stage. A panel of three judges sat on the bench. One of them was Professor Chessman, whose reputation as a hard-edged, Darth Vader-like persona was legendary throughout the university. The second judge was a guest from the New York State Court of Appeals, and the third judge was good old Professor Duberstein who had a reputation for being a good-natured man with a deadpan sense of humor. Students filled the auditorium to capacity, leaving standing room only. The adversaries entered from opposite sides of the courtroom and the tension level, creating its own electricity, crackled through the air as one of them began.

"May it please the court, I am Robert Turner, counsel for the defendant,

Michelle Chandler." Turner's handsome young face lit up from behind the podium, and he gestured with his hands to emphasize his words. "The prosecution instructed my client to stab the mannequin through the heart, the lungs and the ribs as she did that night!"

Jeff smiled when Robert Turner paused for dramatic effect, clearly hoping the jury (and the audience full of students) would react. They didn't, so he plunged bravely on.

"Ms. Chandler, in an extreme state of discomposure due to the effects of the recent trauma she'd suffered at the hands of her brutal husband, along with the State's endless harassing, complied with the prosecutor's request. She stabbed the mannequin for the entire jury to see. Her attorney objected but the court overruled. The frenzy of activity the State's prosecutor created, with Miss Chandler as the center of attention, made her appear, frankly, insane. The demonstration was enough to sway any jury, and most certainly sealed her conviction, thus condemning her to suffer further, first at the hands of her husband and a second time at the hands of the State."

"You mean to tell me you thought the prosecution was too hard on Michelle Chandler?" Judge Chessman demanded. It was obvious to Jeff that Robert's impassioned opening remarks had surprised Chessman. In an authoritarian tone, the judge continued, "At two AM on February 12, 1992, your client got out of bed, went to the kitchen, grabbed a butcher knife, and plunged it into her husband's sleeping body. Not once but repeatedly. Yet you stand there and claim it was self-defense? And further, claim it was improper for the prosecution to have her demonstrate with a mannequin what occurred on that night?"

Taking a long, slow breath, Robert Turner regrouped, and Jeff noticed a more even and less impassioned tone in his response. "Your Honor, it was self-defense! Michelle Chandler endured over two years of physical and mental abuse at the hands of her husband. She stabbed him to death after he returned home in a drunken rage and threatened the life of their two-year-old daughter, Rachael. On the night of the evening in question, Michelle went to bed about midnight. Around one forty-five AM, her husband came home, slamming the door, cursing and throwing things around. He sounded—"

"You expect me to believe it was self-defense?" Chessman cut Turner off midsentence. "She stabbed her sleeping husband to death. She wasn't in imminent danger."

"I respectfully disagree, Your Honor. She was in imminent danger. Michelle Chandler had been beaten and abused repeatedly, and over such an extended period of time that she perceived herself to be in imminent danger. Expert testimony would show that she was suffering from battered woman's syndrome. Indeed, she believed it was only a matter of time before he would kill her. She was a hostage in her own home."

"Expert testimony!" Chessman scoffed, unimpressed. "Your expert's testimony fails to address why your client didn't just leave her husband instead of murdering him in cold blood. If, indeed, the beatings were so unbearable you must concede she had the option to leave?"

The young student abandoned his change in tactics and without hesitation responded in earnest, "Your Honor, the concept of battered woman's syndrome is based heavily on the work of Eleanore Watkins whose research points to a three-stage cycle of ceaseless violence that psychologically traps a battered woman in the relationship. The first stage is the tension-building stage, with only a few minor abusive incidents. The woman attempts to placate her mate, which works with some success at first, thus reinforcing her belief that the situation is under control. The acute battering stage then follows. Attacks become more violent, more severe, more frequent and usually unprovoked."

Some of the students stirred uncomfortably in their seats as they confronted one of the unpleasant realities of life. Jeff was more certain than ever he didn't want to go into criminal law or family law, and get a dose of this misery every day. But now, he noted, the judge was listening. Robert continued:

"Finally, a period of relative calm follows the abuse. During this contrition stage, the abuser shows remorse, apologizes for his behavior and reinforces the victim's hope that he will reform. Continued over an extended period of time, a sense of psychological paralysis seizes the victim. The battered woman believes nothing can be done to alter the situation. Battered women, in effect, become terror-stricken. This abuse is so severe and the sense of fear so constant that it creates a state of mind likened to that of a hostage!"

Turner paused for a moment to catch his breath. He looked down at his notes and flipped through them. He paused, again playing on the drama of the moment. Jeff smiled, appreciating Robert's style. He was working the crowd, holding the attention of the jury and onlookers. Jeff wondered if he'd ever have that much confidence before a judge, in a trial.

This was it, Jeff thought. He had finally gotten a taste of what law school was all about. Counsel on both sides of the case had compelling arguments but Robert Turner was dazzling. After about forty-five minutes, he made his closing statements. "If the expert testimony would have been admitted at trial, it would have clearly shown that Ms. Chandler suffered from battered woman's syndrome. She had to take drastic measures, in the interest of justice. Your Honor should remand this case for new trial on the basis that relevant testimony was not heard by the jury."

Judge Duberstein stood up from the bench and thanked both counsel for their efforts. "We will consider the issues before the court and pronounce our decision tomorrow."

•••

After collecting his belongings and packing them into his briefcase, Robert Turner headed for the stairs to exit the auditorium, barely hanging on to all the folders and files he'd brought with him. The great Roosevelt Auditorium had all but emptied out, but Jeff remained, sitting there in amazement. This guy really kicks ass, he thought. This is what it's really all about. I've got to get to know this guy.

Robert nodded as he passed Jeff, and during that brief moment he lost his concentration and dropped one of his folders. Quickly Jeff sprang to his feet. He picked it up and handed it to the upperclassman.

"Hey, thanks," said Robert.

"My pleasure. I'm Jeff Rhodes." Jeff extended his hand but realized Robert didn't have a hand to give him, burdened as he was by his briefcase and numerous folders. Jeff withdrew his hand. "You were awesome," he continued. "I'm impressed. I'd like to pick your brain a little, if I could. How'd you get to be so good?"

"Well, I—" Robert began. Then a girl in a hurry brushed past them, knocking the folders out of his hand. Jeff caught them just in time. "Hey, Jeff—thanks again," Robert went on. "Looks like we're blocking traffic just standing here. Come on—we can talk while we walk."

Jeff followed him out of the auditorium. As they made their way to the lockers, students and spectators still lingering in the hallway patted Robert on the back or high-fived him.

"So, um, I take it you're a first year here at Livermore?" he asked Jeff after they'd run the cheerful gauntlet of well wishers.

"Yeah, how'd you know?"

"Well, let me see. You just strike me as being all too enthusiastic and well mannered to be anything more than a first year. Believe me, I mean that in a good way. Everyone around here is so fuckin' jaded." Together they piled all of Robert's files into his locker. "Thanks for the help, man. I'm actually in a little bit of a rush."

"Hey, no problem," Jeff said. "I understand. Do whatever you gotta do."

"I tell you what, me and a couple friends of mine are gonna meet for drinks tonight at Dead Scribes. You know the place?"

"Yeah, sure." Jeff knew it was one of the most popular student hangouts on the upper west side. He'd been there a few times.

"Great. Why don't you drop by and we'll talk some more. I'll answer any questions you have."

Jeff grinned. "I'll be there."

•••

The place was packed when Jeff arrived. He went to the standing-room-only bar and ordered a beer and when he got it, he walked casually around the place. He didn't see Robert Turner, but he found a spot where he could lean against the wall near a table full of animated law students, some of whom were in his class with Professor Giles and some he remembered seeing in the moot court that day.

He'd always found the Dead Scribes theme kind of amusing. During happy hour most drinks, named after famous departed authors like Edgar Allen Poe and Ernest Hemingway, were only a dollar—and there were free hors d'oeuvres. The menus, featuring mostly burgers, fries, salads and tacos, were in the form of little books. Jeff was looking through one of them when a stunning girl at the crowded table captured his attention. She'd been in the Roosevelt Room earlier so he knew she was second year. She was tall, at least five-eight he figured, with deep brown eyes and olive skin.

"You know who else is cute?" she was saying. "Robert Turner. He blew me away in moot court today." She was standing behind another second-year student, massaging his neck between taking sips of her drink. Playfully, she slapped at his shoulder. "Don't get jealous, Alberto."

Her hair was dead straight and Jeff loved the way it fell just past her shoulders as she leaned over momentarily to whisper something to Alberto, which made him laugh. Her long slender fingers briefly caressed Alberto's cheeks and worked into his shoulders and neck, making Jeff wish he could trade places, at least temporarily, with Alberto, who was now leaning back in his seat.

"Hey, Monica," said Alberto. "Get over here." He raised his head when she bent to him and gave her a short but sensual kiss.

"Get a room, you guys," said a pretty blond, her carefree tone in complete contradiction to the look of contempt she aimed at Monica.

"We don't need to, Cassandra," Alberto shot back. "We've got nothing to hide."

Cassandra rolled her eyes and went to the bar. A couple at a small side table left and Jeff grabbed the vacant spot. He waved the waitress over and ordered some fries. Cassandra came back from the bar with a beer and Robert Turner.

"Dude!" Alberto called out. "You're late. Come on—you got some catching up to do."

"Nothing I'd like better," Robert answered, taking a place at the table. Then he spotted Jeff and waved him over. "Okay, everybody," he said. "This is Jeff. First year and eager—and he thinks I'm brilliant. Say hello to my little friend."

Jeff smiled at them and nodded as Alberto threw a pretzel at Robert. "You didn't win yet, ass hat," said Alberto. "We'll see how brilliant you are tomorrow."

The girl named Cassandra looked directly into Jeff's eyes, her own flashing with intelligence and interest. "Hi," was all she said, but it was Jeff's undoing. He'd dated a lot in high school and in college but no one girl had held his interest for long—not enough to take his focus off his studies and his ultimate goal. The minute he saw her, Jeff sensed Cassandra would be different, not just because of her beauty, but because of who she was, how she was. If she caressed his neck the way Monica was carressing Alberto's, he might just forget everything.

Part of him knew he had to be careful, to keep his distance from Cassandra (not that he'd ever get a chance to get close), at least until he was on solid footing at Livermore. And part of him wanted to rush headlong into whatever he could have with her and damn the consequences. She was speaking again.

"Come on, Jeff—sit down," Cassandra invited him. "Join us. We could always use a fresh perspective."

•••

The next morning, with only a slight hangover, Jeff was in the Roosevelt Room waiting for moot court to begin. One of the burly university security guards, who was standing in as the court bailiff, entered the auditorium from one of the side doors.

"All rise!" he shouted.

The three judges, all clad in robes, entered the chamber and took their seats and Robert Turner took a snow white handkerchief out of his pocket and wiped his hands before returning it. Jeff thought his palms might be wet. That happened to Jeff sometimes, when he was under pressure—another reason he wasn't interested in becoming a trial attorney.

Professor Duberstein, the acting chief judge, requested that the advocates step forward. Both attorneys answered, "Yes, Your Honor," in unison. As they took their places, there was stone dead silence in the crowd of onlookers.

"We have examined the issues before the court," said Duberstein. "And while both sides have presented very compelling arguments, the court has determined that the expert testimony will be admissible at trial, and therefore this case should be remanded to the lower court for further proceedings, consistent with this opinion. The court now holds that the battered woman's syndrome is a recognized defense in various other states, and should now be recognized in this state as well. The fact that Ms. Chandler, due to the repeated beatings she suffered at the hands of her husband, viewed her situation as one that was life-threatening, and further, one in which she was in immediate if not imminent danger, is the basis upon which the court arrives at this decision."

Jeff watched as Professor Duberstein walked over to congratulate the advocates, and Robert Turner in particular. The professor extended his hand to Robert, a big grin on his face. "You cleared that hurdle. You glad it's over?"

"Yes, Your Honor. I sure am."

"It's only one of many more hoops you have to jump through during your law school and legal career. You won the case! How do you feel?"

"It really feels great, Your Honor," said Turner.

Professor Duberstein let out a hearty laugh. "Cut the 'Your Honor' crap. You can call me Professor Duberstein again. Or whatever you guys call us behind our backs. Come back to reality now. I'm sure you're ready to relax and put away a couple of smoothies. I know I am."

"Yeah, I could go for a beer right now, Your Honor—I mean—Dubey," responded Robert, clearly more at ease.

"Oh, so that's what you kids call me," said Professor Duberstein. "I like that. Less pretentious than all that 'Your Honor' stuff. I mean, you don't have to tell me I'm great—I already know that. I'm isolated on a cliff of my own genius."

"I know the feeling, sir," quipped Robert.

Surprised, Duberstein stared at Robert a moment and Jeff held his breath, wondering if his new friend had gone too far. Then the professor laughed. Robert joined in, and Jeff smiled. In a general hustle and bustle, spectators got up to leave the auditorium, until the moderator tapped the microphone to get their attention.

"One more minute, gentlemen—and ladies," he announced. "Thank you for attending the moot court contest. First, we would like to congratulate counsel on a job well done. Both did wonderful work. Robert, you won this particular case. We hope you have similar fortunes as a litigator in the future. Most important, we'd like to thank all the judges and professors in attendance for taking time out from their busy schedules to be with us. A special thanks to Justice Stern for her invaluable assistance in coordinating this event. A good day to all. Thank you."

•••

That evening, RobertTurner strolled through the entrance of Jackson's Pub which, Jeff learned, was a simple neighborhood joint where second-year students went to celebrate their small successes. On seeing him, two guys jumped up from their seats at the bar.

"Yo, buddy—over here," one of them called out.

"Hey, Red," Robert answered as he went to join them. "How's it going?"

"You tell us," the other one said. "All we know is you won."

"Wait, Cosmo," said Red. "Let's get a drink in him, then he can tell us all about it."

"What's to tell?" Robert replied modestly before breaking into a big grin. "I won. Can you believe it? I'm a fucking genius!"

"Let me be the first to buy the fucking genius a drink," Jeff called out as he worked his way through the crowd.

Robert spun around and waved Jeff over to the table. "Hey, Jeff, how's it going?" he asked, then turned to his pals."Guys, I want you to give a warm welcome to Jeff Rhodes, who's a first year here at Livermore. Jeff, these are my buddies—Cosmo, the tall one, and Red the Russian."

Cosmo and Red took turns shaking hands with Jeff and Jeff realized it was an honor of sorts. He knew most upperclassmen didn't give first year students much attention at all, but he saw these guys weren't like that. Their welcome seemed warm and sincere.

"If you need any advice on how to get through your first year," Robert was saying, "you don't want to ask these guys. They slept and partied through most of it."

"Fuck you, asshole," Cosmo said, and turned to Jeff. "Don't believe it. We worked our tails off. You will, too."

"Yeah," Red chimed in. "You need any advice or support, we're here for you. But right now, we need to hear the shit straight from the horse's ass—"

"No, no, no," Cosmo broke in. "It's horse's mouth."

"But the shit comes from the horse's—" Red started to argue. This time Robert interrupted.

"Ignore them," he said. "They go on like that all the time. Red is from Russia—been here five years but he's still trying to learn to speak American. His English is impeccable. His American slang not so good. Still, he wallows in American culture."

"Yeah, yeah—okay," Red said. "So tell us, big shot—you got them on the admissibility of the expert testimony, right?"

"Yeah," Robert responded. "It was touch and go for a while, but I convinced them."

"Another round of beers for my friends here," Cosmo told the bartender. "Hey, Jeff, what are you drinking?"

"Heineken, and I've got whatever Robert's having."

When the bartender returned with all their drinks, Cosmo lifted his bottle. "A toast, gentlemen! To Robert, a future power litigator and mega-bullshit artist."

"It's all in the presentation," Robert answered with false modesty. "What can I say?"

Through the crowd, Red spotted a woman and nodded in her direction. "There she is," he said. "The one I've been crazy about since I began at Livermore. She makes my Russian blood boil."

In a sarcastic tone, Cosmo added, "What woman doesn't? Red, why don't you forget about it? She's just gonna shoot you down."

"I don't think so," said Red.

"Twenty bucks says you won't go up to her and start a conversation," said Robert. He pulled out a crumpled twenty-dollar bill, smoothed it, licked it and pasted it to his forehead.

Red hesitated for a moment and then replied, "You're on, sucker." He left the bar and, catching the woman's eye, he flashed a smile. She looked at him with an icy stare and gave him a warning:

"Before you waste your time and do what I think you're gonna do," she said when he reached her table, "why don't you turn around and spare yourself the embarrassment." Red opened his mouth to respond but she interrupted. "I'm my own best company, thank you. Why don't you go back and hang out with your immature friends and collect the money pasted to that guy's forehead?"

"Your loss, sweetheart," Red told her, then turned and walked back to the guys. "She really wants me," he said.

Cosmo put his arm around his friend. "Don't worry. Once you pass the bar, you'll have women hanging all over you." He looked at Jeff and added, "Someone's gotta lend the guy support."

There was a smattering of applause as the band ended a Rolling Stones cover song.

"They're playing some really great music tonight," Robert commented.

Cosmo turned toward the band. "Yeah, I know the sax player. We were pals in a previous life. You know, my misspent youth."

At that moment, the band stopped playing and went on break. Cosmo waved to the saxman. At six foot two, with rugged good looks, he clearly stood out, even at the crowded bar. The musician motioned him over.

"He really knows that guy?" asked Red.

"Cosmo knows everybody," said Robert.

It wasn't long before Cosmo was onstage, singing along, in a jam session. Robert Turner and Red shook their heads in disbelief and put away another shot.

"The guy is unbelievable," said Robert.

"So, Jeff," asked Red, "what do you think of Livermore so far?"

"Well . . . I find the classes fascinating," Jeff responded.

Robert jumped in. "C'mon, cut the shit. You must be the first law student in history to find all your classes fascinating. Tell us what you really think. You can be straight with us."

Jeff thought for a moment, then answered honestly, "Okay. So far my first impression has been kind of mixed. I mean, some of the professors seem great in lecture, but after class, if you try to speak with them or ask a question, they're not very welcoming. It's confusing. At lecture, they seem to be inviting discourse and comments, but when the show's over, it doesn't seem they really care about the students."

"Well, that was a mouthful," responded Red.

"Too honest?" Jeff asked.

"Not at all," Robert jumped in. "Can't speak for Red, but I think you're a hundred percent right. I guess, in a perfect world, things would be much different, and they should be different. But you're gonna find that this whole experience—this law school experience—is really tough. I mean, really tough. So my long-term recommendation is, don't take it personally. Learn to just suck it up."

"And your short-term recommendation?" asked Jeff.

Robert smiled. "Have yourself another beer."

"You're right," responded Jeff. "Do me a favor—grab that bartender's attention. And by the way, thanks again."

"For what?"

"Well, I was getting a little depressed about whether I made the right choice to go to law school, but watching you in action renewed my hope. It looks like you love what you're doing."

Robert put his hand on Jeff's shoulder and leaned back against the bar. "Yes and no," he said. "I get a thrill out of arguing a case, but I tell you one thing I'm not looking forward to."

"What's that?"

"Corporations."

"Oh, shit," said Red. "I forgot we have Corporations tomorrow."

•••

The next morning, in another one of the large lecture halls at Livermore, the one hundred or so students who had Corporations made sure to get to class promptly. Not only did they want to avoid Professor Chessman's gaze of death, they also knew it wasn't a good idea to miss any notes on his lecture. There was a lot of chit-chat and conversation among the second and third year students until Chessman walked down the middle aisle of the lecture hall and went to stand behind the lectern. Then everyone fell silent.

Alberto chuckled softly when he saw Red, Molly and Robert Turner come in and go to great lengths to find seats somewhere in the middle of the hall, so as to be as inconspicuous as possible. None of them seemed to be in the mood to get called on today, and Jeff, who was auditing the class, wondered if it was because they were hung over from the night before. But Robert, he knew, would be locked, loaded and ready. Students who obviously enjoyed the attention from Professor Chessman sat at the front, and those who were slackers sat all the way at the back without realizing they were opening themselves up as targets. The middle was usually a wise choice.

Jacob Jefferson, whom many considered one of the most anal students at Livermore, consistently picked a seat in the first row. Highly intellectual, Jacob was a member of the Law Review. He was also an elitist wanna-be. As such, he would never forego an opportunity to kiss up to a professor. By contrast, Alberto Andreo was from one of the wealthiest families in New York and he found no need to be an elitist. He was confident and self-assured and didn't feel he had to prove himself so he took a spot near Robert and Red. He wasn't worried about Chessman calling on him; he almost always had the right answer or comment.

Red leaned over and whispered to Robert, "We better get a study group started as soon as possible. I know this guy's gonna be a real prick. His final will be brutal."

Chessman tapped on the lectern, calling the class to attention. Today the professor was wearing a bow tie, a blue shirt with a white collar (typical banker's attire), gold cufflinks, and a pair of suspenders that hugged his shoulders and pulled his trousers snugly about his waist, which had clearly expanded a few inches since he had purchased the suit.

"Welcome," the professor said. "It's good to see you all this morning." He picked up a piece of chalk and scratched something on the blackboard, then turned to address the class once more. "Arrogant," he continued. "It is spelled A-R-R-O-G-A-N-T, for those of you who didn't know. It has been one of the most frequently used, and may I add, misspelled, words to describe me on student course evaluations."

Tentative laughter moved throughout the lecture hall, and Chessman waited until it subsided before he went on. "I'm not saying whether it's accurate or inaccurate. I just want you to know how to spell it." There was another little pause. "So when you get the student course evaluations sometime during the next several weeks, I do not want to see the word misspelled ten to fifteen times, as I did last year."

There was dead silence, then Chessman laughed—and only Jacob joined him.

"Well, enough with the preliminaries," Chessman continued. "Let's get down to business." He took a quick glance at his student roster and picked the first name on the list. Alberto was almost always the first but this time, he was deep in conversation with the woman sitting next to him and didn't hear his name. Chessman waited a moment, then called again, a little louder. "Mr. Andreo? Alberto Andreo?" His tone became more forceful and impatient. "Is he present?"

"Here!"Alberto straightened up in his seat.

"It never ceases to amaze me how students in my class seem to think they're invisible," said Chessman. "Now, Mr. Andreo—thanks for joining in the conversation, by the way—am I to assume you have read the posted assignment?"

"My apologies, Professor," Alberto said smoothly. "I was out of the country. I arrived back in the States late last night. I wasn't able to do the reading."

The other students were stunned at his answer and Chessman took a step back from the dais. He briefly bowed his head, collecting himself. Then he straightened up and slowly surveyed the crowd. "Being unprepared is unacceptable," he warned them. "I have had students in the past who didn't take their reading assignments seriously. This is a problem—for you and for me. Perhaps when you leave these hallowed halls you'll bump into Livermore alumni who were in my classes. They will tell you that I prepare the most difficult final exam—every year—in all of Livermore Law Corporations history. It's a five-hour exam, but you'll have to complete it in three. I apply a challenging curve as well." He turned back to Alberto. "So, Mr. Andreo—I suggest you catch up on your reading." Then he smiled and addressed the entire class. "I hope we're not going to have a repetition of this incident. Okay, do we have any volunteers?"

In the front of the classroom Jacob's hand immediately shot up.

"Your name, sir," Chessman demanded.

"Jacob Jefferson."

"Okay, Mr. Jefferson. In Devon Inc. v. McMichael & Farmer Holdings, there was a promise by Devon to deal exclusively with Forrester Small in the face of a takeover battle, and a payment of a sixty-five-million-dollar cancellation fee to Forrester if the transaction was aborted. To facilitate this merger, the Devon board agreed to waive the financial covenants protecting the notes. The market value of the notes immediately dropped from one hundred and twenty dollars per share to fifty-seven-point-five dollars per share. Devon's board was threatened with litigation brought by the note holders. Do you think the Forrester option had a damaging effect on the auction process?"

There was a pause, then Jacob cleared his throat. "Interesting question, Professor Chessman," he said at last. "Under the circumstances, I must conclude that the merger agreement with Forrester was unreasonable in relation to the threat posed."

"Is that all, Mr. Jefferson?" the professor asked.

"No, sir—there's more. Lock-ups are not per se illegal under Texas law. Such actions can entice other bidders to enter a contest for control over a corporation, creating an auction for the company, thus maximizing shareholder profit. However, while those lock-ups will draw bidders into the battle to benefit shareholders, similar measures which end an active auction and foreclose further bidding operate to the shareholders' detriment."

Jaws dropped and Alberto was amused by the looks of disbelief on the faces of many students. They hadn't expected such a thorough answer. If someone took a poll, he thought, half them would say they admired Jacob for his meticulous preparation. The other half would simply want to strangle him. Well on his way to an A, Jacob made the rest of the class look like a bunch of idiots. It appeared he'd be able to take on anything Chessman threw at him.

When class was over and students were streaming out of the hall, Red stopped to shake Alberto's hand. "Congratulations," he joked. "That was a brilliant analysis of the course reading—I was out of the country and couldn't be bothered."

"Thanks," Alberto shot back, taking it in stride. "And fuck you."

Red laughed and Robert joined them. They all walked out together and went their separate ways when they reached the rows and rows of student mailboxes, which were actually racks and racks of hanging files containing manila folders. Jeff watched a moment, as Alberto leaned over to look in his folder and two petite hands reached up from behind to cover his eyes.

"Guess who?" she said.

"Well, let me see. I'm hoping . . . Julia Roberts or Nicole Kidman."

"Wrong," said Cassandra, her voice sexy and alluring. "Even better."

Alberto turned to greet her. "You're right. They've got nothing on you."

"You flatter me. Now back to the real world. Can you believe this professor? This is going to be a killer semester—all because of you, moron."

"Yeah, I know," he agreed. "But the way he treated me was totally unnecessary."

"Thank God I've got an awesome outline for his course," said Cassandra, smiling up at him.

Alberto's eyes lit up. "Are you serious? That's great! I'd like to take a look at it."

"I never said I was going to share it with anyone, especially not you," she teased. "You'll have to make it worth my while."

"Trying to be cute? You show me yours and I'll show you mine."

"Oh, now I'm really tempted to help you," said Cassandra, quickly clicking into sarcastic mode. "Why don't you come by my place in an hour and I'll give you a copy."

"Great. See you later."

Yeah, Jeff thought, Alberto Andreo has got to be the luckiest man alive. He let himself linger long enough to enjoy the sight of Cassandra's shapely backside moving away. He shook his head slowly, in appreciation. She really is amazing, he thought as he turned away and headed to his next class.

•••

Cassandra had it all and she knew it. And despite being one of the few Livermore students who had a social life worth writing home about, she was always on top of her game. She didn't try to pass herself off as a Livermore Law intellectual, as many students often tried to do. She could be down to earth and pretentious all at the same time, which Alberto considered sexy as hell. But regardless of the odds and whatever the challenge, Cassandra was always prepared. She really was a star student. There were few things she couldn't get or accomplish once she figured out what she wanted. If Monica were not perfect for him, especially with his family so in favor of the match, he would be tempted to see how far it could go with Cassandra.

Although the neighborhood immediately surrounding Livermore was not upscale and, in fact, could become somewhat unsafe depending on the hour, it was an exciting place to be. Sandwich shops, delis and coffeehouses were open around the clock for students up studying throughout the night. Small conveniences like twenty-four-hour copying and computer services were available. There were bars, movie houses, and every sort of take-out one could dream of, all within a subway stop or a short walk of the university.

Housing, on the other hand—Livermore student housing, that is—was not one of the pluses the university had to offer. Some of the buildings in the area dated back to the 1800s but were well kept with renovated and revamped interiors. Faculty and legal professionals occupied these spaces as they offered an air of classicism commensurate with one of the premier schools in all of academia. But the students' quarters were a bit rundown. The typical unit for a Livermore law student consisted of a small studio with a tiny bathroom and a kitchenette, if it could even be called that. These kitchenettes, separated from the rest of the studio by a sliding door, were often no more than a small stove with an overhead microwave connected to a tiny sink located in the closet.

Cassandra was a little more fortunate. She'd opted for a one-bedroom unit and, through the lottery system, was lucky enough to end up in one of the more modern buildings a block off campus. The doorman ushered Alberto in.

"She's expecting you, Mr. Andreo," he said with a smile. "You can go on up."

Alberto stepped out of the elevator and into the hallway. In the distance he could hear a shower running, and he thought it was coming from Cassandra's apartment. When he reached it he found the door slightly ajar. After knocking and receiving no response, he cautiously peered inside.

"Hello?" he called out. "Cassandra—you there?"

He heard the shower go off, then Cassandra called back, "I'll be with you in a minute. Come on in and make yourself comfortable."

Alberto entered the apartment and quietly closed the door behind him. He turned around to see Cassandra standing in the middle of the living room, wearing nothing but a towel. His heart skipped two beats. "Oh, it looks like you're busy," he said. "Want me to come back later?"

She walked slowly toward him. Moving close, she secured the towel more firmly around her bosom and replied, "No, don't be silly." She smiled up at him. "In fact, you're just in time." She reached up and started unbuttoning his shirt.

Alberto's first thought was that maybe he should grab her wrist or something, and stop her. He didn't need any complications in his life, and Monica would castrate him if she found out. But Cassandra was beautiful, and willing. He found he lacked the will to put up much resistance.

She went on unbuttoning his shirt. Pressing her soft lips against his neck, she kissed her way down to his chest as each button came undone. This is not cool, he thought. He had a girlfriend with whom he was very much in love, but he also knew he'd wanted this to happen since he'd first met Cassandra. The chemistry between them was always there, just simmering beneath the surface. It was inevitable.

An excited shiver raced down his spine. He reached for her to pull her close, but she turned around and walked toward the bathroom. As she entered, she released the towel and it dropped to the floor. Alberto took a step back.

Cassandra turned and smiled at him again, one hand on her bare hip, inviting him to look. Her breasts were firm and perfectly shaped. After what seemed like an eternity, she asked seductively, "Well . . . are you going to join me?"

Slowly Alberto followed her into the bathroom and closed the door. She was already inside the shower stall. Steam rose from behind the shower curtain and all the mirrors were fogged up. He scribbled his name on the mirror above the sink, and hesitated for a moment, wondering again if this was such a good idea. He had a girlfriend. And even though he found Cassandra incredibly attractive, she was one of his best friends at Livermore.

It's never good to fuck up a friendship with . . . well, fucking, he thought. But the sight of her naked, willing body had gotten to him. He quickly undid his belt, unzipped his pants and stepped out of them. When he'd removed all his clothes, he glanced in the full-length mirror hanging on the back of the door. For a moment he regretted that he hadn't been to the gym in over three weeks. He let out a small sigh of surrender.

"I'm waiting . . ." Cassandra called out.

"I'm coming in," he said.

For a moment they just stood there, facing each other in the shower with steam rising around them. Alberto positioned himself with his back facing the shower nozzle. The hot water pelted him, and it took him a moment to adjust to the heat. It was intense. It was also highly erotic. "Do you always shower in boiling water?" he asked huskily.

Cassandra reached up and draped her arms about his shoulders. He stared into her beautiful green eyes.

"I like the heat," she whispered in his ear, her voice low and seductive.

He put his hand on her chin and kissed her cheek, her ear, and then moved his tongue slightly between her lips. His arms around her waist, he kissed her, long and deep. She moaned with pleasure as he moved his right hand over her buttocks, then caressed the small of her back.

His arousal growing more intense, Alberto grasped her hair and pulled her head slightly back for another searing kiss. She lightly bit his neck, then reached up to take a bottle of fragrant body wash from the shower rack. Alberto took it from her and poured soap into his hands, which he then moved slowly, languidly, all over her body as the aroma of coconut and honey blossoms wafted around them. He started at her neck, massaging it, then moved on to her shoulders, her arms and her back.

Still behind her, he got down on his knees. Hot water bounced off Cassandra's back. Alberto paused for a moment to appreciate the view of her perfectly round behind, then he poured more soap into his hands and slowly caressed it. Reaching gently between her legs he washed her there, letting her press herself briefly against his palm before he moved on to massage her inner thigh, her legs and her feet. With his thumb he pressed on her heel, then the arch of her foot, and then he pulled softly on each toe individually. He repeated the same with her other foot, then stood and turned her around.

Again they were face to face. Alberto was tall and Cassandra barely reached his chin, even when on the tips of her toes. Turning her slowly under the water, he rinsed all the soap off her, then bent to kiss her breasts. She leaned back and closed her eyes, sighing with pleasure as his tongue moved from one breast to the other.

She pulled him to her for another kiss, then opened the shower curtain and led him into her bedroom. Neither of them bothered to shut the water off. She removed the comforter from her bed, lay down on top of the sheets and held her arms out to him. A strange feeling welled up inside him as he realized she was even more beautiful than Monica, in that moment. Monica's allure was dark and sultry, while Cassandra's was light, cool, classical, like a white marble statue of the goddess Aurora, enjoying the effect her beauty had on a man while holding herself slightly apart.

As he joined her on the bed, a few small drops of water fell onto her forehead. She laughed softly and opened her legs to him. He covered her mouth with his and thrust himself inside her. She dug her nails into his back and kissed his neck as he pressed deeper into her.

"Wait," she whispered, when he thought he could wait no longer. "It's best for me when I'm on top."

Alberto steadied his breathing and rolled over on his back. She got on top of him and closed her eyes. Placing her hands on his chest, she eased herself down onto his erection.

Alberto struggled with all of his might to maintain his concentration but nothing was working. No amount of thinking about World Cup soccer was going to help him today. With a shudder and a groan, he stopped trying, and it was over.

"Cassandra, I'm sorry."

"Oh . . . you didn't?" she responded. She sounded disappointed. "I was just about to," she added.

"Oh, man," he said. "I'm mortified. I promise I'll make it up to you."

"You better believe you will. We're not finished yet."

Alberto walked back into the bathroom and found his trousers immersed in a puddle of water. Reaching into his pants pocket, he pulled out his cigarettes. The box was wet, as well as most of the contents, but he found one that was viable.

"Ah, one smokeable stogie left," he said to himself. He went to her kitchenette, pulled back the sliding door that camouflaged it and started rifling through her cabinets.

From the bedroom Cassandra called out impatiently, "What are you looking for?"

Alberto appeared in the doorway to her bedroom with two wine glasses, a bottle of Merlot and a corkscrew, the cigarette dangling from his mouth. Cassandra laughed.

"What so funny?" he muttered, the cigarette bouncing up and down between his lips.

"Look at you! You look hysterical. There you are—butt-naked, opening a bottle of wine."

He took the cigarette from his lips and grinned at her. "Yeah—and?"

"You all right now?" she asked. "Recovered from whatever happened to you five minutes ago? You owe me one, you know."

Alberto poured their wine and handed Cassandra a glass. She put it on the table beside the bed, then reached out and took the bottle, which she placed next to it before she pulled Alberto forward to place a kiss on his lips.

"You coming back or what?" she asked.

"I just have a couple of more touches," Alberto said. He left her for a moment to lower the blinds against the afternoon sunlight. Next, he used his cigarette lighter to light a candle on the corner of her dresser. And then he rifled through her stack of CDs, found one he thought would reset the mood, and slid it into the player. "There, that makes it just about right," he continued, turning to enjoy again the sight of her. She looked adorable, tucked away under the sheets now, between the numerous pillows she kept on her bed. He took a final drag of his cigarette, swallowed his wine in one voracious gulp, and put his smoke out in the glass. Then he lowered himself to her, ready to settle his debt.

About twenty minutes later, they lay in bed in a perfect state of comfort and relaxation. With the bedroom shades down the room was dark, except for one candle illuminating the label of the half-empty bottle of wine.

"Well, aren't we off to a great start this year," he said. "I can't believe we've blown off most of our classes for the day."

"Yeah, but wasn't this a little more exciting than going to class?" asked Cassandra.

He responded with a chuckle. "No question about it. You're quite a bit more stimulating than any class I've ever had."

Alberto lifted his head from the pillow to look at the clock on her wall and a bolt of terror streaked through him. He was late and Monica was not going to be pleased. "Oh my God," he said. "I've gotta get out of here. I'm meeting Monica for dinner—with her parents."

"Seriously?" Cassandra seemed incredulous. "You're thinking about Monica after what we just did?"

"Hey, look," he said slowly. "Please don't take this the wrong way, but—I gotta go. I can't stand her up. Not tonight." Alberto rushed to the bathroom, grabbed his pants and scrambled to pull them on. Buttoning his shirt, he felt a moist patch in the seat of his pants, courtesy of the puddle he'd fished them from. Cassandra got out of bed and followed him, watching as he picked up one of his wet socks and squeezed the water out of it. He squirmed around her to get through the doorway and hurried back to the bedroom to look for his missing sock. "Ah, there it is!" He sat on the bed and leaned over to pull on his socks, then his shoes. Standing quickly, he started lacing his belt through the loops of his pants.

"You're a complete asshole, Alberto." Cassandra picked up one of the wine glasses and hurled it at him with all her might. The half-filled glass bounced off of his chest and crashed on the floor, leaving wine stains all over his white shirt and khaki pants.

"Dammit!" cried Alberto. "Now I have to go home and get changed." He strapped on his watch and stormed out of her apartment without a glance in her direction. Cassandra just stood there, a look of disbelief on her face.

•••

"You would think this young man would call if he's going to be late."

"Dad, this is totally unlike Alberto," Monica replied. "He's never late. I hope nothing's wrong."

"He should hope there's something wrong," added Monica's mother as she took a sip of her chardonnay. Monica looked at her in surprise. "Well, this is not making a favorable impression."

•••

Annoyed that he had forgotten to stop at the ATM for some cash, Alberto reached into his breast pocket where he kept his emergency ten-dollar bill. It would cover the cab fare, leaving only a quarter tip for the driver.

"Wow—thanks," the driver mumbled sarcastically. He sped off the instant his passenger closed the door. Alberto straightened his tie and rushed into the lobby to find a line of about fifteen people waiting in front of the elevator that would take them up to the fortieth floor, where Cabrezzi's was located. It was a posh restaurant, and although he'd managed to return to his apartment and change, he was not sporting his typically polished look. His straight black hair, always perfectly styled, was uncharacteristically out of place. He had pulled from his closet the first shirt he could lay his hands on—unfortunately not one of his fresh ones just come from the cleaners. Nonetheless, he was ready to make the best of the situation. He found it exhilarating when he had to fly by the seat of his pants.

Finally the bell went off as the elevator car arrived. The doors slid open and the operator beckoned the patrons to step in. Oblivious to the fact that he was making a spectacle of himself, Alberto pushed his way to the front of the line and stepped aboard the elevator as everyone else filed on board in sets of twos and threes. The attendant turned to Alberto and gave him an icy stare, which brought a grin to Alberto's face.

The entrance to Cabrezzi's was exquisitely decorated yet understated. An elegantly dressed hostess greeted customers as they entered and led them through curtains flowing gracefully from the breeze coming in off the terrace. The restaurant was open and airy with lots of marble columns and minimalist décor throughout. Although there was little furniture, every piece had its place and purpose.

The hostess led Alberto up a grand staircase, past the piano bar and through the main dining area where an amazing chandelier hung from the center of the room. Monica and her parents were seated on the terrace. It was autumn in New York, and a perfect night for a meal outdoors, high above the most amazing city in the world, with the lights of the skyscrapers as the backdrop.

"Sorry I'm late," said Alberto as he arrived at the table.

"Are you normally this prompt?" Monica's father asked, and Monica kicked at him under the table.

"I just had the worst cab ride of my life," Alberto responded. "The driver was an idiot—couldn't speak a word of English—and then he had no clue where the restaurant was." He aimed this last comment at Monica's mother, attempting to draw some sympathy from her. Alberto was a master at this kind of manipulation. He could usually turn a social situation into an opportunity to secure the kindness and affection of others.

"Oh, I know exactly what you mean," said Monica's mother agreeably. "That can be so frustrating."

"I would have been better off driving myself," Alberto said. "I must ask your indulgence a few more minutes—I still feel a bit rumpled." He excused himself to run to the men's room and clean up after his ordeal.

Alberto strode confidently through the restaurant, heading toward one of the side bars off the main dining area, where a waiter with whom he had grown friendly over the years was stationed. Rounding a table near the entrance, he almost collided with a large porcelain vase that held a monstrous bouquet of butterscotch chrysanthemums, peach spray roses and tiny burgundy carnations. Behind the table he knew he would see a familiar face.

"Hey, Mr. Alberto," Giovanni greeted him with a big bright smile. "How are you this evening?"

"Giovanni, can you do me a favor?"

"It would be my pleasure, sir."

"Send that table on the terrace a bottle of your best champagne. Put it on my tab."

Giovanni snapped to attention. "Of course."

"I'll be sure to get you later." Alberto continued on to the men's room where he combed his hair and straightened his tie. Then he went into one of the stalls at the very end of the line, reached into his jacket and pulled out his cell phone. He punched in Cassandra's number.

By this time she had settled herself in for an evening of studying and did not welcome any interruptions. She was sitting comfortably on her couch in a pair of shorts and a T-shirt, her reading glasses on and her hair tied up in a bun. The cordless phone rang once, twice, and just before the answering machine clicked on, she closed her textbook and leaned over to grab it. "Hello," she answered, annoyed.

"Ah . . . that is a classic Cassandra how-dare-you-annoy-me-when-I'm-studying voice." Have you cooled off yet?"

There was a long pause. "You've got balls," she said coldly. She could barely contain the anger she had bottled up over the past couple of hours. She vacillated between unleashing it without mercy on Alberto and just hanging up on the bastard. "You're having dinner with Monica and her parents and you decide to call me?"

"Hey, I felt bad, the way we left things." He sounded serious so she decided to hear him out. She remained silent and after a moment he continued, "So—you still pissed at me?"

"Yes!" she snapped.

"Well, you got your licks in." He emitted a small chuckle. "I don't like getting pelted with wine glasses."

"You think you're so funny. Instead of a wine glass, you deserve a sledge hammer."

"That's what my old college buddies used to call me—the hammer."

Cassandra could hear the laughter in his voice but she was not amused. "You are disgusting. Anyway, you certainly didn't live up to your reputation this afternoon."

"But you still think I'm cute, don't you?" queried Alberto. Again there was a long pause. She knew she should hang up, but he added, "What are you doing with the rest of this evening?"

"I'm going to the dean's cocktail party later."

"Isn't that just for first years?"

In her most biting sarcastic tone, Cassandra responded, "There are so many losers in the third year class I thought I might find myself a cute first year."

"Well, that's robbing the cradle."

"Go to hell."

"So when can I see you again?"

"As soon as you lose Monica and her folks and meet me at the dean's reception," she told him.

"Maybe I'll do that."

CHAPTER 5

Without Remorse

The elderly gray-haired woman sat hunched over in her seat, as if preparing to assume the emergency crash position. One of the flight attendants noticed and rushed over to her, gently placing her hand upon the old woman's shoulder.

"Are you okay?" she asked with a deep sense of concern. "Can I get you anything?"

Marialena raised her head, smiled at the attendant and with a thick Spanish accent uttered the words, "Si, si—yo bien . . . I okay." This was all she could manage.

For a moment her eyes remained fixed upon the flight attendant, and the young woman felt the intensity of the stare. There was sincerity in the old woman's eyes, beneath which were deep, dark ridges, indicating an existence plagued by hardship.

"All right," said the attendant. "But if you need something, you press this button." She showed Marialena where the call switch was. "I'll come back right away."

"Tank you—gracias," the old woman said, and repeated, "Yo bien . . . okay. Okay fine."

Flight 1124 from Caracas, Venezuela, to JFK International Airport was due to arrive on schedule within the next twenty-seven minutes and with each one, Marialena became more uneasy, changing positions in her coach-class seat as she tried to find relief from the pain assaulting her belly.

With ten minutes left before touchdown, the pilot signaled the flight attendants to prepare for arrival. He put the landing gear down, reduced airspeed and positioned the plane for final approach. As the tires hit the tarmac the retro engines fired up, bringing the 747 jumbo jet to a smooth stop. They were now safely on the ground and taxiing to their assigned gate.

When they got there, Marialena grabbed the back of the seat in front of her and unsteadily pulled herself up. The flight attendant started moving toward her but the old woman waved her away.

"Okay," she said again. "Bien, bien . . . okay."

The passenger in the seat behind her reached into the overhead compartment and pulled out her two small bags, which he insisted on carrying out of the plane for her. On the jetway, a gate agent offered her a wheelchair but she refused such a luxury. Instead she opted for a walker and delicately made her way into the airport and to the long line at customs.

The kind passenger who had volunteered his assistance with her bags took his place in line while his wife took Marialena's luggage to the front and informed the agents she wasn't feeling well. Uncharacteristic of the bureaucracy at most major international airports, the customs officials quickly attended to Marialena, whisking her through without searching or questioning her. They merely stamped her passport and welcomed her to the United States of America.

Overwhelmed by their kindness and the ease with which she entered *Gigante el Norte* (the Giant to the North), a teardrop emerged from the corner of her eye, rolled down her cheek and came to rest on her upper lip. She stopped, pulled out a handkerchief and dried her eyes, and then she made the sign of the cross with her right hand. Marialena had safely completed her journey undetected. And with the precious cargo she carried, she could win freedom for her two sons who were falsely imprisoned—for life—back in her homeland. She owed God many thanks.

A bearded man approached her, with a shorter man right behind him. "Marialena?" he asked.

"Si," she responded. "Tu es Señor Mitch?"

"That's me," he said cheerfully. "This here's my friend Vick. We've got a car waiting."

•••

The chill of winter had not set in, yet the bearded man—Mitch—wore a long leather trench coat. As he bent over to pick up her bags, she rested her arm on his shoulder. He turned and looked up at her, and she tenderly stroked his face with her soft, wrinkled hands. "Gracias, mi hijo," she said.

"What'd she say?" asked Vick.

"That means thank you in Spanish, Vick. Don't you know anything?"

"Fuck you, Mitch."

"Watch your mouth, you idiot," responded Mitch with a light slap to the back of Vick's neck. "There's a lady present."

"She don't understand English anyway."

They made their way through the revolving doors and went outside where a shiny new Lincoln Continental, with a tiny chip in the taillight and New York vanity plate that read DMAN-007, sat waiting for them. Its engine was running, with an airline baggage attendant looking on.

"Thanks for keeping an eye out, guy," Mitch told him and handed him a hundred dollar bill. He climbed into the driver's seat. Vick put Marialena's luggage in the trunk and helped her into the back seat, then slid in beside her.

As they exited the airport grounds, heading for the highway, Mitch eased off on the gas and went slowly over a series of speed bumps. With each one, Marialena became more distressed. Drops of perspiration trickled down her forehead, and the palms of her hands became cold and clammy.

"Hey, man, turn up the AC," said Vick. "This woman needs some air."

"I already got it on full blast," Mitch responded.

Marialena leaned forward and grabbed Vick's knee. He patted her arm, trying to comfort her. In a strange sort of way, she reminded him of his own mother, who had passed away several years earlier. "She's sick, man," he said. "I think we gotta take her to the hospital."

"Aw, fuck," Mitch said. "She heaving in my back seat?"

"Never mind your back seat." Now Vick was really worried. "One of the bags must have busted in her belly. I think we gotta get her to a hospital."

"Are you outta your mind? The first thing they're gonna do is pump her stomach. They find fifteen condoms full of coke and we're fucked."

"Then we gotta get her a doctor," Vick insisted. "Don't worry, I know some people."

"You don't worry. I'll take care of this."

"How? What're you gonna do?"

"Whatever I have to," Mitch muttered. "And that'll be the end of the problem."

In the back seat, Marialena writhed in pain. She threw up but none of the cocaine packets emerged. Uttering the names of her children, she fell unconscious.

"Thank God—she finally shut the fuck up," mused Mitch from the front seat. He smiled and looked at Vick in the rear view mirror. "Make sure no one sees her. Keep her head down."

"She's fuckin' unconscious, for Chrissake," Vick replied. "She ain't gonna be poppin' up for anyone to see."

Approximately an hour later, the three arrived at a rundown motel in Queens. It was the kind of motel where the clientele could rent a room by the hour. Mitch walked in and shook hands with the desk clerk. Then, with a circular wave, he signaled Vick who jumped into the front seat and moved the car around back.

Mitch pressed a hundred dollar bill into the eager desk clerk's hand, then walked back to the rear entrance. It led directly to the basement. "Get her outta there," he told Vick, who was gently wrapping the old woman in a blanket. "I'll get her stuff."

Vick lifted Marialena up on over his shoulder and he and Mitch made their way downstairs and placed her on a makeshift mat of old cardboard boxes. Vick leaned over and unwrapped the elderly woman. "She's still breathing—barely," he said hopefully. "If we act now, maybe we can save her life."

"I'm on it." Mitch pulled out his cell phone and tapped in a number. "Hey, Jerry, this is Mitch," he said when someone picked up on the other end. "Yeah—I'm at the place. You know where I can find a fuckin' scalpel?"

Vick knew better than to plead for the woman's life. He might find himself pleading for his own if he made that mistake. Instead he made the sign of the cross upon the old woman's forehead, then stood up. The ultimate act of hypocrisy, he thought. Mitch had offed people before, and not once had it fazed him. Vick knew, when he'd signed up, that he'd be expected to do some things he didn't want to do—and he was a stand-up guy so he did them, even when it bothered him. It was different with his partner. Life or death, it really didn't make much of a difference to Mitch as long as he was getting paid. There wasn't a shred of good left in Mitch's stone-cold heart. Vick stepped aside to let him work.

Amidst the old crates and boxes, Mitch found a plastic bag containing an assortment of nuts and bolts and rusted nails. He emptied the bag and placed it over the old woman's head. After securing it with a tight knot he put pressure on her neck, to speed the process along. She struggled briefly, and then it was done.

"See," he said, a note of pride in his voice, "this way, if her body's found, the cause of death won't be quite as obvious."

"What about the coke, man?" Vick asked. "Won't they find—"

"Yeah," Mitch interrupted impatiently. "They'll find traces in her bloodstream and stomach lining. So we gotta make sure they don't find her. I gotta think."

He let go of the plastic bag and when the old woman remained still and silent, he reached into his breast pocket, pulled out another Marlboro and waved it at Vick. Vick pulled out his lighter and held the flame to the cigarette. Mitch inhaled deeply, getting as much of the smoke as possible into his lungs. Breathing out with force, he pushed the smoke through his nostrils.

"Okay—we gotta get the coke out of her stomach, preferably without making a mess," he said. "But I don't see we have a choice."

"Then what?" asked Vick.

Mitch considered for a moment. "We have our usual options. There's a lot of construction sites all over Brooklyn and Queens. Take 'em about a hundred years to uncover her—after they knock down a building."

"What about that undertaker you got a deal with?" Vick asked. "Wouldn't it be quicker to put her in one of those unmarked graves the city uses? You know—for the homeless who croak with no i.d. on 'em?"

Mitch glanced at Marialena, then looked up at Vick and nodded. "We could do that, no problem, no questions asked. The city of New York has no fucking clue of half the shit that's going on. Only drawback is, if something was to go wrong, the undertaker would have to be disappeared. It's just another complication. I'm not fond of complications." His cell phone rang in his jacket, muffled by the leather and barely audible. He reached into his pocket, grabbed it and tossed it over to Vick. "You answer. I got a headache."

Vick flipped open the phone and put it to his ear. It was Jerry. Vick listened for a moment, then told him to hold on. "Okay," he said to Mitch. "Jerry's already followed up with that medical student he's got on retainer. Bottom line is, we gotta open her up."

"He's fuckin' useless!" Mitch exclaimed. "I don't know why I pay him anymore." He motioned for Vick to give him the phone. "With what, Jerry?" he demanded. "My fuckin' Boy Scout pocket knife?"

"Gimme about forty-five minutes," Jerry said. "I'll be there with a scalpel. Don't worry—we'll get the shit."

Mitch hit the End button on his phone. "He's coming."

"You sure?" asked Vick.

"Yeah, I'm sure." Everyone who worked with Mitch was prompt—always. "If someone's not on time, there's a problem," was his philosophy, on which he readily expounded. "You know someone's in trouble. Either you're being set up, your friend is being whacked, or you're gonna get whacked."

Jerry arrived exactly forty-two minutes later. He put on a pair of plastic gloves and from a linen towel unrolled a set of shiny silver medical implements, all sharper than a shark's tooth. He picked up the longest knife, then undid the buttons on the old woman's cheap, bright yellow dress, which he tossed into the corner of the room. "I don't know what's gonna make me more sick, cutting her open or looking at her wrinkled old body."

"Hey, Jerry?" said Vick.

"Yeah?" responded Jerry, turning to look at him, then at Mitch. He seemed a bit bewildered. "You gonna let him interrupt me now, just as I'm about to get started?"

"She ain't goin' anywhere," said Mitch. "Vick, you got a question?"

"Yeah—didn't she have a couple of sons back in South America?"

"So what?" said Jerry. "They're in the can down there and they won't be getting out any time soon. You don't have to worry about them."

"So, didn't she smuggle the shit into the country in order to spring these guys? These kids of hers?"

"Again—so what?" Jerry made his first incision in the old woman's abdomen. The sharp shiny blade of the scalpel pierced her skin and there was blood. In order to turn a profit, there was always blood.

Vick lit up a cigarette. "Hey, you don't have to cut such a big hole in her, do you? Only big enough to fit your hand in there."

Jerry put the scalpel down and pried apart the layers of skin and muscle before reaching in, first with two fingers, then his entire left hand. "I think I got something."

"What? I bet you're gonna pull a ham sandwich outta there," said Mitch, a smirk on his face. It bothered Vick that his partner was amused by such a spectacle.

One by one Jerry plucked the balloon packets from Marialena's stomach and placed them beside her corpse. He stopped for a moment and turned to Vick.

"What's your problem, Vick?"

"What are you talking about?" asked Vick.

"What do you give a shit whether this old bag's got kids or not?" demanded Mitch. "Or whether they're in prison? Who gives a shit? Is there something we don't know? Was this old lady your secret squeeze or something?"

"I was just–" Vick tried to respond but Jerry cut him off in midsentence.

"Her sons can rot in hell for all I care. What—you getting' soft, Vick?"

"But come on—don't it bother you a little? I mean, this woman was robbed—robbed of her dignity, robbed of her dream of gettin' her sons outta prison, robbed of her last rites and a proper burial."

Jerry scoffed and gave him a look of contempt, then went back to work.

"Hey, Jerry, I apologize," Mitch said. "Don't let this get out. I ain't ever seen Vick act like a retard like this."

"Okay, it's done." Jerry straightened up and pulled a rag from his pocket, with which he wiped his scalpel clean. "I got it all. You guys gotta clean up all this shit. Hey, you hungry? Anybody in the mood for a pizza?"

"You know what?" said Mitch. "I tell you what. A pizza with everything sounds good, but I'd rather clean up, and then sit down for a full meal. And we can either do Italian or maybe some Chinese, whatever your preference. What do you say, Jerry?"

"Sounds good."

"You guys go ahead," said Vick. "I'll clean up here."

"Bring you somethin'?" asked Mitch

"Nah—I'm not hungry."

From the storage closets in the basement, Vick grabbed a couple of industrial size plastic bags—the kind used by sanitation and demolition guys at construction sites. He pulled one over Marialena's head. The other, he pulled up over her legs. Silently he picked up her garments and placed them in the bag with her body, along with the flattened, blood-soaked cardboard boxes. Then he used heavy electrical tape to seal it all in plastic.

In the closet he also found ammonia and a mop and bucket. He filled the bucket with water, added a good amount of ammonia and got rid of the blood on the concrete floor.

Mitch returned without Jerry. He had decided they would deposit the body on the grounds of an abandoned mine several miles outside of Ithaca, New York. Vick sighed but said nothing. He was in for a long night: a four-and-a-half-hour drive, a couple of hours of pick-and-shovel work, and then the return trip.

"We good to go?" asked Mitch. Vick nodded. "Okay—let's do it."

Vick picked up the old woman, hoisted her gently over his shoulder and carried her upstairs. He eased his burden down next to the back door, then went outside and walked over to a van parked nearby, which he slowly backed over to the door. When Mitch opened it, Vick went to give him a hand with the body. By this time dusk had settled in and traffic around the motel was picking up but no one seemed to notice two men carrying an oversized plastic garbage bag.

Marialena couldn't have weighed more than a hundred pounds, but for some reason her lifeless corpse felt like it weighed over two hundred. Together, he and Mitch lifted her, and Vick groaned under the weight. They dropped her in the back of the van like a sack of potatoes. The body crashed onto the metal bed, causing the vehicle to bounce ever so slightly. Vick got behind the wheel again.

"Heading north, right?" he asked.

"Not this time," said Mitch. "I think it would be best to head west into Pennsylvania, out to about Scranton. Then we go north. I've never been stopped in Pennsylvania. I don't want to deal with the New York Highway Patrol."

•••

Idly, during the drive, Mitch wondered how he had come to this. He was a plumber by trade. Years ago he'd started as an apprentice to his uncle, who had built up a prosperous plumbing business in Flushing, Queens. As a young man, however, the prospect of installing pipes and clearing sewer drains for the rest of his life was not terribly appealing. Initially he was attracted to the glamour that surrounded the wise guys in his neighborhood. They always got respect. They had wads of money. And best of all, they always got the prettiest girls. He loved to be around them. Now he was icing old ladies and digging graves in out-of-the-way places. If he had just stuck with his uncle, maybe by now he would have taken over the business, maybe even expanded it and moved into plumbing supplies.

But it was inevitable that he got mixed up with creatures of the underworld. He was on a job one day, installing piping for a new condominium complex. That's when he ran into Jerry Ragusa. They hit it off, right off the bat. Jerry told him he knew of an easier way to make money—not this nine-to-five bullshit with a couple of extra bucks for overtime. Jerry was always so confident and cocky. There was nothing that could make him flinch. He was a tough guy through and through.

At first, when they began working for the organization, it really looked like Jerry was going places. But now, years later, he was still nothing more than a foot soldier. Mitch, on the other hand—it was understood from the beginning—could never be more than a foot soldier. For one thing, he wasn't Italian. Being of German-Irish descent, there was only so far he could go, and he would have to be content with that.

It also didn't help Jerry that he had a reputation for not being terribly swift upstairs. No question he would always get the job done, but he didn't earn the nickname, Blackjack, for nothing. He would drop anything to pay a visit to the casino, even missing his mother's funeral because no one could locate him for four days. He was on one of his gambling binges in Vegas.

"You know," Mitch said, glancing at Vick behind the wheel. "The world's a changed place now. And the organization, trying to survive, has made every effort to adapt."

Vick sighed. He sounded tired. "What're you getting at?"

"Think about it. There's not much room for foot soldiers like you and me, and Jerry. We're still relegated to the bottom rung."

"Yeah—so?"

"And that's it, man. That's all it'll ever be—grunt work."

Vick shrugged indifferently. "What're you gonna do? We ain't changin' the system."

"Because nowadays Wall Street is involved," Mitch said. "That means the days of straight narcotics smuggling and dealing are over. 'Cause these Wall Street wise guys are developing all these sophisticated money games—

that's where the action is now. And they need lawyers and accountants and bankers to help them."

"That's why we're here in this van driving out to no-man's land to bury this innocent old lady?" asked Vick.

"That's what I'm saying," said Mitch. "They think we're useless, not good enough to do anything else."

Vick was silent a moment, then he shrugged again. "Yeah, well—they're probably right. About me, anyway. I'm too old to be startin' anything else."

Mitch quickly scanned through the years of his life, searching for some meaning to his existence. Anything to bring him some brief comfort.

"It hasn't been all bad," he concluded. "I've seen the world, made some cash, got laid on a regular basis, and best of all, I've been able to take out most of my enemies. The emperors of old were plenty content with just that. Who am I kiddin'?" He smiled. "So yeah, Vick—me too. I'm perfect for this line of work. It suits me just fine." He straightened in his seat and took a deep, cleansing breath to wake himself up. "Where the fuck are we, anyway? We been driving for like, two and a half hours."

"About fifteen miles outside of Scranton, near as I can figure," said Vick.

"Okay, then. At Scranton, we head north toward Syracuse."

"Traffic's been light all the way."

"Yeah—it's going smoother than I expected."

"So, ah—" Vick paused as if searching for the right words. "No disrespect for the old lady, but—um—how'd we do?"

"Well, there was no witness saw her at the airport, so no worries there. We lost only one bag. Out of the fourteen recovered we get, say . . . four bags. That's about thirty percent, give or take. So you, me and Jerry, we each get the proceeds from one and a third bags. Not bad for a night's work, hey?"

"Not bad," Vick agreed. "I can't wait 'til this is over so I can catch some rest. You want to get a motel in Syracuse after, and stay the night?"

"Nah—I want to head back. Sooner we turn over the product, sooner we make some cash."

For a moment, Vick took his eyes off the road to glance in the rearview mirror. He saw lights in the distance. "Shit, my goddamn luck—there's no other cars on the road. He's coming for us."

The police cruiser closed the distance between them, its bright headlights illuminating the interior of the van. Vick slowed the van, pulled over and stopped.

"What now?" he asked.

"Got my gun under the seat," said Mitch. "It would be easy. Crack the door, aim and fire. I could take him out before he can reach for his."

"Maybe he called for backup already," suggested Vick.

"Maybe," Mitch agreed. "Anyway, somebody might pass by, and a lotta people got cell phones now. So—not this time. We're gonna have to trust our luck."

The cop stepped out of the cruiser and lumbered slowly over to the van. He was a big man, and cautious as well. His hand on his gun, he leaned over and flashed the light directly into Vick's eyes. He was built like a Roman gladiator. And in his highway patrolman uniform with the high, heavy leather boots, deep-blue shirt and heavy utility belt, he could almost intimidate someone like Mitch—almost.

"Could I see your license and registration, sir?" He was one of those official-sounding officers with a deep voice and polite manners.

Vick, who kept a particular license for moments like these, was well prepared. Clipped to it was a shiny brand-new Police Benevolent Association card. The officer took the items and returned to his cruiser.

"Let's don't fuck around with this guy," said Mitch. "Lot of wise guys been hammered getting loud with the cops. It's a sure-fire way to get your ass thrown in prison. Be cool. Be polite."

"That's gonna work?" Vick sounded worried.

"All it takes is some yes, sir and no, sir and my apologies, officer, and we'll be on our merry way—so long as we're not dealing with a prick."

Mitch was a little worried, too. He knew he had a face that spelled trouble. His friends didn't call him the dark man for nothing. It wasn't that he was dark per se—it was his overall demeanor. Mitch looked like the kind of guy who would be lurking in the shadows waiting for an unsuspecting victim. He thought it was silly. He wasn't a vampire. He just had a face that drew a lot of suspicion.

The police officer returned. "Sir, have you had any drinks this evening?"

"No, officer, I haven't been drinking," Vick responded.

"Whose vehicle is this? Your name doesn't appear on the registration."

"I borrowed the van from one of my friends. I'm just heading up to Scranton to see my girlfriend."

"And this guy?" The officer nodded at Mitch.

"Same thing," Mitch said. "His girlfriend—she's my sister."

The officer flashed his light in Vick's eyes again. "Where'd you get the PBA card?"

"Same friend, officer. My buddy's older brother's with the NYPD. He's a detective."

The officer could see the bag in the back of the van, but didn't bother to question its contents. He handed Vick's license and registration back. "All right, sir. You're good to go," he said. "Thank you. Have a nice evening. Drive safely."

•••

Vick was now frustrated and thoroughly and annoyed. After two hours of digging, he had removed a sufficient amount of earth to allow him to stand hip-deep in the hole. All of the previous remorse he had felt for the old woman was now gone. He now despised her. He was fucking, dead-beat tired. What's more, the soft earth now gave way to impregnable stone. He leaned outside of the hole to reach for the pickaxe. Beside him, Mitch used his shovel to beat relentlessly on the rock, but to no avail.

"That's it," Mitch said. "I'm done. Into the hole, Grandma." He climbed out of the makeshift grave and gave Vick a hand up. Together they lifted Marialena's body and dumped it unceremoniously into the rough cavity they had created. "Get the kerosene," he ordered.

When Vick came back from the car with the can, Mitch poured kerosene over the body and lit a match. They watched it burn for about ten minutes, just enough to make it unrecognizable. They had to be careful not to let it get out of control or all their work would be for naught. They were miles from any residential area, but the smoke could give them away, and there were eyes. No matter how isolated you thought you might be, there were always eyes.

The smoke rising from the hole was thick, and the smell of the burning plastic was toxic. Mitch started to cough as the fumes began to choke him. He turned his face from the flames and gasped for air. "That's enough," he said, when he got the coughing tamped down. "Let's finish this."

Working feverishly they shoveled all the dirt and clay back into the hole. Once the flames were smothered, Mitch poked at the charred mess with a makeshift lance he had constructed with a pocket knife, a tree branch and some electrical tape. He found her face, what was left of it, and was satisfied that the identity of the corpse and the horrible story that accompanied her grisly murder would forever remain a mystery.

"Let's get outta here," he told Vick, who was looking at him like he was some kind of monster. He didn't care. He was too fucking tired to care. Together, they filled in the grave, collected their tools and placed them in the van. Mitch was satisfied. Having accomplished his mission, he was now ready for the long drive home.

CHAPTER 6

The Dean's Reception

Early in the fall, Dean Langhorne started his annual series of receptions at his spacious apartment on Manhattan's fashionable Upper West Side. *It's funny,* Jeff thought. *As you go up the chain of command in the typical law school faculty or administration, the more arrogant individuals you seem to find.*

Strangely enough, this was not the case with Dean Longhorne. In his brief encounters with the man, Jeff had found him to be, by far, one of the most gregarious, amicable members of the law school faculty. In spite of his lofty position, he had a warm personality and went out of his way to engage each and every one of his students as an individual. In addition to participating in the usual functions of a law school dean—namely, fund raising—he seemed sincere about addressing the problems of his students.

Perhaps, Jeff mused, *that's why he's successful at both.* Longhorne was also charming and intelligent. Jeff had read a direct quote attributed to him in a newspaper interview, and it had stayed with him—another reason he'd chosen Livermore:

"In the in the environment of academia," Dean Langhorne had said, "it is always important to be an intellect, but the loss of humanity to achieve that end is an unacceptable tragedy."

So Langhorne sponsored these events at his home, it seemed, because he really cared, and they regularly attracted hundreds of students and their guests.

As Jeff entered the lobby of the elegant pre-war building, the doorman directed him to the elevator banks on the left. It wasn't exactly Jeff's taste, but the building had a feeling of old world opulence. Coming from a blue-collar environment where everything from his home to his high school looked like a worn antique, he preferred modern architecture that was new and fresh. It was a carryover from his desire to part with everything in his old life and move on, to try for something better, and succeed. Still, it was a stylish structure that spoke of wealth and comfort. He took a deep breath as he pressed the elevator button. He wondered if his new friends would be there, like Robert Turner, Red and Alberto—and Cassandra, who probably wouldn't give a first-year a second look. He forced his thoughts elsewhere.

It amused Jeff to hear other students, when they were stressed out over tests or assignments, wish they were back in their younger days, when they had no cares and not a worry in the world. For Jeff it was different. He could never recall a moment when he yearned for the uncomplicated existence of childhood. He'd always felt his ideal could be found in the future. As a youngster his reality, thanks to his mom, was warm and satisfying and created many cherished memories. Still, his happiness lay in forging his way ahead through whatever new adventures life threw at him. And law school was definitely proving to be an adventure.

The elevator opened to a hallway that led to the dean's front door, which was already full of students and faculty members milling about. Some had just gotten off the elevator and were waiting to enter, while others were on their way downstairs. The door opened and a man dressed in a tuxedo and carrying a serving tray greeted the crowd. "Welcome, welcome," he said. "If you'd like to take off your jackets, you can leave them with the attendant in the room to the left. And please make yourselves at home in the study or the living room."

The crowd of guests pressed forward and moved straight ahead. The dean's master study was a large, spacious room decorated in a fashion one would expect from the dean of one of the most prestigious law schools in the country. The walls were wood paneling, lined with shelves spilling over with tome after tome of legal literature. Aside from the extensive library, what Jeff found most interesting was the eighteen-foot ceiling and the scarcity of furniture. Law school professor types (and lawyers like his Uncle Murray) typically had cluttered offices, homes and lives in general. It was the lack of furniture in the dean's study that created this availability of space, and space, most of all, was what appealed to Jeff. Having come from a home where, for a good part of his young life, he had to share a bedroom with his older brother, space was one of those small luxuries he'd always craved. Now he and his cat Yankee shared a small apartment in the Morningside Heights section of Harlem—too far uptown to be fashionable and too small for entertaining. Having a place close to Livermore was the only way Jeff could be sure of making it to his classes on time.

One of the tuxedo-clad waiters approached Jeff and offered him a glass of champagne, which he gladly accepted, hoping to calm his nerves. Another waiter came into the room bearing a large tray of delicious looking hors d'oeuvres.

Exquisite, Jeff thought as he bit into a piece of salmon embellished with some kind of sauce and lying on a thin strip of crispy toast. He washed it down with a sip of champagne, then quickly scanned the room for a familiar face.

There were dozens of professors in attendance. Some he recognized; others he had merely heard of. He noticed a few attractive women but none he would go out of his way to meet.

At that moment, his eyes locked on a vision of feminine perfection. Cassandra stood in the middle of the large room, well aware she was the center of attention. He watched as she sipped from her wine glass and looked impatiently at her watch, as if waiting for someone, anyone, to save her from the fool who was trying to chat her up. Even from a distance, Jeff could see he was completely oblivious to the fact that she was trying to make an escape. Working his way toward her, Jeff heard her excuse herself to go and find the bathroom. But instead of the quick getaway, she backed right into Robert Turner, who in turn backed into Dean Langhorne, splashing red wine all over his crisp white shirt and blue bow tie.

In this, Jeff saw his opportunity. He reached over to one of the waiters, grabbed a stack of napkins and hurried to the dean. "Dean Langhorne," he said, catching the dean's attention and offering the napkins.

Before Langhorne could reach for them, Cassandra and Robert snatched the napkins from Jeff's outstretched hand and started patting down the dean.

"I am so mortified, Dean Langhorne. I'm so sorry." Cassandra repeated her apology four times in succession before the man was able to wave her and Robert off.

"These things happen," he said. "Don't worry. Excuse me—I'll just go and clean up. Not a problem."

Cassandra and Robert stood there speechless and terribly embarrassed. "I suppose this is the last time we'll be invited here," said Cassandra, a slow grin spreading across her face.

Robert shook his head in disbelief, then turned to Jeff. "Hey, man— thanks for the quick save."

"Always glad to lend a hand," Jeff responded. "Or in his case, maybe a little stain remover."

Robert shook his head again. "What a disaster," he said. He gestured to the vision standing beside him. "Anyhow, Cassandra Winslow—meet Jeff."

"Hi," she said sweetly, extending her hand.

Jeff took it and replied, "We've met—sort of—a few nights ago at Dead Authors. But there was a lot going on, so you might not remember."

"I remember," she said softly.

"Tell him about yourself, Cass," Robert said. "I've never known you to hold back with fresh prey. But be kind—he's new."

"Of course," Cassandra said smoothly. "I'm a third year at Livermore, like Robert. Unlike Robert, I'm a total, uncoordinated klutz."

"Not at all," Jeff replied. "I'm first year—I just started at Livermore. It looks like things are even more exciting here than I expected. What do you guys do for an encore?"

"Well," Cassandra said, "since I knocked Robert's drink out of his hand, and since we're standing here attracting even more attention, why don't we all disappear into another room? After I grab some more wine."

When they'd all refreshed their drinks and slipped into the dining room, Robert laughed. "Hey, look—the gang's all here," he said and called out, "Hey—Molly!" Then he said to Jeff and Cassandra, "Those clowns over there are my friends. Come on, you guys. Let me introduce you." He gently placed his arm around Cassandra's waist and steered her in their direction. Glad to be included, Jeff followed.

"No introduction necessary," said Molly as they approached. "Not with Cassandra, anyway." Cassandra's eyes lit up when she saw them, and Molly gave her a welcoming hug.

"But you haven't met the rest of the bozos," Robert put in. "Cassandra, Jeff—this is Cosmo."

"Hey, Cassandra," Cosmo greeted her. "Nice to meet you."

Jeff noticed the subtle wink Molly directed at Cassandra when she added, "You might want to take special note of Cosmo. He's the number one, most eligible third-year bachelor on campus."

From the appreciative look Molly gave Cosmo, Jeff surmised she wouldn't turn down an opportunity to jump all over him herself. Molly, he decided, was the social butterfly of Livermore. She continued to move them around the dining room table, placing a hand on the shoulder of each and every person she introduced. When she was done, she said, "Now, Cassandra—someone just told me you almost got Robert expelled from Livermore. Give it up, girl. Is this true?"

"A slight exaggeration," Cassandra responded.

"Oh, no," Molly said. "This is a story I want to hear—if not now, soon." Then she switched gears. "Can someone find me a corkscrew?" she demanded.

"Uh-oh," said Robert, as she went off to the kitchen in search of one. "Molly's on a rampage. When you mix alcohol and Molly, you've got a sure formula for a spectacle."

"Maybe I'll go and help her look," Jeff said. He felt he was getting a little lost amongst these upperclassmen, so he thought it best to make himself useful. In one of the kitchen drawers, he discovered a corkscrew. "I've got what you want, Molly," he announced.

She looked him up and down for a moment, as if considering. "Maybe," she said. "But in the meantime, you've got what I need. And you are pretty cute for a first-year. I might get arrested for seducing you, but you're damn cute."

She took Jeff's arm and handed him the bottle as they went back to Robert and the others.

At that moment, one of the Livermore professors passed by the dining room. "Quick, close the door!" Cosmo said. "The last thing I need is Professor Davis coming in here."

Molly hurried to the door and closed it. Returning to the group, she said, "So, Cosmo—what's up with you and Davis?"

"All right—look. His wife is a senior partner at the firm I worked at this summer. It was so funny. The firm threw a Fourth of July bash and she brought him along. I swear, for a guy who knows everyone on the Supreme Court, his fashion sense is sorely lacking. No one ever taught him how to color-coordinate. I mean, it was ridiculous. When I saw him, I burst out laughing and made some remark—under my breath of course. Only I think he heard me. Then I found out who he was."

"Oh, that's nothing," said Molly. "I thought you were going to say you were sleeping with his wife."

"Not in this lifetime," Cosmo said. "Why would I? Not much of a looker, and she's a bit of a witch." Jeff noticed the glance of appreciation he gave Molly.

"Why wouldn't you?" quipped Cassandra. "At my firm, the paralegals are sleeping with the associates, the associates are sleeping with the partners, and the secretaries are screwing everybody."

That information really grabbed Red's attention. "What did you say is the name of your firm?" he asked.

"I was at Madden, Karp and Simpson," replied Cassandra. Red quickly reached into his breast pocket and pulled out a ballpoint pen, with which he scribbled the name on a paper napkin. Next to the name, he penned five stars. Cassandra looked up at Robert. "Where did you spend your summer, Robert?"

"Oh, no place consequential, he said casually. "Just the office of the United States Attorney. What about you, Molly?"

"Well," replied Molly, "I was on a margarita tour that my firm sponsored."

"Margarita tour? What's that?" queried Red.

"It's a tradition at Berman and Stinner. It goes back at least ten years. It got pretty wild last year so I don't think they're going to do it anymore.

Someone wrote an editorial in some legal journal that firms shouldn't be sponsoring public debauchery."

Red threw up his arms in exasperation. "They might as well take all the fun out of life. So what is this margarita tour?"

"You start off in the Village with a list of bars you have to hit. At each place, you're required to have two margaritas. The final stop is at three-fifty-five AM at a place called Hogs and Hyenas. You've never seen such a place. It's in the meat-packing district and animal heads adorn the walls in the entire place—but you can't really see the heads because they're covered with bras."

Red jumped to his feet and placed his hand over his heart. "I love America," he said solemnly. "But please tell me—why are they covered in bras?"

Molly continued, "Any woman who takes hers off and leaves it at the bar gets free drinks all night."

"My kind of place," said Red.

"And if you walk in there with a tie, they cut it off," added Molly. "Anyway, one of the partners at the firm ended up dancing on top of the bar with a busty bartender. It was quite a scene. The funny thing is that the next morning at the office, everyone pretended nothing happened. I really liked the firm. It was pretty much my style."

"Me, too. I wish I was there, but, um, I'm a loser," said Red.

"Nah," Cosmo offered, patting his friend on the back for sympathy. "You'll get a spot."

"Molly, do you think they're going to extend an offer to you?" Robert asked.

"Of course. They know a good opportunity when they see it."

From the corner of his eye, Jeff saw Alberto coming over to join them. "Good opportunity," Alberto repeated with a grin. "That's me. Here I am."

"I see you took your modesty pill this morning," Cassandra fired back.

"Yeah, with a glass of red wine," said Alberto. He winked at her and then turned to address everybody in the group. "I'm Alberto, by the way." Then Robert introduced him to Jeff, Cosmo and Red.

"Cassandra and I have been so fortunate as to have had the pleasure of Prince Alberto's company on previous occasions," said Molly. Jeff caught a note of sarcasm in her tone.

"If you're talking summer experiences," offered Alberto, "I have a story for you. I was with Molly at Berman and Stinner."

"Yeah," Molly agreed. "Champagne and caviar for the entire summer."

"We'll see how long that lasts once you start as an associate," said Robert. "Is anyone taking Bradley for Evidence? He didn't show the first day of class. Not like I'm complaining."

"He's so old. He probably croaked or got lost on the subway. He's got to be at least ninety."

"Anyway," Alberto continued. "I got a chance to work with a divorce attorney for the summer. The guy was really sharp. But he ended up in negotiations with opposing counsel, who, by the way, happened to be a total knockout. So he's trying to settle this thing because it was getting really nasty. I'm in the office late one night and I walked past his office to grab a cup of cold, stale coffee and you wouldn't believe—"

"Don't tell me," said Robert. "He was getting busy with opposing counsel?"

And to add emphasis, Alberto tapped on the wooden table. "Right there on the desk!"

"I have been so deprived," grumbled Red.

Finding an opening into the conversation, Jeff spoke up. "Wouldn't that be a violation of some ethical considerations or disciplinary rules?" he asked.

Alberto started to answer but Red jumped in. "Not if no one finds out."

"I can't believe stuff like that actually goes on in a professional environment," said Jeff. "I mean, it seems like such hypocrisy. On one hand the partners expect the utmost loyalty, responsibility and dedication from their associates, but once you become senior enough to get away with it, it seems the rules no longer apply."

"You're right, Jeff," said Molly. "I mean, we're drawn to the law because of the prestige and the notoriety. And let's be honest—the chance to make some big bucks. But it seems we're sacrificing the very essence of what it means to be a lawyer."

"Like what, the pursuit of justice?" Alberto asked.

"Yes—shouldn't that be the primary reason we're here?" Molly responded. "Or what's it all for? I mean, we all know this isn't the glitz and glamour we see on TV where cases are won and lost in an afternoon, and research and due diligence get done over drinks at the local bar. That's not the life we're going to lead. Not even close. The truth is, it gets about as exciting as a high-profile chess match or reading the back of a cereal box." She paused and took a breath, then added, "Oh God—this is supposed to be a party. Someone give me a beer."

Cassandra leaned over and poured Molly another glass of wine. "I hope that'll do."

Two new arrivals burst into the room. One, Jeff could see, was a Law Review type—the typical nerd who hadn't done enough partying in college, and whose contributions to class were as factually dry as the scholarly journal. The other guy was wearing an expensive looking suit with a turtleneck and Italian loafers (without socks) that looked even more costly. He thought them a curious pair.

"Hey—where's the little boy's room?" asked the tall, well-dressed one. He had a bandage on his hand and his arm was in a sling. Cassandra pointed the way, then she and Molly looked at each other and laughed.

"That was interesting," said Cassandra.

"No, it was obvious," Molly observed. "That guy—the one with the bandage?"

"What about him?" asked Cosmo.

"His name is Keith. He's a third-year, working his way through law school selling nose candy."

"No way," said Jeff. "You sure?"

"Yeah," said Cosmo. "That's why they call him Candy Man Keith."

"So we shouldn't consider him much in the way of competition?" asked Jeff.

"Not many attorneys like Keith make it into the top New York law firms," said Cosmo. "He's from somewhere in the south. He can be charming all right—but he doesn't like New Yorkers and he's got a chip on his shoulder. His dad coaches for major league baseball. He used to be head coach for the Alabama Slammers. Now he's with the Philadelphia Flames."

"Yeah," said Molly. "His father pays his tuition, but nothing else. So he supplements his income by being the campus connection."

"How do you know?" asked Alberto. "You one of his customers?"

"Not me," she replied, lowering her voice a little. "But I know some people who are. And why do you think he and the nerd went into the bathroom together? 'Cause they're gay?"

"One would assume," said Jeff.

"Nope," Molly replied. "Not at all. He's got a customer on the line and he's letting him sample the product. You want to stay away from him."

"You know what," Alberto put in. "This conversation has gotten far too serious."

"Sure has," snapped Molly. "Especially for those of us who will leave this place with no student loans to repay and a ready-made job anywhere they want, so save your comments, Prince Alberto."

The bathroom door opened and the two men stumbled back out into the hallway. The Law Review type was brushing something away from his upper lip. Smiling, they made their way outside.

"Hey, Molly," Robert said. "You're definitely going to be a litigator, right?"

"You know I am. Why?"

"Because you have the uncanny ability of silencing your opposition without batting an eyelash."

Alberto raised his glass. "Hear, hear. A toast to Molly and her uncanny . . ." he paused for an instant. ". . . Mouth."

Everyone laughed—Molly most of all.

"I plan on practicing law for a couple years," she said. "Then, if I can't get an in-house position at some corporation, I'll strike out on my own. We're young, ambitious and creative, so when we see an opportunity, we grab it."

"I hope you're right. I don't want any part of this Habitrail," declared Cosmo.

Perplexed, Red asked, "What is this . . . Habitrail?"

"If you were fortunate, as I was, to have a hamster when you were young, you would know that it is one of those little homes you put your hamster in," Robert explained. "The hamster runs on a wheel in order to get exercise. So—it's like we're a bunch of little rats caught up on this wheel, and we can't get off."

Cosmo, who seemed perfectly content sitting back in his chair sipping his wine, volunteered his opinion. "Red, you were in Russia. You guys didn't have Habitrails."

"Okay, you got me," Red admitted, and everyone laughed again. "But it's a good analogy. It applies here perfectly."

Robert spoke again, thoughtfully. "It seems to me there's more to life than working hard until retirement, and sacrificing family, friends and social life to the god of the big-name law firm. One of my buddies told me what goes on at his firm. He says at night, the city becomes a parking garage for Lincoln Town Cars. Thousands of professionals going home in limo services, well after dark. It's indentured servitude. Making a big salary just isn't that important to me."

"Robert's right," added Molly. "Sometimes I wonder if these people are human. I heard that at one firm, one of the partner's secretaries—and I know, everyone professes to love their secretary. Well, this secretary came down with a brain tumor. Fortunately, it was benign but she assumed, like everyone else, that she would be taken care of. It turns out the firm offered her the opportunity to go back to work when she recovered, but in the meantime, she was laid off and running out of money."

"That's fucked up," Cosmo said.

"So what are we doing all this for?" asked Jeff.

"Hey, look at that," quipped Cassandra. "The first year wants an answer, which—after two or three years of the most grueling schooling you can imagine—no one can provide."

"Why do we do it?" Cosmo stepped up to the plate, and he wasn't trying to be funny. "To prove we can, Jeff," he said. "To prove we can."

CHAPTER 7

Semester's End

A spate of cold weather heralded the beginning of autumn. Jeff was invited to a couple of Halloween parties but he had to decline. He couldn't even go home for his mom's annual Thanksgiving feast.

He had to study. That's what his life—his entire life—had become. Going to classes and blocks and blocks of nothing but study.

Early Monday morning he got up with a splitting headache. Waking up had never been easy for him so he utilized a combination of alarms. First, he set the radio alarm to go off at about seven with soft music to allow an easy transition from slumber to an active day. Then, half an hour later, the buzzer alarm (which he'd set on a separate clock) would go off and shock him toward wakefulness. In a semi-conscious state, despite having two alarms, he would stumble to the radio, hit the snooze button and stagger back to bed, only to wake half an hour later to knock the buzzer alarm off his bureau with a quick swipe of his pillow. Pulling himself out of sleep was always an ordeal, and Jeff frequently missed the first five minutes of class.

But today he was instantly up and awake; the radio alarm blaring a Latin salsa version of *Jingle Bells,* and Yankee's insistent meowing had done the trick. He wouldn't be late today, but he would pay the price. His head was throbbing, and it wasn't because he was hung over. It was the third week in December—exam week—and he'd been up past four AM, cramming for his first set of law school exams. *Twelve rounds with the heavyweight champion of the world, he thought, would have been more merciful on my skull.*

With Yankee following him, still demanding food, Jeff went to the bathroom, straight to the medicine cabinet. Breakfast this morning would be extra strength Bayer Aspirin and a strong cup of coffee, black. The other casualty of the long nights and early mornings during exam week were his eyeballs. His late-night study routine left his eyes extremely sensitive to early-morning light, so a vial of Visine and a pair of sunglasses were his companions on his way to school.

Jeff washed his face, brushed his teeth, combed his hair, and got dressed—all in about five minutes flat. Just as he was about to open the front door, he caught himself. He'd forgotten his house keys, and as he stepped back inside, he heard again Yankee's insistent meowing. Running into the kitchen, he pulled the cat's feeding dish out from under the sink, grabbed a can of gourmet cat food off the shelf, filled it, and put it down for Yankee. Then he dashed into the hallway and grabbed his keys and his shades off the table near the door. Before placing the sunglasses carefully over his eyes, he took one last quick look at himself in the mirror.

"Damn, Jeff, you look pale—but hey, still not so bad." He closed the door behind him and raced to the corner to catch the bus into Manhattan.

Once on board, he reached for his notepad and a pen and started jotting down his assignments and chores for the day:

> Drop off dry cleaning
> Xerox notes for Civil Procedure
> Pick up cat food – 2 cans.

He stopped for a moment. Two cans of cat food, he thought. How the hell do I afford this cat? He only eats gourmet. Fifty cents for one of those mini-cans. I gotta take him to get groomed and shaved every couple of months or his hair gets knotty—another seventy-five bucks. There was also the ten dollars he gave his elderly neighbor, Mrs. Bentley, to look after Yankee on the rare occasions he could go home to see his mom. Then the teeth cleanings! The cat gets regular cleanings, and I see the dentist maybe once a year. Go figure.

But like any good lawyer, Jeff tried to analyze issues from a number of different perspectives. It occurred to him that although Yankee was expensive, he was an even more reliable alarm clock than the buzzer and the radio combined. There's nothing more annoying when you're dead asleep than having a cat swat you in the face and purr in your ear. If it weren't for Yankee, he figured he'd sleep his way through three-quarters of his legal education, which would be a real waste of a super expensive education. Also, the cat was always there for moral support. Somehow Yankee always knew when Jeff had a hard day or needed some encouragement. Okay, he concluded, and turned his thoughts back to exams. It's settled. The cat's a bargain.

All throughout college, Jeff had not opted for the study group method of learning course material. For him, the political science stuff was a breeze compared to the technical workings of the law. He could study a week for an exam—study hard—and do smashingly well. He'd been a straight honors student throughout college, but law school was different. Livermore students were just plain brilliant. Even in the study groups it was hard to keep up. Without them, clearly, Jeff would have been lost.

The material was voluminous and the time allotted in which to digest it was constricted. Already some of his friends at other law schools were second guessing their decision to pursue a legal career and considering other alternatives. He knew some would leave law school before the end of their first year. But Jeff was a fighter. He wasn't going anywhere.

Other schools provided a schedule that gave their students a two-week study period after their classes ended, but not Livermore, especially in the first semester. Classes continued right up until the day of exams, with maybe a day or two in between. And that was if the faculty decided to be merciful. Other exams were scheduled immediately after the return from holiday break; thus, there was no holiday, so Jeff wouldn't be going home for Christmas.

But he didn't care. He put his to-do list away and looked out the bus window, letting his mind wander back to his valedictory speech in high school. He remembered the look of pride in his mother's eyes and the cheers he received from his classmates as he finished it. He remembered his pledge to become a lawyer, and to use the law as a tool for the betterment of society. Those weren't empty words. Maybe coming from someone else they would have been, but not from Jeff. He meant it. From deep within his soul he meant every word, and someday he would make good on that pledge. No matter how difficult law school became, he would continue.

But it was frightening. Virtually everyone in his class came from top schools, and although many of them were financing their education with student loans, most of them had parents to fall back on. Jeff had no such safety net. His mom had made enough sacrifices to help him fulfill his dream as had his brother and sister, because of her determination. He wouldn't let them do it anymore. Now it was up to him. He'd saved almost every penny he'd made with part-time jobs in high school and college to see himself through the three years it would take to get through law school.

And it was turning out to be one of the most difficult things he had ever attempted. The study process in law school begins from day one, with taking copious notes which, on a regular basis, must be translated into a comprehensive outline of the entire semester. And from that outline each member of the study group would draw what they felt to be most important, then coordinate their outlines to create a master outline covering every concept, every case, every legal premise touched upon during the course of the semester. Without these outlines, Jeff knew, the information would have been more than he could manage. And without a group contributing to this end, there was no outline. In this respect, powerful bonds were created amongst fellow classmates during law school.

However, in every group there were the teachers and there were those who were taught. The taught, in which group Jeff regarded himself, did their damnedest to keep pace with the teachers. But in the end, it was always the brilliant students, those who stood out, who would communicate to their fellow classmates the reasoning behind the most complex legal concepts. Some teachers were patient. Some teachers actually learned through the process of teaching. But others were clearly arrogant, and just as bonds were created during these study sessions, enemies were also made when personalities clashed. And the clashes occurred not only between the teachers and the taught, but also amongst the teachers, especially when one of them failed to acknowledge a valid point another teacher had made.

But what, Jeff wondered, was the key? Did these people have a higher intellect? Did they have more innate ability? Or was it the fact that many of the better students came from families with a long tradition of law firm partners, lawyers and judges? From what Jeff could ascertain, no one was working harder than he was—and it wasn't an issue of whether or not he would get by. He knew he would do well, as he had always done in everything he'd ever undertaken. But why was it so damn hard? Why did it come naturally for the teachers, and yet so painfully for others?

He knew he could learn by tying together concepts to legal cases; in other words, if he could recall the fact pattern of a specific case, he could remember the concept the professor was trying to communicate in class. The problem was that there were hundreds upon hundreds of cases. It was impossible to memorize them all and thereby master the legal concepts or remember the fact patterns. But that was the way he caught on to the legal principles. If he remembered the peculiarities of an individual case, some of which had hilarious outcomes and ludicrous circumstances, he could then recall the legal principle the case was meant to stand for—and often have a laugh at the same time.

The better students, however, found memorization of cases to be irrelevant because they were able to master, digest and manipulate a few dozen legal principles and concepts covered throughout the semester, which made it easy for them to cite the cases. Once he could identify the legal principals, Jeff knew, citing the cases was just a matter of filling in the blanks.

This was the disadvantage with which he struggled. His brain simply had it backwards because, unlike any other exam throughout his entire education, a law school exam was a completely different animal. A law school exam involved a story—a chain of events that took place. It wasn't enough to memorize dates, names and places, nor was it even enough to memorize the concepts themselves. One had to manipulate.

The type of ludicrous story that might appear on an exam was a fact pattern that included a young boy who purchased a chemistry set and then used the internet to gain information on how to build a bomb. Then he shipped that bomb to his best friend, who had just moved across country with his parents, using a next-day courier instead of the U.S. mails. And the boy who received the package was too afraid to detonate the weapon, so he buried it in the back yard of his new home. Then fifteen years later, after that same home had been sold on three separate occasions to three different owners, the final owner decided to put a pool in his back yard. So, if the contractor, who didn't have the proper work permits, was injured (along with his employees), who was liable? That was where manipulation came into play.

Manipulate. Identify the legal issues and manipulate. In class, it was Jeff's mission to discuss the liability of each and every party, each and every individual, and the reasons for and against attaching liability to such persons, in addition to discussing who would have standing to sue, and for what sums of money. It was enough to drive a sane man mad, especially in the two hours allotted to discuss all the relevant issues that under normal, ordinary, circumstances, could require weeks to discuss.

Okay—enough, Jeff thought during his morning commute to Livermore. No more feeling sorry for myself. I'm going to make a success of this, no matter what it takes, no matter how little I sleep, no matter how many all-nighters I have to put in, no matter whether I have to wake up each day looking like a vampire or a zombie from *The Night of the Living Dead.* It's all going to be for the best. It has to be.

Surprisingly he got to class on time and was in his seat before the professor took his place at the podium. That was a treat. He'd made it just in time to witness a spectacle he had only heard about from classmates. This particular professor, older than most (perhaps in his eighties but still, definitely not the oldest on staff), went into a coughing fit, complete with spasms. The student in the seat next to Jeff leaned over and queried, as the professor pulled a handkerchief from his back pocket, "Did he just hack up a phlegm ball?"

Dismissing the disturbing visual image from his mind, Jeff tried to focus on the lecture, but there were too many distractions. The most prominent of all was what the professor was wearing.

Who taught these people to dress? Jeff thought. You could pretty much characterize a professor's style of dress by the type of law he or she practiced or taught.

Professor Chessman, the university's prominent Corporations scholar, dressed for the board room (as one would guess) in a gray pinstriped suit complete with suspenders, a blue shirt with a banker's collar, loafers and a bow tie or a highly conservative light blue tie.

This morning the Law and Economics professor, who Jeff couldn't help but stare at, was wearing a confused ensemble. Because of his age—and Jeff could only assume it was because of his age—it consisted of clothing from a number of different decades. The man was wearing checkered slacks straight out of the 1950s. His jacket was tweed, probably expensive, maybe even a recent gift from someone who was making an attempt at upgrading his wardrobe. They didn't succeed, because whoever bought him the jacket forgot to buy him the rest of the outfit. His shoes were an ordinary pair of loafers—at least he hadn't gone wrong there. For the finale, the professor had topped off the ensemble with a bright, neon-red turtleneck, the origin of which, Jeff could only conclude, was alien, as if from another planet.

Jeff thought his theory was actually pretty solid. His Family Law professor was well dressed; in fact, she was rather normal. The professor who taught Transnational Law and the European Union was a fabulous dresser. Her wardrobe was exquisite. The only exception was the Contracts professor. She showed up to class every day, rain or shine, heat or cold, in a pair of green slacks with sandals on her feet. The T-shirt that accompanied this getup did change (fortunately) on occasion. Jeff would have thought a Contracts professor would dress more along the lines of Professor Chessman. But then again, no theory is perfect.

Later, on his walk home from the bus stop, it hit Jeff again—almost like a punch to his solar plexus—that exam period was closing in on him. Each of the study groups with which he had been working had determined it was time for everyone to break off and start cramming individually. So, with an outline for each course in hand, he began the final phase of preparation for semester's end.

He felt pretty comfortable with Torts and Property, and with Contracts as well, except that his Contracts professor was so damned theoretical it would be tough for him to get a handle on what she might ask on the exam. For now, he decided as he unlocked his door, he would have to concentrate on Constitutional Law. He took a deep breath and pulled the two-inch-thick outline from his backpack. He went to the kitchen, poured himself a cup of coffee and seated himself at the table. It was four PM.

Thirty pages and four hours later Jeff stopped to take a break. He opened his refrigerator and scanned its interior. There was a nice steak in the freezer, but he didn't have time to defrost it, let alone cook it. Instead he reached for a can of Diet Coke and a microwaveable meatball sandwich. It wasn't a good idea to eat anything heavy, which would put him to sleep right away. But he was starving so he popped the meatball sandwich into the microwave and put another pot of coffee on to brew. He flicked on the tube and watched the news while he wolfed down his dinner. Then it was back to the trenches.

It was eleven o'clock. Jeff could feel his eyelids getting heavier, yet he knew it was far too early to quit. He had gotten through Article Three, the Power of Judicial Review, the Jurisdiction of the Supreme Court, Political Questions, Legislative Power, Congressional Spending Power, the Commerce Power, the War Powers, and Executive Privilege. But this was all introductory fluff. He had spent the last four hours studying but had yet to scratch the surface and get to the real meat of what his professors had covered in class. He still had to get through Interstate Commerce, the 13th and 14th Amendments, Due Process, Fundamental Rights, and most important of all, The Regulation of Speech and The Freedoms Of Association, the Press and Religion. It was overwhelming.

As midnight drew near, even the multiple cups of coffee that passed through his lips had lost their potency. Slumped in his chair, he felt like passing out face down in his Con Law book. *No,* he thought. *Instead of packing it in, I will cram as much into my head as possible before I crash for a couple of hours.*

With less than a week left and five outlines to completely digest, every minute, every second, counted. The only good night's rest he would get would be the day after exams. Jeff rose to his feet. If he was going to continue studying, it would have to be standing up. Otherwise, he would be tempted to crawl under the table, curl up into a little ball next to his cat and fall asleep. Jeff stood, and leaning over his desk he started reviewing material in his Constitutional Law book.

At four AM, he clicked off the coffee machine, closed his book, tabbed the last page he'd reviewed in his outline, pulled off his shirt, slipped off his sweatpants, and collapsed onto his bed. As soon as he got under his covers and put his head on the pillow, he fell asleep with Yankee curled contentedly beside him.

At six-thirty the alarm clock next to his bed went off. The horrible buzz droned on for ten minutes but his body demanded more sleep. His brain refused to fire and come to life, continuing instead in a state somewhere between consciousness and slumber. Waking up this morning seemed even more painful than usual. The bed was so warm and his pillow was positioned perfectly between his head and shoulders, providing the perfect support. His room was a tranquil cocoon with no light and no sound, a peaceful sanctuary sealed against the cold blast of winter.

The alarm clock was an invader, a ruthless barbarian, turning his bliss into a nightmare. He was caught in a tug-of-war between his effort to subdue the physical necessity of a trip to the bathroom and the desperate yearning for a few more moments to dream. He procrastinated, imagining for a moment what it would be like to spend an entire morning and afternoon in bed.

Turning slowly toward the invader, Jeff opened one eye ever so slightly, only enough to allow his right arm to locate the alarm clock, in order to end the torture. Although he opened his eye only a fraction of a millimeter, it was enough to allow the ray of light coming through the blinds to pierce his eyeball for an instant. That instant was enough to jar him out of slumber and into consciousness. Just as he shut off the first alarm, his back-up, located on the other side of the room, started shrieking like a heavy metal band, and his radio came on blasting *Rudolph the Red Nosed Reindeer.* That did it. He was finally awake. Yankee took his cue and immediately—loudly—begged to be fed.

Jeff left the comfort of the cocoon and stumbled into the bathroom, where he first relieved himself, then washed his hands and splashed cold water on his face. Peeking through the kitchen blinds, he saw a gentle flurry of snowflakes had begun to collect on his windowpane. He decided a little caffeine and a jog around the monastery was what he needed to jump-start his morning and get him through the rest of the day.

It was important to keep in shape—or at least try to keep in shape. Or at the very least, to convince himself he was trying to stay in shape. He quickly brushed his teeth, slipped on a pair of sweatpants, laced up his sneakers, and threw on his heavy sweater and ski jacket. It wasn't the prettiest collection for a jogging ensemble, but it would do just fine.

Jeff took to the streets, enjoying the crisp December air. He could see the monastery in the distance. Erected over a century before, it was a beautiful piece of architecture. The building was indeed majestic and in its presence, even in this cold weather with snowflakes softly falling on his nose and forehead, he felt warmth and a sense of peace. A heavy iron gate extended for eight blocks around the entire perimeter of the monastery gardens. Although a portion of the main structure had burned to the ground in an electrical fire several years earlier, it was still awesome, standing strong and solid for decades. The sight of it gave Jeff strength to move forward, literally and figuratively. Today, he aimed for ten laps around the property, probably the equivalent of three and a half miles.

His mind was racing. Going for a run was a marvelous idea, but time was precious, and he knew he was still procrastinating. *I need to focus,* he thought. *I need to remove all the clutter from my mind so I can function. So I don't let fears or doubts or insecurity make me so anxious I start doubting I have what it takes to get into a big New York law firm.*

If all his efforts came to naught—that was the most worrisome—he had no backup plan for what he would do with his life. All he had ever wanted to be was a lawyer.

After rounding the perimeter ten times, Jeff turned and ran home. Fully awake and energized, he was ready to take on another full day of studying. Without these breaks during exam time, night would run into day and day would run into night, and keeping track of time would become impossible. But now he was ready. His mind was in the right place. He would dedicate this day to attacking Civil Procedure.

Civil Procedure really amounts to the nuts and bolts of trial law, Jeff knew; and although he aimed to become a transactional attorney as opposed to a litigator, Civil Procedure was a required course, as it was for all law students. It taught them the procedure of practicing law, the rules and regulations governing attorney conduct in the courtroom, and all facets of conducting a trial including pretrial discovery, court rules, and appellate rules.

Before he'd started his marathon cram for exams, he'd complained to Robert Turner over a drink at Dead Authors. "There's so much minutiae to be mastered in order to understand civil procedure," he'd said. "At least I don't have to memorize actual case law for this class."

"Civil Procedure is difficult because you either understand the concepts or you don't," Robert replied. "So get it together, my friend. If you don't, that'll translate into a low grade. You'll get it. In my first year, I read my Federal Rules from cover to cover—all two hundred pages of it—over and over. Then, a few nights before the exam, I had a sudden epiphany. Out of nowhere, it all fell into place. Suddenly it was crystal clear."

Jeff had finished his drink, thanked his friend and gone home to study.

The Federal Rules of Civil Procedure was (by law book standards) a short manual, light reading as far as most legal works go. It was the playbook from which lawyers pulled the necessary legal tactics for courtroom battle in civil court, not criminal. Sure, there was much more drama in criminal practice. But Jeff knew the real money was in the hotshot big law firms that engaged in large-scale corporate litigation. Partners in those firms were the hired guns for corporate America. It was those guys—the corporate honchos—who really pulled the puppet strings, and Jeff wanted to be one of them.

He was finally beginning to understand Civil Procedure and he paused in his studies to bask in the apparent epiphany that was beginning to occur. Then the phone rang. It was Robert.

"Hey, Jeff—how's it going? Just thought I'd call and see if you need any help. I know your first big exams are coming up."

"Thanks, man," said Jeff. "It's really cool of you. Yeah . . . maybe you could kinda let me bounce some questions off you, just to see if I'm really starting to understand Civil Procedure or whether I'm deluding myself."

"Yeah, that's fine," Robert responded enthusiastically. "I'm just curious, though, Jeff. You're not doing a study group for Civ Pro?"

"Well, I did for Torts, Property and Contracts. Especially for Contracts, because my professor's a little whacked out, and no one in the class really understood what was going on. But all my groups came to the mutual decision that it's time for individual study. Otherwise, you know, you spend the evening listening to other people talk—and some of them have never heard anything as lovely as their own voice. Not to mention, they get way off track."

"I hear you. If you're with cool people who like to give and take, that's great. But when you get stuck with people who monopolize the conversation to get their own questions answered, that's counterproductive. So—what do you want to ask me?"

Jeff fired off his first question, "Well, do you think the exam will be on a federal question or a diversity issue?"

"Professors usually make it a diversity issue. It makes the fact pattern a little more complicated, therefore less cut and dried. They want to make you think. Just remember, the aim in Civil Procedure is to get the defendant into court. You always have to ask yourself, how can I get jurisdiction over the defendant? If the issue involves a federal question—a question that has to be resolved within the federal courts—that would be like pitching you a softball. But diversity involves two litigants from different states. Then the question is, what Rules of Civil Procedure can you use as plaintiff's attorney to claim jurisdiction over a defendant from an entirely different state? You following me?"

A smile breaking across his face, Jeff leaned back in his nice, comfy, thrift store La-Z-Boy and put the footrest up. "Yeah, I'm following. First you have to look at the wrong that has taken place. For the exam, it probably won't be a simple car accident. It'll be something grand, like a plane crash, a train wreck, toxic spill or defective product put into the stream of commerce."

"Right," said Robert. "So then what?"

"Then you look to see if you can get jurisdiction over this defendant. If the entity or person lives in the same state, great. But that probably won't be the case. I'll bet the only way to get them into court will be based on some form of specific jurisdiction, like does the entity transact any business in the state? Have they committed a tort within the state? Or at the very least, does the entity solicit business within the state?" Getting more excited because he really was beginning to grasp it, Jeff paused and took a breath. Then he continued. "Next, you gotta determine if the statute of limitations has run out, if proper notice has been filed—and proper venue."

There was a brief silence, and Jeff felt his spine begin to tingle. He was hoping for an immediate response from Robert but silence—that wasn't good.

At last Turner spoke. "Fuckin' A, Jeff! That's excellent, man!" he exclaimed. "That's it, man! You've got the big picture. The difference now between a good grade and an excellent grade is just filling in the gaps. But the big picture—that's the most important step."

"Thanks, man," Jeff said. "When it's all over, let's grab a bite somewhere—my treat."

"You got it, kid."

Jeff breathed a tremendous sigh of relief and decided he was going to catch a brief nap, eat a little something and then put on a pot of coffee. By his estimate, he could be ready to study again at about eight, in bed by midnight (early for a change), repeat the whole routine the following day, and then pray to God for the courage and focus to kick some ass in exams.

It was nice to have positive reinforcement from someone as together as Robert Turner. Instead of trying to doze off with that anxious feeling in his stomach, Jeff hit his comforter and pillow and was instantly sound asleep.

CHAPTER 8

Exam Day

Jeff looked at his watch as he stepped off the bus outside the gates of Livermore. He had just enough time to grab a bagel and a cup of coffee and get settled at his desk before the exam started. The lights adorning the trees that lined cobblestoned College Walk were still on, heralding the coming holidays. In the evenings, their cheery glow was breathtaking; in early morning, it was comforting.

It wasn't a cold morning, but occasional gusts of wind cut through Jeff, chilling his extremities. In his haste to make it to the exam on time, he'd grabbed a light jacket and forgotten gloves and hat. Not too bright, but at least he was there on time, and he'd be indoors in a couple of minutes. His ears and fingertips were turning red but he figured some hot coffee would warm him up. Fortunately there wasn't a long line at the deli across the street from the law building.

"What can I get you, chief?" asked the young man behind the counter. *He can't be more than twenty-eight,* Jeff thought. Yet, he was ambitious. His deli was in a great location and got all the business from Livermore law students, isolated as they were on one end of the campus. He provided quick service with a smile, and had excellent chicken cutlet sandwiches besides. He probably pulled in a good hunk of change every day.

There were anxiety-filled days, when Jeff was about to lose his mind, that he considered trying to open some kind of deli with a twist instead of spinning his wheels following an impossible dream. But he couldn't think about that now. Now he had to focus on exams. It was going to be a long, long week.

"Let me have a bagel," he said. "Light cream cheese. And a cup of coffee with skim milk and two Sweet'n Lows."

The young man quickly filled his order. "Exam time, huh?"

"Yeah—how'd you know?"

"Man, you got major luggage under your eyes, and it looks like you got a lot more gray hair since the last time I saw you."

"Yeah, exams'll do that to you," Jeff responded with a smile.

The exam was scheduled in one of the larger halls, and there were no assigned seats. Tension mounting, he selected a spot in the back, near the exits. Some students were flipping through their notes, taking in last-minute information. Others, confident they would master the exam, sat back, drinking their coffee and relaxing. Still others, realizing that if they didn't know the material by now last-minute reading wouldn't help, sat resolute as all waited for the proctor to distribute the test.

The proctor, a young woman dressed in an ill-fitting tweed skirt and faded sweater, called for everyone's attention. "This is the Civil Procedure exam," she announced. "Do not open the exam until instructed to do so. You will have three and one-half hours to complete it, and you will be notified one-half hour before the exam ends, which will be promptly at one o'clock, at which time your test booklets will be collected. Once we call for them, you must turn them in immediately. If you continue to hold onto them longer than the allotted time, your exam will be disqualified. It is now nine-thirty. You may begin."

The room went silent except for the rustling of papers and the sound of students putting pen to paper. As time passed, the panicked feeling in the pit of Jeff's stomach receded. As he had expected, the test was a diversity question involving multiple parties from different states and involving a manufacturer who put a defective snow blower into the stream of commerce. In many instances, the machine failed to shut off, and users (believing it was off) lost fingers to its internal mechanisms while trying to dislodge snow. The object was to show the professor how the plaintiff could get the manufacturer into federal court, and to discuss the multiple possible outcomes.

Three hours later, Jeff was still writing when the proctor spoke again. He flinched in his seat, his tension mounting.

"It is now twelve-thirty," she said. "You have half an hour left. You may continue for thirty minutes. If you feel you have completed the exam, please turn it in and exit the lecture hall now. If you do not leave at this point, you will be required to remain in your seats until the end of the exam."

A number of students got up and made their way toward the exits. Jeff couldn't help but wonder whether they were leaving because they had aced the exam, or because they were so frustrated they couldn't bear to continue.

He took a moment to scan through the fact pattern again, and he noticed that one of the parties wasn't a resident of Virginia as he had previously thought, but lived in Vermont. He had only twenty minutes to correct the mistake. Instead of spending that time putting finishing touches on his arguments, he had to re-read everything he'd written, to make sure the different residency didn't destroy his central argument.

The proctor's voice again startled him and caught him in mid-sentence. "Time is up," she said, her voice full of irrefutable authority. "Please turn in your exams."

He continued to write feverishly, pretending he was so caught up in his work he hadn't heard the announcement. With his peripheral vision, he could see her coming toward him but he went on writing.

"Please turn in your paper right now," she ordered. "Or you risk getting an F on the exam."

In response to her stern warning, Jeff put his pen down, placed his exam inside the answer booklet and turned it over to her. He gave her a smile, which she returned. Relieved, he took a deep, refreshing breath. Although he didn't get to finish his last thought, it was over and he felt confident in his work. He collected his belongings and threw his backpack over his shoulder. He was famished. It was time for one of those chicken cutlet sandwiches at the deli across the street.

Jeff followed the crowd into the hallway, down the corridor and out through the front door of the law building. As he descended the stairs, someone snagged his arm. It was Red.

"Hey, Jeff—you got exams today?"

"Yeah, my first. Civil Procedure. I just got out."

"Awesome. How do you think you did? You kick ass?"

"Well, I don't know if I kicked ass," Jeff replied. "But, at least for the moment, it feels like a huge burden's been lifted off my back."

"Tell me about it. C'mon, let's celebrate." Still holding Jeff's arm, Red started up the stairs again.

"Wait," Jeff said. "To tell the truth, I was kinda hoping to catch the bus and go home. I'm exhausted like you wouldn't believe."

"No, I do believe it. That's why I'm dropping some stuff off in my locker and you're coming with me to my place for a drink."

"A drink? Are you crazy?" replied Jeff. "I'm beat. I just got out of an exam. The last thing I need is a drink. Did you look at your watch? Do you know what time it is?"

"Listen, it doesn't matter what time it is. It's always a good time for some real Russian vodka."

"Aw, shit," Jeff said. A drink did sound good. He followed Red to his locker, and then went with him to his apartment.

An hour later, they were still sitting at Red's kitchen table. Red was a mess. His complexion, rosy from alcohol, blended nicely with his fiery red hair. His necktie was loosened and tossed over his shoulder. He had just returned from an interview, he'd told Jeff, who was half-baked himself by this point.

"I came to America to be a liar," Red mumbled. "No—I mean lawyer. No—liar." Leaning heavily to one side in his chair, he seemed to find this comment hysterical. Laughing loudly, he corrected his balance before his chair tipped over, then he reached for the half-empty bottle of vodka. He poured them each another shot. They were drinking from paper cups. "Fucking economic slowdown," he concluded.

"What'd you say?" Jeff took a sip from his cup, while Red quickly threw his back and poured himself another.

"Jeff, my friend, I'm gonna teach you the ways of the world, right here and now." Red slammed his fist down on the table, then playfully slapped Jeff on the side of the cheek. His eyes now glassy, he leaned back in his chair and gazed at Jeff. Without flinching or even blinking, he let out the loudest belch Jeff had ever heard, then burst into a fresh round of raucous laughter.

Jeff couldn't help but laugh as well. It was a bit juvenile—like the stuff he'd done back in high school—but it was funny. He wasn't about to pretend he was above it, because he wasn't. If he was back home in New Jersey, hanging out with Bernie and other buddies he'd grown up with, he'd probably be doing the same thing.

What the heck, he thought. There's no harm in acting like an ass for a little while.

He was getting a serious buzz on but Red, who'd been slugging back shot after shot, was almost incoherent, even talking about how tough it was to be the campus stud. Transfixed by the spectacle, Jeff figured he had to be joking. Red had become downright entertaining.

"You want to get rich quick?" he asked. "I know how to do it."

"Sure," Jeff responded. "How?"

"It's a scam—we could pull it off using those nine-hundred numbers. It would be easy money, my friend."

Jeff decided to humor him. "Sounds interesting," he said. "And fascinating. But Red, if it's a scam and you get caught, all your hard work and effort—I mean everything you've gone through, from getting out of Russia to getting through Livermore—God, wouldn't it all be one big massive waste?"

"You're right, kid," responded Red. "I don't have the balls to do it. But I wish I did." He never explained what the scam was but he mumbled to himself, "Yeah . . . 1-900-LAW-SCAM."

The conversation got increasingly weirder and more twisted, running the gamut of a story about Red's date with a Louisiana woman who, while wearing stiletto heels and sitting in the front seat of his car, decided to put her foot through the windshield, to his gripes about the legal profession, his summer internship, recent economic downturns, and his inability to nail the internship of his choice or the cute receptionist who worked there.

"Well, maybe it would be a good idea not to have two shots of vodka before an interview," Jeff ventured. "Skipping that little ritual might help. What do you think?"

"No—I need it to take my edge off."

"Your edge off what?"

"You know—a little something to ease the tension. It's like this: during my summer internship, I was working for this dick. One minute, he was slapping me on the back, telling me what a great job I was doing, then yelling at me at the top of his lungs the next. He was a real schizo."

At least, Jeff thought he said schizo. With Red's Russian accent, his words now slurred with vodka, it was hard to make out.

"Anyway, my friend—I'll make short a long story," Red continued. "The guy ended up giving me a great recommendation and encouraged me to come back to that firm once I graduated—but I'm not going back. You know why?"

Jeff shook his head and shrugged his shoulders. "Not a clue," he said.

"Because he told me. He told me how it is at that firm. Young attorneys get paid the big bucks to get yelled at. To take shit and get yelled at."

"That's nonsense."

"You know it's nonsense," Red agreed. "If I wanted to get yelled at, I would have stayed in Russia and joined the military. My family came here to pursue a dream, and I came here to become something, to become someone, an individual, somebody with dignity. Not some puppet who gets paid to take abuse. I don't care how much they pay me."

"So that's why you're so tense?"

"You got that right. And I need a hit."

"You mean another shot? Here, I'll pour you one."

"No, I mean a hit. I got some blow. You want a hit?"

Surprised, Jeff watched Red as he went to the cupboard above the refrigerator, reached in the back, and withdrew a teapot. He sat down again with Jeff, and from the teapot, he took a playing card—the queen of hearts—and a glass vial half-filled with white powder. He screwed the top off the vial, gently tapped it on the table, and with the card began to form two thin lines of white dust. Jeff couldn't believe what he was seeing.

He knew Red was a prankster and wondered if he was waiting to see Jeff's reaction. If he'd set this whole thing up so he could have a good laugh.

Well, Jeff thought. I'm not falling for it. That's gotta be a vial of sugar. He decided to play along.

Red leaned over the table and snorted loudly and one of the lines disappeared up his nose. He threw his head back and closed his eyes, enjoying the rush. Jeff dipped a finger into the second line of powder and touched it to his tongue. It wasn't sugar. His mind racing, he asked himself, Does Turner know about this? He has to know—these guys are best friends.

Red slowly lowered his head. Smiling, his eyes bright and glazed, he motioned to Jeff that it was his turn. He had white dust on the tip of his nose and even on his forehead. Jeff saw him in a different light now. He was no longer funny. Now he was pathetic.

Drugs had never been a temptation for Jeff, not in high school and not in college. As an athlete who needed scholarships to complete his education, he wasn't about to let anything mess up his game.

His Uncle Murray had told him that, as he pursued a career in the law, there would be moments that could overtake him, moments for which he was entirely unprepared, and during those moments the decisions Jeff made could change the rest of his life. Jeff had never thought those moments would include drugs.

"Red, I gotta go." Jeff stood up from the table, walked over to the sofa and grabbed his backpack.

"What do you mean, you're going? No, man, it's cool. Come on—we got to party."

Jeff stopped at the door, his hand on the knob to ensure his escape. He turned it and opened the door, then stopped to take one last look at Red who seemed confused and bewildered. He couldn't understand why Jeff was leaving. "Later, man," said Jeff. "I gotta get home and study."

It was becoming clear to Jeff that there were some students in law school to whom he would never be able to relate. Caught up as they were in the esoteric world of the law, they had little else to contribute. Others—like Red—were completely off the deep end. He was glad he could count Robert Turner as a friend.

Once Jeff hit the pavement outdoors, the brisk air on his face felt great. Still in shock, he wondered who else in Robert's crowd was into cocaine. He hoped Robert wasn't one of them.

CHAPTER 9

One of the Top Firms

"Congratulations, Jeff!" exclaimed Robert, his tone enthusiastic, when he ran into Jeff in the corridor outside the Roosevelt room a few days later. "I heard you got some solid grades this semester."

"Two As and two Bs. Not stellar, but they should get me in the door at some of the big-name law firms."

"No doubt. With a Livermore degree, even if you had Cs, you could still line up some good interviews. But with these grades, you'll be able to play with the big boys. Just keep up the good work."

"Yeah, I will," Jeff said. After a moment he added, "So . . . Red tell you we had drinks the other day?" He hoped Robert was oblivious to what he had witnessed at Red's apartment. *He can't know,* Jeff thought, *because if he does, he'd do something to intervene.* Unless he was also doing blow.

"No," said Robert. "I'm surprised I wasn't invited."

"Oh—it was a last-minute thing," responded Jeff. "I ran into him after the exam."

"So did he tell you? Did you hear the good news?"

"No, he was—" Jeff paused. "Well you know Red. We were drinking vodka, and he got to telling me about one of his get-rich-quick schemes. So what's the good news?"

"I got into Darby and Blackstone," Robert announced. "I guess that makes me one of the big boys."

"Wow—I'm impressed," Jeff told him honestly. "If anyone can handle it, you can."

"You know, it was never really my intention to go to one of those sweatshop New York firms where they work you into the ground, but when they said they'd start me at a hundred and seventy-five grand, I couldn't refuse."

"Is that the going rate?" Jeff was stunned. It sounded like a small fortune.

"Yeah—and there's a signing bonus on top of that. It's one of the top five firms in the country. They expect a lot, so they pay a lot. The best part is, they're going to let me work there while I finish my last semester, and make some extra money before I start there in the fall."

"That'll be some nice pocket change."

"Oh, yeah, and I'm gonna use every last cent of it to hook myself up with a nice pad, and a nice vacation after I pass the bar."

"That's amazing—you are the man," said Jeff. "And yeah—congratulations."

"Well, listen. You keep doing what you're doing and in two years, when you're ready to graduate, I can put in a good word for you."

"Thanks, Robert, but I'm not Law Review. I don't think I'm exactly cut out for Darby and Blackstone."

"That's nonsense. Just keep pushing forward and we'll see what happens. Don't get lax."

•••

And then the holidays were upon them, and Jeff was able to get home to Jersey for a couple of days. His mom celebrated his good grades with a special Christmas Eve dinner, with the whole family in attendance. His brother and sister came with assorted spouses and offspring, and Uncle Murray brought his new girlfriend, who was half his age. Even Jeff's childhood friend Bernie was included in the feast. After dessert, when the men were nodding out in the living room, the kids were watching Santa videos back-to-back, and the women were cleaning the kitchen, Jeff and Bernie took a walk around the neighborhood, reminiscing over old times.

"And look at you now, college man!" Bernie said. "You're really gonna make it, Jeff. Make all of us proud."

"You don't look like you're doing too bad yourself, married man with a kid on the way. And you bought a house already."

Bernie shrugged, modest. "Well, you know—I make do."

Bernie didn't have a real job. He held the honorary title of mayor of the block, a position he'd inherited from his father, who knew everybody and could hook people up for almost anything they were looking for. Bernie didn't have Jeff's education, but Jeff knew the connections, knowledge and street smarts he had were invaluable.

"So, how's things at Livermore?" Bernie asked. "You got everything you need?"

"Yeah, I'm good. But something I want to ask you. You know anything about drugs on campus?"

"What kind?" Bernie asked.

"I heard some students are into cocaine. And at least one student is dealing."

"You on the stuff?"

"Of course not," Jeff said. "You know better than that. I just . . . well, I found it hard to believe until one of my friends—"

"Believe it," Bernie cut in. "Livermore's no different than any other college. Yeah, there's a market for it at Livermore. Lot of students—even some teachers—are into it. You watch your back, Jeff."

•••

With the onset of a harsh winter and the increasing demands of his classes, Jeff put aside his worry about Red's drug habit. Clearly, Robert didn't know anything about it. That was a relief, and Jeff was happy to take his friend's advice. The next five months were a tension-filled blur of study, classes, and more study as Jeff continued to push forward. He sometimes wondered what it was all for. He was looking for fulfillment yet not finding it—but sacrifice had to have some meaning. Law school was demanding, not fun, and Jeff had been fully aware it wouldn't be. The payoff would come, he knew; the day would come when he would be able to sit back and realize it was all worth it. At least, he hoped so.

•••

As the months went by, Jeff's friendship with Robert Turner grew. Here was a guy, Jeff knew, who would undoubtedly be a success. Tenacious, insightful, well-mannered and well-groomed, Robert would be partner material at any law firm. He had a sense of humor. He was a good person and, without a doubt, well-intentioned. These traits were uncommon in a typical law student, because although they claimed they wanted to save the world or win big cases in the interest of justice, Jeff believed most of the ones he'd met so far didn't always get how to treat people on a day-to-day basis. The typical law student, as far as he could see, would rarely extend a hand to anyone unless there was something to gain, even if it was just to pump his or her own ego.

But Robert Turner was different, and in him Jeff had found someone after whom he wanted to model himself. Robert was a genuine person, and a serious intellect. Their frequent midnight chats were invaluable to Jeff, and assisted him in targeting the right courses, the right professors, the right outlines—in total, advice that helped him maximize his chances at some solid grades.

As his first year drew to an end, Jeff again scored two As and two Bs, and he was getting interest from some top law firms for a summer associate's position. He landed a spot working in the compliance group of an investment bank in Manhattan. He was feeling more secure about his choice of career, more confident that he would continue to do well at Livermore.

His temporary job allowed him to keep his apartment in the city instead of going to stay with his mom in Jersey and working as a busboy at some beach hangout. He was able to make some decent cash over the summer while building his resume with experience that had substance. Many students, despite having good grades, ended up going back home or to their native backwoods in some no-name town, to clerk for a local judge.

Robert was working crazy hours at Darby and Blackstone but every couple of weeks he and Jeff were able to meet for drinks or a late dinner. He'd told Jeff the firm had him rotating through different groups so he could become familiar with all areas of its practice and its clientele. He was also excited about going on his first business trip to the Caymans.

"Man, I couldn't believe it when my boss invited me," he told Jeff. "I guess it's time to start drinking in all that glamour and excitement we've heard about. Makes law school worth it."

"My job's boring, next to yours," Jeff said. "But it's pretty easy." More importantly, since he planned to do transactional work, having a position at an investment bank on his resume would boost his chances to get interviews with the bigger law firms.

When he got his first paycheck, Jeff took his Uncle Murray to lunch to celebrate. By now Jeff had become interested in doing deals.

"So, you want to do the big deals," said Uncle Murray over his steak. "That's wonderful—you'll be good at it. You're a bright boy, Jeffrey. I knew you would do well in law school. So you'll work hard. You'll learn to do deals and you'll be successful. It's good to be enthusiastic about your work, and about the deal, but the work shouldn't be your entire existence. You have to be equally enthusiastic about life."

"Who has time?" Jeff responded cheerfully. "It's taking every minute I have to get through law school."

"But you need balance. One should not come at the exclusion of the other. No extreme can produce happiness. Remember, balance. You can have the law—but you can also have a life. Take some time to . . . what do they say . . . smell the flowers. Kiss the girl. Spend a day at the beach. Have a life."

"Yeah," Jeff said. "That sounds great. And I'm gonna do it all—as soon as I finish law school."

•••

Jeff turned from his alarm clock and stumbled, in a haze, toward the ringing telephone. Who in God's name could be calling him at four in the morning?

It was Robert Turner.

"Hey . . . what's up?" Jeff mumbled into the phone, more awake now.

There was silence on the other end of the line.

"Robert . . . you there? You back from the Caymans already?"

"Yeah. I left a day early—"

"How was it, man?"

"It was . . ." Robert paused a moment, then: "Jeff, listen. I can't talk now, but—" He paused but Jeff had heard the anxiety in his voice. It was uncharacteristic. Robert was always in control, always in command of any situation thrown at him.

"Hey, man—you okay?" Jeff asked. "Where are you?"

"At the office—at D and B—trying to figure something out."

"Maybe you should get some rest."

"Listen," Robert said, lowering his voice. "A lot of crazy shit's been going on. I can't talk right now—I don't know who might be listening. Just do me a favor. Come meet me this morning, before you go to work, at my place. You're the only person I can trust. Will you come?"

"Of course. Yeah. You know I will."

"Good. I knew I could count on you. I feel better already. See you soon."

•••

Jeff's alarm clock went off three hours later. He rolled out of bed, his brief, weird conversation with Robert still fresh in his mind. He grabbed his phone and called in at work. He would be late this morning. Within an hour, he was in the foyer of Robert's apartment building, impatiently ringing his doorbell.

Where the hell is this guy? he thought. *If it's so important, he should be here.*

Robert, clearly distressed, had said he was worried about someone listening. What the hell was that all about? It was out of character for Robert Turner to panic, but that's how he had sounded. It was also out of character for Robert to miss an appointment. He was too responsible to leave anyone hanging.

Jeff's first instinct was to call the police, but he knew what they would say. Robert was an adult and he would have to be missing for a couple of days before they would even try to track him down.

After wrestling with the idea for a few minutes, he decided to wait, at least a full twenty-four hours. He didn't want to send out a false alarm. Robert was solid, and he was an adult. Maybe he was jet-lagged after flying home from the islands, and now he was sleeping it off. Jeff didn't want to embarrass him with a search party.

For the rest of the day, Jeff was able to put it out of his mind. But by the following day he still hadn't heard anything. He decided to call Red. If Red didn't have any answers, Jeff's next call would be to the police.

He couldn't explain the uneasy feeling he had in his stomach. It prevented him from enjoying a sound sleep and caused him to wake up even before his second alarm went off, and that never happened.

As he reached for the phone and began to punch in numbers, his clock radio came on. It was set to the local news broadcast.

"Police are baffled by the appearance of a body floating face down in the East River early this morning. Officials would not comment on the case, but will say only that a special detective unit is investigating. The tragedy involves a student from the prestigious Livermore University, who has been identified as Robert Turner. An anonymous source at the university has informed us that it was an apparent suicide."

Jeff doubled over and sank to the floor in disbelief. He felt sick to his stomach and numb, all at the same time. It couldn't have been suicide. Robert had an amazing, bright future ahead of him. He would never have taken his own life. Jeff called Red and Cosmo but they had no information either, besides what they'd heard on the news. He even called Darby and Blackstone and told them he was a friend of Robert's. Pretending he was helping to organize the funeral, he asked if there was anyone he could speak with about Robert's last few days at the firm, or if they had any photos of him for the memory wall.

"No, I'm sorry," replied the impersonal voice of some receptionist or intern. "His superiors at the firm have already given a statement to the press. That's all that will be forthcoming."

The multitudes of people who attended Robert's funeral gave evidence of his popularity. Professors Duberstein, Chessman and Giles, along with numerous deans and members of the student body, came to say goodbye. The pastor who gave the eulogy said it was more than a funeral. It was a farewell for one of their best. Jeff agreed. Robert Turner was one of the best, and not just as a law student. He was one of the best human beings Jeff had ever met.

In his beat-up old Jeep, Jeff drove to the funeral with Red and Cosmo, and Red's emotions issued forth without restraint. His eyes were bloodshot from crying, and there were dark shadows beneath them. He told Jeff he hadn't slept for two days. Tears streamed down his cheeks and came to rest on his chin, and he didn't bother to wipe them away. He simply stood there, gazing at the casket. When Molly's hand came to rest gently on his shoulder, he ignored it.

Jeff looked down at her. "How are you feeling?" he asked.

"You know how I feel," she responded dully. "I feel like shit—excuse my language. How are you doing? You guys were so close."

Red shivered slightly and turned to Molly, finally aware of her presence. He put an arm around her waist and drew her to him for a brief hug.

"Okay," Molly said. "You've got to pull yourself together, Red. He'd want us to be strong."

Cassandra stepped out from behind Molly and grabbed Jeff's hand. Leaning down to her, he whispered, "I'm really glad you're here."

"We didn't want you guys to go through this alone," she responded softly. "We didn't want to go through it alone."

After the casket made its descent to Robert's final resting place, his parents came forward. Consumed with pain, his mother sobbed softly as she and Robert's dad each tossed a handful of earth onto the coffin. And that was it. Robert was gone. The great Robert Turner was no more. Jeff felt empty, all his emotions drained. He joined the line of mourners going to offer condolences to Robert's parents, but he could only shake their hands. He couldn't trust himself to speak without breaking down.

"I can't take any more of this," Cassandra told him as the crowd began to disperse. It was a beautiful afternoon, with a soft, late-summer breeze teasing the flowers around the grave. "Look—there's Alberto and Monica. Let's go to Jackson's so we can have a drink and get something to eat. And then I just want to go home."

"I'm gonna go with Alberto in his car," said Red. "We'll follow you."

"Well, I'm going with Cassandra," said Monica. "With all the blasted tests and studying, I haven't seen her in ages. We've got some catching up to do." She flashed Cassandra a big grin.

"Oh?" Cassandra looked at her—surprised, Jeff thought—and then returned her smile. "You and Alberto have set a date then?"

Monica shook her head. "Not yet, but we're looking at venues. You know, a big wedding takes a lot of planning. It's going to be so awesome!" She hooked her arm through Cassandra's and they piled into the Jeep, along with Cosmo, as Jeff got behind the wheel.

He pulled away from the cemetery and made a left at the first light. He glanced into his rear-view mirror to make sure they were behind him. "Hey, Monica, is that Alberto back there?"

She turned to look. "No, that's not a BMW."

The black Lincoln Continental caught up to Jeff and pulled alongside him. The driver, a heavy-set bearded man, rolled down his window. Staring at the people in Jeff's car, he lit a cigarette and threw his match out the window. "Hey, you little shit," he said, his voice threatening. "You almost rammed into me back there. You better watch yourself, you know what's good for you."

"No way—" Jeff began, but, the guy sped off. Jeff couldn't help noticing his vanity plate: DMAN-0077. "Asshole," Jeff muttered. There was still no sign of Red and Alberto when they parked in front of Jackson's Pub.

Jeff and the rest of the group, tired of waiting, went ahead and ordered their meals. After an hour, when they were finished eating, Red and Cosmo arrived.

"Where the fuck were you guys?" asked Cosmo. "We're already having our cappuccinos."

Red sank into the booth and put an arm around Molly. "I wasn't in the mood to eat. We just drove around for a while."

Alberto pulled up another chair and opened a menu. "Well, I'm hungry," he announced. "You guys aren't in a rush to leave, right?"

Red, however, was finding it difficult to remain still. He suddenly stood up and excused himself to go to the rest room.

"This is all so morbid," said Cosmo. "What an incredible waste of such tremendous potential."

"A tragic waste," agreed Cassandra.

"So what happened?" asked Molly. "Robert had everything going on. Why would he kill himself?"

"He wouldn't," Jeff said simply.

"The official word," said Alberto, "at least, according to Darby and Blackstone, was that Turner wasn't living up to their expectations. But that's weird. If they were disappointed in his performance, they never said anything to him. If they had, he'd have told me."

"Maybe it was Robert's expectations that weren't being met," said Molly.

"What do you mean?" asked Cassandra.

"Well," Molly replied, "Robert—being Robert—would not stand for anything less than excellence, especially from himself."

"So when this reality—the possible reality he wasn't perfect—came crashing down on him, he slit his wrists and hurled himself into the East River," Alberto put in. "That's the official word, according to the PR department at Livermore."

"I'm not buying it," said Jeff. "Nothing about it rings true. Robert wouldn't do that. He just . . . he wouldn't."

"I told you, it's all so morbid," said Cosmo as he took a sip of his cappuccino. "It's all so fuckin' morbid."

•••

There was dead silence on the way home. They had stayed longer at the pub, had some more coffee and then a round of drinks, and now the sun was setting on the worst day in Jeff's life. He dropped Cosmo off first, and as soon as he was out of the car, Molly rolled up her sleeve and peeled a nicotine patch away from her arm.

"I need a cigarette," she said. "It'll calm me down." She reached into her bag and pulled out a pack of Marlboro Lights.

As she placed the cigarette into her mouth, Cassandra reached over and snatched it away. "Real mature, Molly. I thought you quit."

"I did, but if there was ever a moment to start up again, I'd say that would be now. Wouldn't you?" Molly grabbed her cigarette back and lit it. Immediately, Jeff started coughing.

"Oh, shit—you gotta put that out," he said. "I think I'm gonna be sick. I gotta get out. I gotta pull over."

"There's a service station up ahead," said Molly, pointing at a sign that read Food and Fuel. It had a Sunoco logo, with a McDonald's logo attached beneath it.

Jeff slowed for the exit and pulled into one of the handicapped spots. He opened the car door and leaned over, but instead of throwing up, he started weeping, his shoulders heaving with sobs.

"Why?" he agonized, his tears streaming uncontrollably. "Why the fuck would he kill himself!"

Cassandra opened the glove compartment, searching frantically for a tissue. She settled for a coffee-stained Dunkin' Donuts napkin. "Good," she said, handing it to him. "Let it all out. Don't hold back. You don't have to be embarrassed with us."

Molly reached over from the back seat, placed her hand on Jeff's shoulder and gently squeezed it. "Is he gonna be all right?" she asked. "Should we get an ambulance or something?"

"He'll be fine," said Cassandra. "It's been a rough day. I'll look after him."

"No," Jeff protested. "I'm okay. That's really not necessary."

Cassandra looked up at him. "It is," she replied softly. "You shouldn't be alone tonight. You're staying with me."

•••

Upon entering her apartment, Cassandra kicked off her shoes. "Interested in some TV?" she asked Jeff. "I've got cable." Jeff collapsed on her sofa. She sank down next to him and reached for the remote control. "What do you feel like?" she asked. "News? A mindless sitcom?"

Like a lost child, Jeff nuzzled his head on her shoulder and gazed at her feet. They were small and pretty and perfectly shaped. Gently, she ran her fingers through his hair. Then slowly she lowered his head onto her lap and stroked his forehead.

"How can you be so strong?" he asked, a touch of wonder in his voice.

"I'm not strong," she said. "I just thought it would be important to Robert that we get through today with some dignity—"

"How?" he interrupted. "How do we get through this?"

"I don't know," she said, tears filling her eyes. "We remember him, and we celebrate his memory. We take comfort where we can."

He was still staring at her feet. *They are perfect,* he thought randomly. His gaze lingered on her toes before moving across the deep curve of her arch. Her toes are perfectly sized and each aligned, one just a bit longer than the other. A prettier foot, he concluded, could not have been carved by Michelangelo himself. Then he sat up and held his arms out to her. She went into them and he kissed her with all the passion that had been building in him for weeks.

•••

The soft cooing of pigeons outside Cassandra's window slowly coaxed Jeff into wakefulness. It took him a moment to remember where he was. At some point, they had moved from the couch to her bedroom, where they'd fallen asleep, comforted at last in each other's arms. Sunlight streaming through her window told him a new day had arrived.

Motionless, Cassandra was still sleeping, her head on the pillow and her long blond hair curling around her shoulders. Seeing her like that, innocent and vulnerable, almost made his heart stop. He couldn't imagine what it would be like to make love to her. He pulled the comforter up around her shoulders, then dressed and left as quietly as he could.

As soon as he hit the sidewalk, the bright sunlight assaulted him. He hated it when he forgot his sunglasses. Shielding his eyes against the piercing rays with his right hand, he made his way down the block. His vision thus impaired, he almost stumbled over a young boy who couldn't have been more than eleven years old.

"Sorry, mister," said the kid.

"No—I'm sorry," Jeff said. The boy took off down the block.

"Sorry, mister!" The loud, mocking chant came from a group of five other boys who were chasing the kid. They all looked to be about the same age. "Sorry, mister! Sorry, mister!"

Jeff stood and watched as they caught up to him. Clustered around him, they taunted and pushed him. One even took a full swing, slapping the palm of his hand onto the back of the boy's neck, knocking him down. Jeff heard the loud smack half a block away.

"Hey, leave that kid alone!" he shouted.

One of the gang of five leaped onto the hood of a parked car and brazenly flashed his middle finger at Jeff. Jeff took a couple of steps toward him, and the gang quickly dispersed, taking off in all different directions. The young victim jumped up from his knees and ran to Jeff.

"Hey, thanks, man!"

"You don't have to thank me," said Jeff. "What's your name?"

"I'm Joey. What's yours?"

"I'm Jeff. Nice to meet you, Joey. Take care." Jeff turned and headed toward his car. The boy tagged along, a couple of paces behind. Jeff stopped and waited for him.

"Hey, you mind if I walk with you?" Joey asked. "It's just—I don't want those guys to beat up on me again."

"Why are they giving you such a hard time?"

"Because I struck out with the bases loaded and lost the game. They won't leave me alone about it."

Nothing angered Jeff more than the pack mentality of any group pouncing upon someone vulnerable. "How many games do you have left?" he asked.

"A couple more before the summer's out."

"Believe it or not, I used to coach Little League," Jeff told him. "What do you say I give you some pointers sometime?"

"For real?"

"For real, man."

"That would be great," said Joey.

"For now, how about an ice cream?"

CHAPTER 10

The Interview

By the time Jeff's second-year summer arrived, the economic climate had changed. The free-for-all heyday prevalent when he'd started at Livermore had given way to a somewhat tighter job market. His professors assured him positions were there for Livermore graduates, but it meant more competition, more interviews and fewer offers.

During each and every interview period, all the top law firms in the nation descended upon Livermore in an effort to grab the school's best and brightest. Jeff's grades were solid. He was a strong candidate, but he wasn't Law Review. He thought his first round of interviews, including one with Darby and Blackstone, went well and he had amassed some callback interviews. Ironic, he thought, if he ended up working in Robert's last job.

His first interview was with Markham and Broadstreet, on the twenty-sixth floor of the Financial Center. As he entered the lobby, he paused for a moment to appreciate the view the massive bay window offered, with the Statue of Liberty in the distance.

"Hello, Mr. Rhodes. We've been expecting you," the receptionist greeted him when he stepped off the elevator. She gestured to a plush leather sofa. "Please take a seat. We'll be with you shortly."

Figuring they would make him wait, Jeff got comfortable. He noticed the firm's brochure on a table beside the couch. The caption on the front cover caught his attention:

A Tradition Of Assisting Clients In Achieving Their Goals

This particular firm had ten offices throughout the United States; the New York office was their flagship. Jeff had done everything he could think of to prepare for this interview. He had run a number of different Lexis/Nexis searches to determine in which prominent transactions and litigations the firm was currently involved, and which partners ran them. *And I know my resume like the palm of my hand,* he thought. *Speaking of which, both of them are damp with nerves.* He pulled a handkerchief from his pocket and clenched it into a ball in his fist, blotting up the moisture before he returned it to his pocket.

After a few moments, the receptionist smiled and called him to her desk. "This is a list of whom you'll be meeting with today," she said, handing him a sheet of paper. "Take a moment to look at it, then our recruitment coordinator will take you down the hall to the corner office. You'll begin with Todd Handley. He's a partner in our general corporate group."

On his way to the corner office, which was down a long corridor, Jeff passed a number of secretarial stations and small offices he assumed belonged to the associates. As promised, Todd Handley was waiting for him.

"Hi, Jeffrey—I'm Todd. Please come in and have a seat." He welcomed Jeff with an outstretched hand and a warm smile.

"Thank you," Jeff said. "This is a breathtaking view you have here, Mr. Handley."

"Well, one of the many benefits of working in the Financial Center."

A wry response came to Jeff's mind. He wanted to say, "Yeah, but how's security?" Instead, he caught himself and simply smiled.

"And please, call me Todd," Handley continued. As he glanced briefly at Jeff's resume, his phone rang. "Excuse me," he said, and then into the phone, "Have you heard from the client? And what did they say?" Todd's conversation continued for an additional fifteen minutes, as Jeff patiently waited. Todd fired off a couple of questions, briefly paused, scratched his chin, and grunted to show his agreement. "Well, Bill, got to sign off now. I have a candidate in front of me and I've probably screwed up his entire interview schedule. See you next week." He turned his attention back to Jeff. "So sorry—" he paused for moment as if struggling to remember Jeff's name before glancing again at the resume. "—Jeff! Important phone call— you understand. So tell me, what area of the law are you interested in?"

"To be honest, Todd," Jeff said, "I'm interested primarily in transactional work; however I would welcome the opportunity to do some litigation." Robert had briefed him months ago that it would be good to play both sides of the fence in order to secure a position with any firm.

"Do you think you would enjoy litigation, Jeff?" Todd asked.

"Again, in all honesty—probably not. But I do want to work for a top firm like Markham and Broadstreet."

"I'm impressed by your honesty," Todd responded. "Transactional work is important at Markham and Broadstreet. We do general corporate, finance, M&A, and even real estate. But it's only a small part of what we do."

"Yes—I looked at your website—"

Todd flashed him a big grin. "We're quite proud of that. You know, there's only a couple of thousand companies that have set up sites on the web. I'll bet in ten years, it'll be a gazillion."

Jeff smiled. "I'll bet you're right."

"Well, what did you think of it?" It was obvious Todd Handley was excited about being on the ground floor of this new technology.

"Very interesting, and colorful. The broad range of services you offer your clients appeals to me."

"Your resume and the courses you've taken, like Corporations, clearly show that transactional is the direction you want to take. I see here you even did some internships with investment banks. Not bad. However, our needs right now are in the litigation department. When we bring in our summer associates and our first-year associates, we rotate them through all our practice groups—including litigation. This gives them exposure to everything we do here."

"Yes, I'm aware of that," Jeff responded pleasantly. Although his experience was limited, he had come across a few different types of interviewers. Some preferred hearing themselves talk as opposed to listening to the interviewee. That wasn't so bad. It meant you could get through it unscathed. Some interviewers asked vague questions and allowed you to fill in all the gaps. Others asked questions with such a level of detail that you knew they wanted you to respond with the focus of a laser beam. Those were the highly technical types, and the scariest.

Todd Handley was more laid back, as partners go. His questions seemed to come from his gut, on instinct, and Jeff didn't get the impression he was interviewing for quality. The fact that Jeff was from Livermore had already earned him a seal of approval. No, Todd Handley was putting feelers out to see if Jeff was the right fit. He seemed content to sit back and see where Jeff would take the interview.

Jeff answered his questions as candidly as possible. Although it might be best to tell the interviewer what you thought he wanted to hear, that's not what Jeff was all about. He thought it best to be honest.

"So Jeff, you've told me a great deal about yourself," Todd concluded. "And surprisingly, about your background. Not everyone who comes in here wants to admit they come from a blue collar background. You strike me as someone who has real fire in the belly. You had to work hard to get to Livermore, and that's wonderful. Are you willing to put in that much effort, and a whole lot more, in order to become part of this firm?"

"Yes—without a doubt."

"Where do you see yourself in ten years?"

"Well, sir, without sounding presumptuous, I'd like to be exactly where you are. I'd like to be a partner at a prestigious law firm"

Todd Handley leaned back in his brown leather chair and took a good long look at Jeff, as if trying to see through him. "That's good," he said. He then leaned over and pressed the intercom button on his phone, summoning his secretary. "Stacy, could you take Jeff in to Marius?"

To Jeff's surprise, the associate conducting the next interview was warm and personable, at ease, and soft-spoken. Marius Walden was a Livermore graduate as well. He was tall, a little on the lanky side, and wore thick glasses. His blue pinstripe suit, starched white shirt and suspenders were definitely Wall Street but he didn't have that Wall Street cockiness.

"So, Jeff, I'll bet you're sitting here wondering what kind of nonsense I'm going to feed you about this firm. I'll tell you what. Our firm believes associate interviews should be about telling you guys the pros and cons of this place. After all, we're going to work long hard hours and it makes sense to have a good fit, both from your side and our side. So, fire away. What burning questions do you have about our firm?"

"I do have a couple," Jeff said. "You brought up the issue of long hard hours. Typically, what kind of hours are you billing?"

Marius leaned back in his chair and thought for a moment. A beam of light penetrated the window blinds and ricocheted off his watch, causing a disc of light that resembled a flying saucer to appear on the ceiling. "Well, typically—it's tough to say. Some months—like last month for instance—I billed about two hundred and sixty-five hours doing documents for a real estate transaction. It was multi-state, multi-property, and it had tons of due diligence. Most of that stuff I passed on to the first years. There was intense negotiation on every point, so that translated into more hours. Other months, things are more reasonable. I might bill anywhere from a hundred and seventy to two hundred hours. For a large practice, that's not too bad. I think this year I'll probably bill about twenty-three hundred hours, which will allow me to take advantage of our bonus system. Anybody told you about that?"

"No," Jeff responded. "What's the bonus system?"

"In terms of base salary, we tend to pay a little bit less. But if you do the hours and qualify for the bonus system, you can take home anywhere from twenty-five thousand to seventy-five thousand dollars in bonus, depending on what class year you're in."

"Sounds good." Jeff tried to keep the excitement out of his voice. The thought of killing his huge student debt with a big fat bonus check was more than welcome. A seventy-five-thousand-dollar bonus, he thought. That would go a long way toward wiping out the student loans he'd had to take to get through law school. He'd made it through college without owing a penny in debt, thanks to his scholarships. But that damn law school debt, a hundred thousand plus, was unbelievable. His mind was racing. *I'll have to work for it, and it'll take me a couple of years before I start making the big cash, but it's nice money all the same.*

"Jeff, it's been a pleasure." Marius ended the interview. "Here's my card. Call me if you think of any other questions or if you'd like to schedule another day to come visit with us." He gave Jeff a warm handshake and walked him down the hall to the office of another associate. Jeff felt pretty good about the way the interview had gone.

That afternoon he met with three other associates and another partner. Some even kept him talking longer than the twenty-minute period allotted for each interview. He thought that was an excellent sign.

But he wasn't going to wait around to hear from them. He continued his interviews, hammering away at some of the top law firms, but none seemed to go as well as the first. The chemistry just didn't seem to be there. Still, he met with everyone who would grant him the opportunity, went on callback interviews, and followed up with letters and phone calls. He was still waiting to hear from Darby and Blackstone. Although his on-campus interview with their recruiter had not gone well, he'd leveled an all-out blitz to their recruitment office, sending his cover letter and resume three times. He wasn't Law Review, and Darby and Blackstone typically took only Law Review types. But his grades were solid. With some luck, he thought, I might have a chance. The only question is, if I get the call, should I mention Robert Turner's name?

The economy was inching toward a recession, and many firms were freezing their hiring. Other practice groups, except those that specialized in bankruptcy, were reducing their number of new recruits. Tension continued to build within Jeff as he waited to hear something, even though a Livermore degree virtually guaranteed employment with a large firm. After all, the employment rate for a Livermore grad, right out of law school, was somewhere around ninety-eight percent. You either worked once you graduated, or there was something wrong with you. Despite the gloomy economic picture, he still hoped he would get a callback from Darby and Blackstone.

The next time he went into the law school cafeteria it was bustling with activity, as it usually was between classes. There were students on cell phones and public phones, students at tables discussing outlines, paper deadlines, and even some occasional law school gossip. Jeff saw Cosmo and Red at a table. He grabbed a cup of coffee and went to join them. He could hear Jacob Jefferson's big mouth at the next table, boasting about his success.

"I have a choice between five firms," Jacob was telling the equally nerdy guy sitting next to him. "The top five as rated by *American Lawyer* magazine, of course. So I developed a sophisticated evaluation system to determine which offer I want to take. Five points for overall reputation, four points for compensation, three points if I liked the practice area they're going to put me in, two points if I liked their offices, and one point if I liked the people. I settled on Tidley and Stanley. They're number two on the *American Lawyer* magazine list."

"Either I'm going over there and smash that muffin in his geeky face," said Red, "Or I'm going to bend over right here and hurl in front of everybody."

Jeff laughed. "Why? Just because he's arrogant and obnoxious? When did that become a crime?"

"So how's it going?" asked Cosmo. "You hearing back from anybody?"

"Yeah," said Jeff. "Just not the one I want. This fucking wait is damaging to my ego." He opened his backpack and pulled out four days of mail he hadn't had time to open. "You know, he continued, "I have to wonder whether all of these coordinators at all of the firms we interview with are genuinely that perky, or if they're putting on an act."

"It's an act," said Cosmo. "Designed to torture applicants by getting our hopes up."

Jeff was tearing thorough his stack of envelopes. "Bill, bill, another bill," he said. "Bullshit mail—oh, wait. This is interesting." He tore it open.

"What?" probed Cosmo. "You get an offer?"

"Yeah," Jeff said. "I . . . I believe I did. Listen to this. 'It is our pleasure to offer you a position as an associate,'"he read. "'Please inform us within two weeks if you plan to accept our offer. We look forward to hearing from you soon.'"

"That's awesome, man!" exclaimed Red. "Who's it from?"

"Markham and Broadstreet," Jeff replied. "I guess the first interview was a charm. Let's see what the rest of these say."

One by one, he ripped open all the letters bearing the crest of the law firms with which he'd interviewed, and one by one, he tossed them aside.

"Rejection, rejection, rejection," he said. "Good thing I opened the acceptance first. It made my day." He folded the acceptance letter and put it in his breast pocket, then used his other hand to crush the rejection letters in his palm. Taking aim at a nearby trash bin, he hooked it. The paper basketball nearly struck Jacob's head before landing on target. Jacob turned and stared indignantly at Jeff, who gave him a wink in response.

"Later, guys," he told Red and Cosmo. "Gotta get home to see if I have even more rejections waiting for me." He got up, threw his backpack over his shoulder, picked up his coffee and sauntered out of the cafeteria.

Nearly two weeks had passed since his first interview, and the rejections kept rolling in. It was time to make a decision, although it wasn't a difficult one, with only one offer on the table. He hadn't heard back from a handful of outstanding interviews with firms that had excited him. He had just a few more days to accept the offer from Markham and Broadstreet before it expired, so he had to get back in touch with them soon. Yet something prevented him. It was every Livermore law student's hope to get an offer from one of the top five.

They want the Jacob Jeffersons of this world, not me, he thought. *Who the hell am I kidding?* But there was a faint glimmer of hope that someone might recognize a special quality in him, one that made him stand apart from his brilliant and competitive peers. *I'll give it one more day,* he decided. *One more day, and that's it. And then I'll accept that offer.*

Before he left campus, Jeff stopped by the computer terminals on the second floor of the law building behind the escalators. The line to get a terminal was ten-deep but he needed to check his e-mails. It was a cumbersome process, but he had no other choice. His computer was beat-up and antiquated. The modem didn't work properly and it was a pain in the ass. *This is all just bullshit,* he lamented to himself. *It sucks being poor.*

Finally, after twenty minutes, he got one. Should I kiss the keyboard, he wondered. He logged on, typed in his password, and quickly scanned through his e-mails. The law students were regularly bombarded with correspondence about job placement, local events, exam and paper deadlines, and general Livermore news bulletins. A symposium on the development of legal thought in ancient Greece. End of the week keg party with the Legal Eagle Association. He deleted both of those and continued scanning until one caught his eye. It was from Dean Weissman.

"I understand you are interested in transactional work," the dean wrote. "It has come to my attention that Darby and Blackstone is looking for a new associate to do general corporate work. You are among a handful of students to whom I am forwarding this message. Please contact me if you are interested. I am anxious to respond, and to place one of our own with them."

Jeff leaped up from his chair and started off in the direction of the nearest phone booth. The girl at the terminal next to his called after him, "Hey, you forgot to log out."

"Do me a favor and log out for me."

"What about your backpack? Do you want that?"

Jeff ran back, grabbed his backpack, gave the girl a high-five, then turned again toward the phone booth. He made an appointment to see Dean

Weissman that afternoon.

Darby and Blackstone needed a transactional attorney, the dean told him, and they were planning to pull in a summer associate to groom for that position. It was a long shot—they were also looking at top students from other top law schools. So Jeff resolved to remain unemotional and accept whatever happened, but he gave the dean his resume with a renewed feeling of hope. He didn't even have to include a cover letter. The dean would send it over as part of a package that would include resumes of other Livermore candidates. "You probably won't hear from us," the dean told him. "I imagine you'll hear directly from Darby and Blackstone if they're interested."

There's no way—absolutely no way I'm going to lose any sleep over this, he thought but as the week went by, each passing day was more agonizing than the one before. If only they would go ahead and reject him he could get on with his life.

The end of the week came and went. *First thing on Monday, that's it,* he thought. *I'll have to take Markham and Broadstreet. But enough worrying. I'm gonna go to Wendy's and get myself a big fat burger and forget about this mess.*

Jeff unlocked the front door and bent over in his hallway to pick up his most comfortable sneakers. All his shoes were lined up in a neat row down the hall. He was pretty anal about that. Organization was everything, so everything in life had its ordered place. He certainly didn't have time to go looking for shoes when he was usually late for classes.

At that point the phone rang. Instead of racing down the hallway to answer, he proceeded at a slow, steady pace. He just couldn't take any more anxiety. His answering machine picked up, and he stopped and listened. Then:

"Shit!"

He fumbled through his pockets for the keychain engraved with an elaborate bald eagle and the inscription *United States Senate* underneath. It was a gift from his mom just before he left for Livermore. It stayed with him at all times. Quickly, he unlocked his door, then raced to the phone and snatched the receiver from its cradle. He pressed the talk button. The green light came to life.

"Hello?"

"Jeff Rhodes, please."

"This is Jeff," he said.

"Hi, Jeff. I'm glad you're at home. I was just leaving you a message. I'm Terry Summers, and I'm the recruitment coordinator with Darby and Blackstone."

He was so excited he could hardly speak. Realizing he'd better play it cool, he quickly composed himself. *Just keep it sweet and don't put your foot in your mouth,* he told himself.

"We'd like to bring you in to interview with some of our partners and associates in the corporate group. We have one more position available than we had anticipated. I know it's short notice, but would you come and visit with us?"

"Yes, of course. Whenever it's convenient."

"But before we bring you in—I know it's late in the season—we want to make certain you haven't already accepted a position elsewhere."

"No, I haven't. However, to be honest, there is a firm awaiting my reply. I have to get back to them soon or I may lose my position."

"Well then, that settles it. How about tomorrow? I'm sure I can fit you in, although it might get a little hectic squeezing you in to see all the partners."

"Oh, I understand. Their schedules must be crazy."

"Without a doubt," Terry responded. She sounded pleasant and had a quality about her that would immediately put anyone at ease. Most recruitment coordinators had that quality. It was a prerequisite to dealing with frenzied lawyers all the time. "Excellent," she concluded. "I'll get back to you later this afternoon with your itinerary. We look forward to seeing you."

Jeff spent the rest of the evening at the campus computer terminals on Lexis/Nexis, pulling up information on Darby and Blackstone. The firm had a ninety-eight-year history, ten domestic and international offices, and five hundred partners and associates—and the starting salary was over a hundred eighty thousand a year, plus bonus. Its corporate clients included General Electric, General Motors, Lockheed, Morgan Stanley, Merrill Lynch and Citicorp. The list went on and on and on.

The recruitment coordinator had scheduled his appointment for 11:30, but he built in extra time so he could sit quietly in the library for a while reviewing his notes before heading over to Darby and Blackstone's offices on Manhattan's exclusive east side.

For the interview, he wore his best pinstriped suit, and he added suspenders to enhance the corporate touch. His shoes were a couple of years old and a little worn, but they were polished, and they were a good brand that had cost him (on sale) almost a hundred bucks. Before leaving his apartment, Jeff stopped and looked in the mirror. One last time, he practiced asking all the questions about the firm he already knew the answer to, by virtue of his research. He would have to sound genuinely interested, well informed and inquisitive. Jeff threw on his jacket and picked up his briefcase and was out the door. He reached into his pocket for his lucky key chain, locked up and headed out.

It was a beautiful morning. The sun was climbing but the temperature, only about sixty-eight degrees, was comfortable. He stepped off the front porch of the old brownstone and looked up at his second-story window. As expected, he saw Yankee sitting on the window ledge, looking down like a young prince greeting his admiring subjects. Jeff waved to his little friend. The cat was sometimes a pain in the ass, but he always knew when to show support.

He took the bus into the city so he wouldn't have to work up a sweat over finding a place to park the Jeep, and so he could look over his notes one more time. He had researched the personal histories of each of the partners he was scheduled to meet, and he knew their areas of practice, the schools they attended and any transactions of note with cases they'd worked on. He also reviewed bullet points about his resume, the classes he had taken, and what he considered his unique qualifications for the position. And last, were his lists of questions for each interviewer.

The bus pulled into Penn Station and Jeff collected his belongings, shoved them into his briefcase, and started filing out with the other passengers. He was the last in line.

"Watch your step," the bus driver cautioned an elderly woman who was taking her time. Jeff followed the old woman but didn't heed the driver's advice. As he stepped off the bus, he felt the heel of his left shoe scrape against the curb and he felt the wobble as he walked away. Turning back, he saw the heel sitting on the curb. Walking over to pick it up made the nails that had secured it push against the sole of his foot, and he could feel them scraping against the concrete. *Fuck me,* he thought grimly as he put the heel in his pocket, limped to the nearest pay phone and dialed information. He couldn't wait until he could afford a cell phone.

"Yes, New York Telephone," answered a pert female voice.

"Hi—I'm at Penn Station in Manhattan. Can you give me the location of any shoe repair shop in this area of the city?"

"Do you have a name?"

"No, I don't. Any will do."

After a moment, the voice said, "Sorry, I'm not picking anything up—although I do have something under shoeshine shop. Would you like that number?"

"Whatever," responded Jeff, completely overwhelmed. He glanced at his watch. Thank God he had built in an extra half-hour. That's all the time he had left to make it to Darby and Blackstone.

"Vito's Shoe Shine, located on West Thirty-Sixth Street. I believe that's just off Seventh Avenue. Would you like the number?"

Jeff hung up the phone and did a kind of awkward tip-toe shuffle with his left foot, trying his best to prevent the nails from scraping against the sidewalk. On his way to Thirth-Sixth Street, he passed two shoe stores. One was a sneaker shop, so he couldn't have purchased anything there. The second, however, was upscale. The cheapest pair of loafers on display was two hundred and fifty bucks. With only twenty-five dollars in his pocket, he had no choice but to hope Vito's Shoe Shine also doubled as a repair shop.

Two-and-a-half blocks later, with sweat dripping from his brow and enough embarrassment to last him a lifetime, Jeff made it to Vito's and limped through the front door. One of the shoeshine men, wearing a red vest over a white shirt, leaped out of his chair. "Hey, what happened to you?" he asked with a thick Brooklyn accent. You get shot in the foot?"

"Hey, buddy—you gotta help me." Jeff pulled the heel from his jacket pocket and slipped off his damaged shoe. Holding it out, he looked at the man, his panic growing. "Can you fix this?"

"Whoa—how'd that happen?"

"I really don't have time to explain, my friend," Jeff replied. "I've got an important job interview today and—"

"Only guy who can fix that is Vito, and Vito's not here today."

A man sitting in one of the shoeshine seats puffing on a Marlboro dropped the sports page of The *New York Times.* "Nah, he's here," he said. "Came in when you went out to get coffee. He's in the back. Hey, Vito!" he yelled. "You got some guy out here looking for ya."

"Man, you're in luck," said the shoeshine man.

"Thanks, guys."

A short Asian man stepped out from the back room. "Who's got a problem here?" He had a thick Chinese accent.

"You're Vito?"

"Yeah, I Vito."

He didn't look like a Vito, but Jeff stepped forward and handed over the shoe. "Please, I'm in a rush. Can you help me?"

"Yeah—five minutes," said Vito, holding up five fingers.

A few minutes later, Jeff bolted out of Vito's like all the demons of hell were after him. Time was precious. He absolutely could not arrive late for the interview of a lifetime. That would be inexcusable—but his luck was holding. A Yellow Cab was heading his way. He held one arm up and yelled, "Stop!"

The taxi came to a screeching halt. Jeff opened the door and jumped into the back seat. "Thanks," he said. "I have an important interview in fifteen minutes, and I've gotta get my butt all the way over to East Forty-Fourth." He hoped his anxiety would dissipate by the time he reached Darby and

Blackstone.

"No problem," the driver assured him. "Hang onto your hat, pal!" He whipped the cab into a wicked U-turn and sped through two yellow lights and one red before reaching Jeff's destination. "That'll be thirteen-seventy-five," he said as he pulled to a stop ten minutes later. Jeff handed over fifteen dollars, which left him with barely enough to make it back home. As he stepped out of the car, the driver rolled down the window. "Good luck, kid."

"Yeah, by the looks of things today, I'm gonna need it."

CHAPTER 11

Darby and Blackstone

Jeff arrived at the posh east midtown address with only five minutes to spare. The building was relatively new, and the interior décor was modern, featuring lots of marble and glass. There was a single security desk at the center of the lobby, the only structure in that area besides the numerous silver columns stretching thirty feet into the air, floor to ceiling. Massive windows encircled the space, and delicate white curtains prevented the intense light from assaulting all who entered there. The lobby would otherwise be unbearable during the summer months.

Jeff checked in with the security guard, who directed him to the fortieth floor. The elevator door opened and Jeff stepped out, his heart pounding. The elegant black and gold marble nameplate, Darby and Blackstone, hung above the firm's entrance. He took a deep breath to settle himself. There was no time to be nervous. He would just have to wing it. It was time to kick some ass.

The receptionist buzzed him in and greeted him politely. Throughout his interviews the offices of many firms had impressed him, but Darby and Blackstone was different. The entry way was unlike anything he had seen so far. This was real class. The floor was marble tile. A large, circular glass table sat across the room, opposite the main reception desk. Majestically, at its center, sat a huge Chinese porcelain vase, filled with the most dazzling bouquet Jeff had ever seen. The delicate perfume of the flowers permeated the reception area. A few minutes after Jeff made himself comfortable in a small leather chair Terry, the recruitment coordinator, came out to greet him.

"Jeff—wonderful to see you," she said. "Did you have any trouble getting here?"

"No, none at all," he responded calmly. *If she only knew.*

"May I get you something? Sparkling water? Tea or coffee?"

"No thanks, Terry. I'm fine."

"Well then, let's get started. Come with me to my office and I'll brief you on who you'll be meeting with."

Jeff followed Terry down a spiral staircase with shiny, solid brass banisters. Again, the décor was spectacular. The stairs were the same expensive marble as on the floor in the main reception area. Once they arrived at the bottom of the staircase, he looked to his right and peered down the long corridor.

"Impressive, isn't it?" said Terry.

"It sure is," Jeff responded.

"When you're working long, hard hours, it really is nice to be in an environment that's aesthetically pleasing. Let me take a few moments to show you the conference area. And one of the associates you'll be meeting with today will show you the library. I think you'll find it equally impressive."

The corridor, unlike the entrance area and the lobby, was dimly lit but it had little reading nooks set into the wall every ten feet or so. Within each nook was a comfortable chair with a small painting directly above it. They reached the end of the corridor, where a spectacular painting of Versailles hung on the far wall in a brightly lit foyer. The contrast was breathtaking.

"The conference area is excellent for entertaining clients or impressing opposing counsel," said Terry.

"I'm sure," Jeff responded, trying not to sound overly impressed himself.

She turned a brass doorknob on a large oak door, then opened it just enough to allow Jeff a peek inside. There was a meeting going on, so he couldn't see much. Terry quietly closed the door, then spoke in a whisper. "Sorry—I wasn't aware there was a meeting in there. That's the Blackstone conference room. Let me see if the Darby room is available." She led him to the other side of the large foyer and ushered him inside.

"Wow," Jeff said, no longer able to restrain his enthusiasm. It was unbelievable.

The large doors opened into a massive space with a table that stretched from one end of the room to the other. It could easily seat fifty people. Large portraits of Darby and Blackstone graced the walls on either side of the conference table, and below them were framed photos of various partners with CEOs of Fortune 500 companies, Cabinet members, representatives of the United Nations, and the heads of state of various countries. Huge bay windows allowed in dazzling bright light that nurtured two large palm trees in each corner of the room. The ceiling was about twenty feet high, contributing greatly to the prominence of this room.

Terry motioned for Jeff to follow her, and she took him past a bust of Blackstone and through a side panel in the wall that slid open to another long corridor.

"Pretty cool, isn't it?" she quipped, smiling broadly. "Like something out of a James Bond movie."

Jeff was speechless, taken in by the aesthetics—the beauty of design combined with the sumptuous furnishings. The place was magnificent. It even smelled rich.

They arrived at the end of the corridor and made a left turn into Terry's office, where she invited him to take a seat as she settled behind her desk. "This is your itinerary," she said, handing him a sheet of paper. "You'll be meeting with Sean Witherspoon. He's one of the most prominent partners, and he's the chair of our corporate group. You'll also see Raymond Alexander, another senior partner in corporate. Both have impeccable reputations and serve numerous Fortune 500 companies in some of their most complex transactions. Unfortunately, Franklin Barro, one of our star junior partners, will not be able to meet with you today. He regrets having to cancel. It would have been great for you because he made partner only a year and a half ago."

"That would certainly lend a different perspective," Jeff said.

"Do you happen to know any of these partners?"

"No," he replied, puzzled by her question. "Why do you ask?"

"Well, I detect a certain degree of excitement amongst them in meeting you. So I thought either you know them, or you're one of the hottest new students to come out of Livermore."

Carefully watching her expression, Jeff wondered if he should mention he'd been friends with Robert Turner. She was still smiling, which gave nothing away. He decided against it. He flashed her a quick grin and said, "Oh—obviously, the latter."

She laughed, and he joined in.

They ascended the dazzling spiral staircase and took the elevator five flights up to Sean Witherspoon's corner office.

"We occupy ten floors in this building," Terry told him. "If you count word processing, our central mail room and our IT department, it's actually eleven." As she stepped off the elevator she asked Jeff to have a seat in the reception area. During his brief wait, Jeff looked at the firm's brochure which profiled the recent redesign by Coffman, Reeds Architects, P.C., of the downstairs lobby. The caption under the photo read, "The elegant lobby now has a ceiling perimeter of stained glass by an artist selected by the Museum of Modern Art, custom bronze lighting sources, an embellished terrazzo floor pattern, stylized elevator entrances, a two-hundred-foot-long planter, and an oversized marble high-tech concierge desk, which all contribute to the new, distinctive look."

Terry emerged from Witherspoon's office, still smiling, and Jeff got to his feet. "He's off the phone now and ready to see you."

"Thank you so much for everything," he said.

"Good luck, Jeff. We're aware that you have a deadline to meet with another firm. The partners are having a recruitment committee meeting tomorrow morning. All decisions are made rather quickly, as far as New York law firms go. You should have an answer shortly thereafter."

Jeff thanked her again and started down the corridor to Witherspoon's office. He was surprised to find the door open. He tapped on it anyway.

In his high-backed black leather chair, the partner swiveled around, then rose to shake Jeff's hand. "Mr. Rhodes, how are you?"

"Very well, Mr. Witherspoon. Thank you for having me."

"Oh, let's drop the formality, Jeff. Have a seat over here next to me on the sofa."

Jeff had never had an interview conducted on a sofa, but he had no problem with it. The more laid-back the environment, he thought, the better. *The only thing is, I don't want to fall into a trap. Maybe he's trying to see how comfortable he can make me to see if he can sucker me into saying something stupid.* The key, he knew, was to exude confidence and stay sharp, but to also show a sense of humor.

"So, Jeff, you want to do deals?"

"Yes—I've always been interested in the transactional side of the law. Litigation has never really appealed to me."

"Well then, you're in the right place. Although the economy has been a little slow of late, Darby has remained busy, very busy. Our clients want quality and they know they can find it here with us."

The interview continued for about thirty minutes. Although it wasn't an easy one, Jeff felt he had Witherspoon in his corner. The man had an interesting style, first pointing out a potential flaw in Jeff's resume, then turning it around and saying something positive, which put Jeff off balance for a split second. Then Witherspoon built him back up to a level where he felt comfortable again.

"Normally here at Darby we take only Law Review," the partner said. "But as I mentioned earlier, we're incredibly busy, and we need warm bodies in our corporate group. Your resume is solid and, on the whole, better than many of the candidates I've seen thus far."

Now that's what I like to hear, Jeff thought. *But dammit—why does everyone characterize my resume and my transcript as solid? Why not spectacular? Damned lawyers—always so understated. They find it so difficult to give a compliment. Still, it was going well. Really well.*

But what he said was, "Thank you, sir. I appreciate that."

"It also didn't hurt that one of our associates put in a good word for you."

Jeff was surprised. "That's good to hear. I'll have to thank him before I leave, if you'll tell me who—"

"Oh, that won't be possible," Witherspoon said quickly. "He, uh, he's no longer with us. But his recommendation was solid."

Immediately, a warm sensation swept through Jeff. Of course it was Robert—Jeff didn't know anyone else who'd had anything to do with Darby and Blackstone. Robert had been serious about recommending him. That was a true friend.

At the conclusion of the interview, Witherspoon leaned over, picked up the phone and told two other partners that if at all possible, he'd like them to see Jeff. That was a good sign. There was no reason he would ask two other partners, in addition to those already scheduled, to see Jeff if he didn't like him.

After four and a quarter hours, four partners, three associates, and a final debriefing with the recruiting coordinator, Jeff exited the downstairs lobby and stepped out onto the street again. He felt good, and for the first time in a long time, he felt like all his hard work would pay off.

He arrived at his apartment an hour and a half later, opened his door, went straight to his bedroom and collapsed on his bed. Yankee hopped up and greeted him with a nuzzle under his arm.

"Are you happy to see me, or do you want me to feed you?"

Jeff already knew the answer. He got up, took off his jacket and undid his tie. Whenever he wore a suit, it was always a race to get his clothes off as quickly as possible before Yankee rubbed against him and got cat hair all over everything. As he undid the buttons on his shirt, he noticed the light on his answering machine blinking. Probably his mom, he thought, calling to find out how the interview went. He pressed the button and fell into his La-Z-Boy.

"Hi, Jeff. I hope you get this message as soon as you get home." Jeff immediately recognized the voice—Terry—but he tried to suppress his excitement. "We know you need a prompt response, and in all honesty, this is probably the quickest response I've ever seen in all my years at Darby. You must have knocked the partners' socks off, because the firm is pleased to extend you an offer, and we await your response. A confirmation letter will go out immediately and should arrive at your home within the next two days. We look forward to hearing from you soon."

It took a few moments for the words to sink in. Jeff jumped out of the chair, picked up his phone and began to dial. "Mom, you're not gonna believe this," he said as soon as she picked up. "I did it! I got the job!"

"Of course you did," she replied. "What did I tell you? Persistence counts."

He laughed. "You're not even surprised."

"Not at all. You deserve it. You've worked hard, and everything you want in life will come to you because of it. I'm proud of you, my son."

"You too, Mom," he said. "You worked hard, too, to get me here. I'm going to make sure it wasn't for nothing."

CHAPTER 12

A New Beginning

"My man! Good to see you," said Cosmo as Jeff approached the bar in Mario's café in the heart of Soho. Cosmo held out his hand, which Jeff took with both of his. He turned around and stepped straight into Red's bear hug.

"Congratulations, big shot!" Red said, then turned to the bartender. Waving a fifty-dollar bill, he motioned for another round of shots for the three of them.

"This feels like old times," said Jeff with a smile. "Just a little more upscale." He appreciated the warm reception. He hadn't made a close connection with anyone else at Livermore, except Robert Turner. No one he could call a real friend. He'd run into Red at the library that afternoon, and when he'd shared the news he'd landed a position at Darby and Blackstone Red had insisted on a celebration. Jeff was happy to oblige.

He noticed Red's eyes were somewhat glazed and there were dark shadows beneath them, which meant he was working long into the night— every night—or he was doing coke again. Jeff hoped it was the former.

"A toast!" Cosmo pronounced enthusiastically. "To Jeff Rhodes, the hardest-working man at Livermore."

"And he ain't seen nothin' yet," added Red as the bartender poured all three of them a shot of Sambuca. They tossed them back quickly, and Cosmo motioned for another round.

"Not that I'm not ecstatic to see you guys," said Jeff. "But how are Cassandra and Molly? I was sort of hoping they'd be here."

Cosmo coughed. "Well, excuuuuse me!" he said "Why don't you just kill me now?" He leaned over slightly so Red could plunge an imaginary knife into his back. "Mind you, I gotta go back to the office tonight, and I slipped out to have a couple of drinks with my old friend from Livermore, only to hear him say he's more interested in the ladies than in hanging out with me."

The three men laughed. Cosmo put his hand on Jeff's shoulder, then grabbed him by the back of the neck. It sent a tickling sensation down Jeff's spine. "Cassandra sends her love," Cosmo continued. "She wishes she could join us, but she's stuck in the office all night."

"I had a sneaking suspicion about you and Cass," Red commented.

"What do you mean?" Jeff asked. "She say something to you?"

"No, but we can tell," teased Cosmo. "You always get those puppy dog eyes when you guys are in the same room. You have a thing for her."

"And you're a pair of idiots," Jeff shot back cheerfully.

Cosmo's cell phone rang and he rolled his eyes. "This better not be the office." He flipped open his phone and answered with a brisk, "Yeah, Cosmo here." Then, "Yes, the new Darby and Blackstone man is standing right beside me. He paused a moment. "Fine—I'll turn the phone over to him, since you have no interest in how I'm doing and what I've been up to." Another pause, then with a chuckle: "Okay, I'll remember that." He gave the phone to Jeff. "Here, it's for you."

With all of the noise in the bar, Jeff could hardly hear her, and now that the pressure was off, he realized how much he'd missed that beautiful voice. He held the receiver tight to his left ear and plugged his finger in the right one, but he still couldn't make out what she was saying. Frustrated, he moved away from the bar to find a quiet corner in another room.

"Where the hell is he going?" asked Cosmo.

"He doesn't want to miss a word," replied Red. "I think the boy's in love."

"Did I miss something? I mean, I knew he liked her, but I didn't think it bordered on—choke, gasp—love."

"If only he knew she was dating that prick Alberto."

"I wouldn't call it dating. She's his piece on the side."

"Which makes him a prick," Red agreed.

"Yeah—a real obnoxious jerk-off," said Cosmo.

"He barely had two words for me last time I saw him and Monica," Red told him. "He's up for partner this year and will probably make it, so he thinks he walks on water."

"Cassandra's too smart to put up with that shit."

"Yeah, well—you know what they say. Love is blind."

"And stupid," Red commented. He sniffed, took out a handkerchief and wiped his nose. "Which is why I don't bother."

•••

Jeff found a quiet spot near the kitchen. "Okay, that's better," he told

Cassandra. "I can hear you now."

"I'm sorry I couldn't make it tonight. I'd really love to see you."

"Oh, that's okay. It's nice you made time to call."

"I always have time for a friend."

That stung a little. A friend. He knew what it meant. It spelled out the sentiment that even though a woman liked you, maybe even cared about you, she wasn't interested in anything else. He shouldn't be surprised or hurt, he knew. They'd had that one special moment in time, comforting each other after Robert's funeral, but that's all it was. What with studying, tests and interviews, he hadn't spoken to her in weeks, and they hadn't seen each other. Jeff had called her a couple of times but she'd been busy and so had he, and time got away from them.

"So what have you been up to besides work?" he asked her.

"That's a depressing question," she said. "I haven't been doing very much of anything besides work."

"That's even more depressing," he said. "But I hear you. I've been busy, too."

"I know—and congratulations on D and B."

"Thanks, but you've got to have some fun—" he was leading up to something but she cut him off.

"Well, I have been trying to get away once in a while," she said. "You know—weekend trips to Florida, or the Hamptons. About two weeks ago I went to a bed and breakfast up in Maine for an overnight. That was fun."

It sounded like there was a significant other in the picture, but Jeff wasn't about to give up. "So when can I see you?" he asked. "Do you get to take lunch outside the office?"

"Yeah—and when you start at Darby, you'll be right in my neighborhood. We can definitely get together for lunch. I would love that."

"Well, I better get back to the guys. They're gonna wonder where I went for so long."

There was a brief silence. He felt there was something more to be said. He didn't want to hang up.

"Jeff, I just want you to know I'm really proud of you. Robert would have been proud of you as well."

"Yeah . . . thanks. I try not to think about it but I wish he was here. And I wish he was at Darby with me. If I dwell on it too long, it overshadows the happiness I'm feeling right now. And that's the last thing I want."

"That's the last thing Robert would want, too. Anyway, I'm so happy for you, and we will get together soon, okay? Keep in touch."

"Good night. Don't work too hard."

"Good night, Jeff."

Jeff folded up Cosmo's cell phone and walked back to the guys at the bar, both of whom were smiling broadly. "What's so amusing?" he asked as he handed the phone back to Cosmo, who slipped it into his interior breast pocket.

"Don't get mad, now," Red told him. "We didn't say a word." He and Cosmo looked at each other, and then at Jeff. They both started blowing kisses at him.

•••

"Shit! I'm gonna be late!"

Jeff quickly did his tie, threw on his jacket and ran out the door. He had to be on time for his first day of orientation. Stopping at the base of the stairway, he pulled his itinerary out of his pocket and unfolded it.

Breakfast in the Darby Conference Room, 9:00 A.M.

Library Tour, 10:00 A.M.

New Associate Seminar, How to Succeed as a First Year Associate, 11:00 A.M.

Lunch and Tour of Corporate Group, 12:30 P.M.

Office Assignments, 1:45 P.M.

Jeff couldn't wait to see his office.

As he walked to the corner of his block, a bus bound for midtown Manhattan blew past him and came to an abrupt halt at the stop. In the distance, he could see the doors fly open and a couple of passengers disembark. Running at full speed, he arrived just as the doors closed and the bus started off again. "I know you saw me, you son of a bitch!" he shouted, frantically waving his arms. Suddenly the driver pulled to a screeching stop and Jeff heard the welcome sound of the doors opening again.

"Thanks, chief," he said to the driver. Then he made his way down the aisle to a seat all the way in the back, promising himself he would get an apartment near his office as soon as he had amassed enough pay checks to cover the move.

A nervous tingle of excitement followed him as he walked down the long corridor to the entrance of the Darby and Blackstone conference room. There was also the beginning of a knot in his stomach. He turned the brass knob of the large oak door and the tantalizing aroma of breakfast hit him instantly, causing his mouth to water. He realized he was hungry.

Each of the high-back leather chairs arranged around the massive table had a name tag and a packet of information on the table before it. Jeff made his way through the crowd of new associates and found his place. Jeffrey Rhodes, Livermore Law. Determined not to feel like an outsider, he decided to work the room and get some conversation started. Sizing up the competition, he took a quick scan of his new co-workers. "Law Review nerds, all of 'em," he mumbled.

"Excuse me—did you say something to me?"

He turned to look at the woman next to him. "No," he replied. "Just thinking out loud, I guess."

"I'm Dahlia." She gave him a tentative smile and looked down at his name tag. "And you must be Jeff from Livermore."

"Nah . . . that's my alias," he quipped. "My real name is Double-O-Seven."

Dahlia looked at him with a blank stare, then turned to greet another associate as Terry, the recruiter, entered and asked all the associates to be seated so Ray Alexander, one of the partners, could deliver a few words. But first, she said, she wanted to encourage the second year associates to give the new associates a real Darby and Blackstone welcome. In the meantime, she added, an attendant would go around to each of them to take their breakfast order. Jeff was famished.

He watched to see how other associates interacted with the attendant. Some were gracious and considerate, taking a moment to look at the man, acknowledge his presence, and thank him once they had placed their order. Others barely looked at him, ordering quickly and brusquely as if he were interrupting an important discussion they were having with the associate next to them.

Fuckin' obnoxious assholes, Jeff thought. Then he felt a tap on his shoulder.

"Hey—do me a favor and pass the Sweet 'n' Low," whispered the guy on his right. "Thanks. I'm Phil."

"I'm Jeff—Jeff Rhodes."

"Phil Ginsburg." They shook hands and Jeff slid a gold-plated dish of Sweet 'n' Low over to Phil. It also held packets of sugar. "Did you notice it yet?"

"What?" asked Jeff.

"Everything in this place is golden."

"Golden?"

"Yeah," Phil said. "Golden doorknobs, golden fixtures, golden silverware." He lifted his spoon. "Golden dishes, golden everything."

"Yeah, you're right."

"Do you see the golden bars on the windows?" asked Phil.

"Bullshit!"

"Right—well, maybe you don't see them now, but you will."

"What do you mean?"

"This is it—this whole place," Phil explained. "It's our golden prison, complete with golden handcuffs—or diamond, if you walk the walk. My dad's a partner at Chase and Barney, and I'm in my second-year here. Trust me, I know the drill. This is your new home for the foreseeable future, Jeffy boy. Welcome to D and B."

The knot in Jeff's stomach loosend a little. "That's cool," he said. "At least it's a nice home." Phil seemed the type of guy who tells it like it is, which Jeff appreciated.

Those comments brought a rush of memories pouring into his consciousness, memories of his struggle, all the little sacrifices he and his mom had to make over the years, even doing without some of life's necessities, in order to get him to where he was at that moment. He didn't think he'd mind a prison, as long as it was as luxurious as the offices here. Ray Alexander came in then, and Terry gave him a quick introduction before he started speaking to the group.

Jeff glanced around at his fellow associates. Their eyes were transfixed on the speaker as if he was imparting some great philosophical knowledge or giving them the keys to unlock the deepest mysteries of the universe. He droned on about how they should stop every so often and smell the roses, or bathe in the sea, or look up and marvel at the clouds. It reminded Jeff of Uncle Murray's advice, then his mind wandered.

My mom has never pushed me to do anything, yet her strong influence is always there, he thought. *My family all say I have exceeded their expectations. I know they all think I'm going to be really big someday.*

How was that possible? He was over a hundred thousand dollars in debt.

It was so weird at graduation. So many professors who'd given him a hard time made it a point to go up to his mom and tell her what hard a worker he was and how he was a real person. They had raved to Mrs. Rhodes about Jeff's work ethic, his compassion and his demeanor, some even saying he was an extraordinary student who tried his best to remain an ordinary person and to treat everyone around him with dignity and respect.

He wasn't sure exactly how to take the compliment, because compared to their comments about Jacob Jefferson, some of which he overheard, maybe ordinary wasn't so good. Those same professors said Jacob was a brilliant student who would be extremely successful in law, and if he continued on the right track, he could even mold the law. They had no doubt he would make partner, or perhaps even become a great judge. Still, Jacob almost had three cows when he found out Jeff was going to Darby and Blackstone.

The grand hall had been electric that evening. Adding to the excitement of graduation, an Associate Justice of the United States Supreme Court was there to deliver the keynote address. Jeff's entire family was present and gave him their enthusiastic support, but it was his mother, above all, who'd been glowing with pride.

Thanks in large part to her, Jeff had made it. He'd landed a position as an associate in one of the biggest, most successful law firms in the country. Despite the sense of urgency and the certainty of the long hours to come, there was something exciting about it all. Very exciting. He still wasn't quite sure how he'd pulled it off.

He snapped back to attention when another associate entered the room and interrupted the presentation. The man had a glazed, blank look on his face and appeared a little nervous, as though he had something on his mind but was uncertain about how to address it. He stopped for a moment, scanned the crowd, and then tapped the speaker on the shoulder before whispering something in his ear.

Phil turned to Jeff again. "I don't want to get you all worked up, but I think it's time for your exciting library tour. Come on—finish your breakfast and I'll show you around."

Jeff's first three days at the firm were an uneventful routine of orientation seminars, facility tours and paperwork—lots of paperwork. There were forms to fill out, including health and dental benefits, and even a life insurance policy equal to two times an associate's salary. Not bad, he thought. If I kick the bucket, Mom will make a nice piece of change.

He settled easily into his office, which had a kick-ass view, and he had quickly become acclimated to his secretary. Adrienne was a no-nonsense character who could type about five hundred words a minute. A couple of the other associates had told him he'd better get on her good side early on. Otherwise not much of his work would get done. She was good, they'd said, but only if she liked you. If he'd had any fantasies about a bombshell secretary with long legs and tight skirts, Adrienne dispelled them. She tipped the scales at over two hundred pounds, and all her skirts went to mid-calf. Jeff figured he was better off with that situation. A bombshell would be a distraction he didn't need.

The intercom on his phone buzzed, and he sprang forward to pick up the receiver. "Yes, Adrienne?"

"Franklin Barro would like to see you in his office. He said you just got staffed on a transaction and he needs you right away."

"Thanks, Adrienne."

Franklin Barro's office was at the other end of the long hallway. Between him and Jeff were several associates' offices, secretary cubicles, and a massive file room. Jeff walked toward Barro's big oak door with a mixture of excitement and trepidation and arrived there to find it shut. He read the nameplate to make certain he was in the right spot. He was. Taking a deep breath, he knocked on the door. He waited a moment and when he didn't hear anything, he opened it just enough to peek inside. Barro was behind his desk, leaning back in his leather chair, rocking gently back and forth, the telephone to his ear. A heavyset man with thick eyeglasses and thick black hair slicked back with some kind of pomade or gel, he was wearing suspenders. Jeff noticed a thick gut hanging over the front of his pants where his belt would have been.

Barro waved him in and motioned for him to take a seat on the couch. Three other attorneys were there—one partner and two associates. "Tom, if you don't mind I'm going to put you on speaker," he said into the phone. "I have everyone here. Joining us on this call is a new addition to the group— Jeff Rhodes, another hotshot from Livermore. You should put his name on the distribution list. He's going to be doing a lot of the legwork on this transaction."

"Welcome, Jeff," said the voice over the speaker.

"Thank you. It's good to be here."

That drew a round of laughter from everyone. One of the other associates leaned over and handed Jeff a transaction background. Barro spoke again. "Ray, why don't you catch Jeff up."

"Of course," Ray said. "Gamma Enterprises. A four hundred sixty-two million dollar purchase of Plateau Inc. Plateau is an Arizona-based conglomerate whose assets may be divided into three primary components: real estate, which includes hotels, multifamily housing and retail shopping centers; aircraft and equipment, which includes a fleet of four small aircraft and engine parts as part of Plateau's charter flight division; patents, which includes patents for fuel-efficient automobile engines and significant research and development to secure an additional three patents within the next three years. Plateau is heavily in debt and unable to meet its debt service payments. Facing a possible Plateau bankruptcy, Gamma proposes to secure a loan in the amount of six hundred million to pay off outstanding creditors and purchase all of Plateau's assets. The projected closing date is mid-November."

Barro listened intently as Tom Williams, executive vice president with Gamma, outlined the company's issues of concern for the transaction. "Franklin, we haven't wrapped up the financing yet. We have some of the big banks interested, but we're getting the best rate from Reed and Reed."

"I have no problem with that, Tom, but if you go with one of the investment banks—even if they do quote you the best rate—for the real estate portion of the transaction, you know they're going to want to securitize it. That means you get the rating agencies involved, which means you'll have to deal with a whole range of bullshit requirements. That could slow us down, and I know your target date is mid-November."

"I understand, Franklin, but I have the utmost confidence in you. You could wrap this up in your sleep." Another round of laughter.

Several hours later, after a conference call it seemed would never end, Jeff went back to his office and collapsed into his swivel chair. Already, he had file folders stacked on top of his file cabinet and papers strewn about his desk. Exhausted, he picked up the phone. He needed to speak with a friendly voice.

"Mr. Ginsberg's office."

"Hi, Marcy. Could you put me through to Phil?"

"Is this Jeff?"

"Yes."

"Just one moment."

"What's up, asshole?" Jeff asked when Phil came on the line.

"This is Phil Ginsburg. Asshole already left for the day. Can I help you?"

"It was you, wasn't it?"

"Me what?" said Phil, trying with all his might to disguise the fact that he was about to burst out laughing.

"Every time I come back to my office, I have to unscrew those little screws that hold my nameplate in place, flip the damn thing over, and then screw those damn screws back in."

"You mean someone keeps turning your name upside down?"

"Yes, among other things."

"Other things?" Phil responded, and he no longer sounded amused.

"Like . . . I couldn't find my mouse this morning. And then it miraculously reappeared this afternoon."

"Really?" Phil feigned surprised.

"Oh, and I almost forgot—this morning I left my desk for about twenty minutes to go to the fax room. When I came back, I found that someone drank half of my glass of orange juice and took a big bite out of the bagel I left on my desk."

"Barbarians. You'd think at a firm like this people would behave themselves."

"I don't think it has anything to do with behavior," said Jeff. "Maybe this mystery bandit has a little too much time on his hands."

"I think you should have that bagel dusted for fingerprints. Did you keep any of it for evidence?" asked Phil, and they both laughed. "Are you swamped with that mega-deal?"

"Phil, I don't know whether I'm coming or going."

"If it makes you feel any better, I just got staffed on a monster deal myself. I'm gonna be here all night. You want to order Chinese, Italian, or go downstairs to the cafeteria?"

"Before I do anything, I need another cup of coffee."

At approximately eleven P.M., Jeff decided to take a breather. He put down his pen and looked up from his desk to find Phil standing in the doorway with a big grin on his face. "Nice socks, Phil," he said to his shoeless friend.

"Never mind casual day. If it were up to me, we'd be allowed to walk around in our robes and slippers past nine o'clock—and women in T-shirts and panties. I figure at the very least, I should be allowed to roll up my sleeves, undo my tie and take my shoes off."

"Are you out of here soon?" asked Jeff.

"Maybe another forty-five minutes and then I'm gonna call a car."

"I can't figure this shit out."

"What the hell is that? What are you working on?"

Jeff picked up the twenty-five page title insurance commitment sitting on his desk and grabbed three canister tubes, which he put under his arm. "Follow me."

They walked down the hall to the main conference room. Empty cartons of Chinese food, half-eaten slices of pizza, chips, dip, salsa, fruit and cans of soda were strewn about the table. "I guess the cleaning crew hasn't arrived yet," remarked Phil.

"What I can't believe is how much food is wasted," said Jeff. "It's what my mother would call a sin, with millions of starving people out there, and tons of food around here that's just thrown away. You'd think we—the practice, I mean—would have some kind of relationship with a soup kitchen or something. Look at this. Veal parmesan—not even touched. All this should be boxed up and delivered to a soup kitchen or homeless shelter."

Phil looked at Jeff as if he had just dropped out of the sky from Mars. "Get real, Jeff. Now show me what you're working on." Jeff unplugged one of the canisters and unrolled a nine-page survey. It stretched across half of the conference table. "Awesome!" Phil continued. "So now you're an architect."

"I wish. I gotta figure this thing out."

"Didn't anyone tell you what to do?"

"No, and I have no fucking clue. Maybe if they communicated with each other—"

"That doesn't seem to happen at Darby and Blackstone," Phil broke in. "It's rare that one partner knows what another partner is doing, or having the associates do."

"Yeah," Jeff agreed. "The clueless associates are expected to take on any work given to them. And the partners—most of them—are so impatient.

That creates a lot of tension in the office."

Phil laughed. "Oh, you've noticed. Well, it's not likely to change anytime soon. That's why you gotta blow off steam every chance you get. So, by when do they want the review done?"

"Tomorrow!"

"Man, you're screwed."

"Thanks for the words of inspiration, Phil."

"All right now. Don't get sensitive on me. I'm gonna stick around and help you. Okay—so what do you know?"

"Survey and title work is the most basic review any lawyer working on a real estate transaction would conduct," said Jeff. "The first thing to be checked is whether the legal description on the survey matches the legal description on the title report."

"Because—?" Phil prompted.

"A survey isn't a blueprint of a building. It's a mapping of all of the buildings on a piece of property, showing their footprints."

"And the attorney's job?"

"It's to ascertain whether what is claimed to be owned by a certain individual actually is owned by that individual or entity, and properly documented. Further, if there are easements or rights of other parties to come onto a property, and thereby burden the title of the owner." Jeff tried to keep the frustration out of his voice. "There's more. It's from a book—Land, Title, Surveys and the Wonderful World of Real Estate."

"Not a bad book, Jeff. If only it were worded in plain English."

Jeff cracked a smile, but at almost two-thirty in the morning, that was all he could manage. He didn't know how much more of this he could take.

"You know, this is so ridiculous," he said. "I mean, this is basic stuff. It's easy. And I know I can figure it out. I just don't understand why the powers that be can't take fifteen minutes out of the day to properly point things out. I mean, never mind the billables it would save. It's just more efficient, and courteous to boot."

"Look, there's lots of shit that can be done better," Phil agreed. "Lots of stuff we would both do differently. But some partners barely let out a grunt to acknowledge you when say good morning. It's no way to foster a nurturing work environment, but who cares? It's all bullshit. Let's get this done and go to bed."

They reviewed the survey and all its easements, checked for encroachments, reviewed the legal descriptions, checked zoning requirements, marked up the title commitment, and requested various affirmative coverage. Phil looked at his watch. "It's almost four," he said. "I'm calling a car and we're going home. You still out in the 'burbs?"

"Yeah," responded Jeff. "If you call Morningside Heights the 'burbs. Dude, I live in Harlem. I haven't had time to go apartment-hunting. The only thing I've had time to do is get my own cell phone."

"You definitely need a place closer to the office."

"Yeah—one of these days. Thanks, buddy. I really appreciate your help."

"What are friends for?" said Phil. "But don't worry—I'm running a tab. I'll get you to return the favor at some point."

The next morning, Jeff stumbled into work at well after nine. In order to keep his eyes open, moist and clear, he had his indispensable pocket-size bottle of Visine with him. When he opened his office door, he could see his phone's message light blinking. He picked up the receiver and the system instructed him: "To check your messages, press one. To record a message, press two. To delete an old message, press three—" Jeff quickly hit one and his messages began to play.

"Hey, Jeff, it's Franklin Barro. I heard you were here all night. Good—you've been de-virginized. Get your ass into my office as soon as you have a chance. Thanks."

There were two messages left but Jeff didn't wait to hear them. He picked up a pad and pen and raced over to Barro's office. As usual, Barro was leaning back in his leather chair, gently rocking. Two other partners—Ray Alexander and Sean Witherspoon were in his office, sitting on his couch, and they were all on a conference call. No one moved as he entered the room, except Barro, who glanced at him for half a second and motioned for him to take a seat.

The voice of a client was blaring on the speaker phone. Barro reached into his briefcase, grabbed a document and tossed it onto Jeff's lap. Jeff flipped to the last page. It was a hundred fifty-two pages long. Barro hit the mute button and looked at Jeff. "All right, Chief," he said. "Get started."

That was it. Those were the instructions. Ray Alexander, one of the old guard of the firm, was sitting like Rodin's The Thinker, with his head balanced on his fist. He wore a bow tie and suspenders, and for some reason, he always left the buttons on the wrist of his shirt undone. Staring straight ahead, he seemed deep in thought. Physically, he was there, participating in another New York mega-deal, but Jeff thought his mind was somewhere else, like maybe on a beach in Bali. "This the new guy?" he asked, his lips barely moving.

Barro rocked forward and put his finger to his lips in order to keep everyone quiet as the client rambled on about the deal. Beams of light ricocheted off Barro's cufflinks and struck the ceiling of the room. Ray got out of his chair and stretched. "Old bones," he mumbled under his breath, and then placed a hand on Jeff's shoulder. "You should get started," he whispered.

Jeff excused himself, but before he left he made eye contact with Barro, who gave him a thumbs-up. That small gesture was enough to inspire him to tackle another assignment he didn't have the slightest idea how to start.

Back in his office, Jeff played his remaining messages, including another one from Barro. "Jeff, I want you to take the offering memorandum I'm going to give you and proof it. Review the tables and make sure all the reps and warranties conform with our standard model documents. Also, I want you to compare it to a prospectus I worked on a year ago. You'll find it on the system. Make sure there isn't anything in this memorandum we missed. Highlight any provisions in the old prospectus and bring them to my attention immediately."

Well, that's a start, Jeff thought. *My first clue, at least. I should consider myself lucky.*

Although the turnaround time for the project was twenty-four hours, he knew Barro would want it in two. The pressure, with one assignment after another, was on. Time passed in a blur of memos and reviews and phone calls.

Three weeks went by and Barro the Taskmaster, as the junior associates called him, kept a steady stream of work flowing to all the associates working on his deals. It was great to be part of such large transactions, and interacting with people who were on an intellectual level far beyond anything Jeff had ever encountered. But it was a grind, and it was as exhausting as it was invigorating.

It still amazed him that he was actually doing it—the New York law firm thing. He was making a real nice starting salary, and he was billed out at two hundred forty-five dollars an hour. And then there were the perks: extravagant lunches with clients, cars home in the evening, cheap-as-hell lunches in the company cafeteria, free snacks (from nuts to fruit to pastries) in the break room, an in-house gym and spa with a masseur and a valet who'd pick up your dry cleaning. Jeff had heard there would also be occasional travel to exotic places, and he was looking forward to that. But if you broke down his billable hours and stopped to think about the number of hours he was working, he was making about as much as a clerk somewhere working two jobs—and this, after he had invested tens of thousands of dollars on law school. That was the contradiction. He was elated he was learning so much, often without direction, and he was making more money than he ever had—but he had no time to spend it. Not even on a flashy new apartment. He didn't have time to even look for a place. He hardly had time to take a piss.

He certainly didn't have time to worry about taking on new clients, except those the partners steered his way. Not even when people obviously of humble means came in off the street looking for an attorney—but he tried to help them anyway. He was determined to remember where he came from.

Late one afternoon, after Adrienne had left for the day, he heard a light tap at his office door.

"Come in," he called, and a young Latin man in coveralls entered. Jeff recognized him as one of the night cleaning crew. He appeared a little embarrassed and uncomfortable. "Hey," Jeff said pleasantly. "Come in, have a seat. What can I do for you?"

The young man hesitated, and then gave a tentative smile. "My English no so good."

"That's okay. I understand a little Spanish. I'm Jeff."

"Juan Encinosa."

"Nice to meet you, Juan," said Jeff. "What's up?"

Juan explained that his wife and two children in El Salvador were having immigration problems, and he was having trouble getting them into the country. "I no want bother you," said Juan. "But I don't know what to do. I see you nice—kind—to workers. So I think is okay to ask you."

"Okay—well, I don't know much about immigration law," Jeff replied. "But I can refer you to an immigration attorney I know—up in the Bronx. He might even take the case pro bono. If that doesn't work out, I know another attorney in New Jersey, and she's wonderful. And if all else fails, I'll make some phone calls. Don't worry—I'll find a way to help you."

"Gracias, senior," Juan said, his eyes clouded a moment with tears of gratitude. "You have give me hope, sir. Gracias."

Juan left Jeff's office, closing the door behind him and Jeff's thoughts went immediately to Robert Turner. He didn't care that he'd just wasted half a billable hour, or that D and B probably would not approve. He thought that's what Robert would have done. He remembered all the times Robert had helped him, encouraging him and giving him tips on how to survive law school and the interview process. He didn't think he ever wanted to become so successful he wouldn't take a moment to help people like Juan.

On another occasion, a woman came in who was exasperated, depressed and overwhelmed. She confessed to Jeff she'd been so desperately in need of money that she was wishing she'd get hit by a car so she could sue for damages. Then she did get hit by a car—an unlicensed taxi in the Bronx—but she couldn't find an attorney to take the case. All she had was a statement from one witness and the car's license plate. Jeff promised to see if he could track down the taxi owner and find out if he had any insurance or property that would make a lawsuit worthwhile.

By eight that night, Jeff was famished. He had been munching on a bag of stale pretzels that had been in his drawer since the day he'd arrived. His phone rang and he picked it up. "Food da lobby."

"Excuse me?"

"Food da lobby," said the man on the other end of the line. He had a thick accent, probably Chinese since it was Chinese food Jeff had ordered.

Thank God, Jeff thought as he raced out the door to the elevator banks. The elevator doors sprang open, and out bounced Phil. He immediately grabbed Jeff's arm. "We're going out tonight, guy," he announced.

"No way, man—"

"Hey, it's almost Thanksgiving," Phil interrupted. "Odds are ten to one you and I will be stuck in this hellhole while everyone else is pigging out on turkey and pie. Give yourself a break."

"Sorry. I've got a ton of work."

"You remember I spent that all-nighter here to help you, to coach you through the pain in your hour of need? Do you remember?" Jeff remained silent. "So I ask you for one favor, one minor favor, like a pal, to accompany me out on a night on the town." There was a pause. Jeff was hoping with all his heart this was another of Phil's gags. "You disappoint me," Phil finished. You're a young, sharp guy, but you act like a pussy."

"My food's in the lobby."

"Yes, but life awaits you outside the hallowed halls of this golden prison."

"Come on, man, are you serious? I don't have time for this."

"That may be true, Jeffy boy, but you need this so no more excuses. There's a new club—Primo—opening tonight. I'll swing by your office in about an hour."

"I don't know, Phil. Like I said, I've still got a lot of work—"

"This is work," Phil interrupted. "The company that's buying this club—Primedia—is our client. So we're checking out the property and the potential for profit."

Jeff laughed. "Sounds like a bit of a stretch to me."

"No, seriously. And because it's work, I can charge it all to my expense account, from the car to the last drink. You're going." Phil disappeared through the double doors before Jeff could protest again.

How the hell does he do it? Jeff wondered as he ate his mushu chicken. Where the hell does he get the energy?

Phil could stay out all night, drinking almost to the point of passing out, make it to the office on time the next morning and act the perfect professional. No way could Jeff compete with him. Phil was a genius. A mad genius, but a genius nonetheless.

Jeff had to admire his raw ability, even though he had the tendency to be over the top. Even if he waltzed in every morning with his hair sticking up and uncombed—like Einstein—no one would make a comment. He was a natural and everyone knew it, so he could always get a pass. He was familiar with both legal concepts and the transactions themselves. After all, he'd grown up hearing this stuff discussed at the dinner table.

I have a great work ethic, but it goes just so far, Jeff thought. This guy, he's got the tools. I have to find some way to fashion my own.

"I still don't know why I'm doing this," he told Phil, who had a car waiting for them downstairs.

"Get in and stop whining," Phil ordered cheerfully as he and Jeff climbed in. "Here, have a cigarette. It'll keep your mouth shut."

"No thanks. I quit. So where is this place?"

"In the seventies, on Columbus," replied Phil, a cigarette bobbing up and down between his lips as he searched through his pockets for his lighter.

Jeff rolled down his window and eased back in his seat. Autumn had eased gracefully into the city and the chilled air caressed his forehead and sent shivers down his spine. He started to relax. "This is nice."

"What is?"

"Hanging. Hanging with you. Maybe this is a good idea. Thanks."

"You have to listen. You have to listen to the man when he's right."

"You're right," said Jeff.

"You're too stiff. I'm gonna make a partier out of you yet."

"Be patient, Phil. It'll take me a little time."

"I have spoken," responded Phil. "And so it shall be."

Jeff looked at Phil and shook his head. They both laughed. "So what have you been working on?" he asked.

"Ray Alexander's been keeping me busy. You know, Jeff, someone should slip that guy some Prozac in his morning coffee."

"What do you mean?"

"He is perpetually cranky," Phil explained. "He's so grumpy. It's depressing to work for the guy."

"Really? So far, I haven't had the pleasure."

"It's funny," said Phil. "When I interviewed at Darby, I met with Ray, and he put on a good show. He was like, all upbeat. He even tried to sell me this bullshit that billables at Darby weren't so bad. What a bunch of nonsense. He was even talking about having balance—the people at Darby and the partners encouraging the associates, you know, to work hard and to play hard and all this nonsense. I mean, I know I'm gonna work hard and play even harder. But Ray Alexander can barely crack a smile. It's pathetic."

"Yeah," Jeff agreed. "He's pretty stoic."

"Stoic, shit—you know what happened to me this afternoon, Jeff?"

"What?"

"I had this terrible itch on my back. I'm leaning back in my chair, and like I said, I had this terrible itch. I was tempted to go and ask my secretary to scratch it. So I'm trying to hit the spot, and I just couldn't reach it. So guess what I did."

Jeff wasn't entirely sure he wanted to know the answer but he said, "Beats me. What did you do?"

"I grabbed a pen, right? And I started just reaching back with my arm and scratching my back. But like an idiot, I was doing it with the pen cap off, which I didn't realize! So later I walk into a meeting with—get this— Sean Witherspoon, Ray Alexander and Art Swede."

Jeff laughed. "Oh my God—the Three Horsemen of the Apocalypse."

"Exactly," Phil continued. "Witherspoon, who you already know has the foulest vocabulary in all of fuckin' human history–"

Jeff interrupted. "Unlike you."

"Exactly. Anyway, I walk into the room, and Witherspoon takes one look at me and goes, 'What the fuck happened to your back?' Obviously, I couldn't see my back, so I didn't know what the hell he was talking about."

"So what happened?"

"Ray Alexander actually laughed. Can you believe it? He must have taken his Prozac, because I don't think I've ever seen him crack a smile, not even once. So anyway, Art Swede's sitting there, and he starts laughing hysterically. So now they're all laughing and I still don't know why."

"Did Swede drop to his knees and say a prayer for you or something?" Jeff asked.

"I know, the guy's such a hypocrite. They say he's in church like three days a week, but for the life of me, I can't understand it. He treats everyone like shit. And meanwhile, he's so far up Witherspoon's ass you'd think he's gonna shoot out Witherspoon's mouth if he burps. It's like—if he's so righteous, don't you think he'd say something to Witherspoon about groping any woman with a pulse who gets near him? Anyway, my secretary finally pointed out that I had scribble all over my back. I had to run over to Barney's to pick up another shirt."

"You're awesome, man," Jeff said. "I don't know anyone else who could get away with half of what you do."

"Yeah—everyone at D and B thinks I'm a nut but it doesn't matter. You know why?"

"Why?"

"Because I am the Rain Man of legal concepts. For some reason, I pick 'em up quickly so they overlook my shortcomings—of which there are many."

"Not me," Jeff confessed. "I've got to watch everything. You know—

work hard just to keep my head above water. Do you remember the last deal I was working on, when I spent three weekends in a row in the office?"

"What weekends don't you work?" asked Phil.

"Well, my client lost the document package so he asked me to do another distribution, to everyone on the list. I gave it to a paralegal. That's when Frank Barro saunters into my office."

"For what, to give you an assignment?"

"Yeah. He asked why I looked so annoyed. I told him about the documents being lost—and what do you think he did?"

"No clue."

"No reaction. No fuckin' reaction at all."

"As if you're retarded for being annoyed."

"Exactly."

The black Lincoln pulled up in front of Primo. Jeff filled out the voucher for the limousine service, then he and Phil stepped out and headed for the entrance. Already there was a line forming behind the velvet rope, where a throng of people were all clamoring to get in.

"I'm on Michael's list!" one guy yelled from the back of the crowd. A man wearing a green cap and purple-rimmed glasses examined a couple of sheets of lined paper attached to his clipboard. The bouncer, who stood at least six-foot-six and weighed approximately two hundred eighty pounds of solid muscle, stood directly behind him. His arms were folded and his distinctively trimmed goatee somehow managed to make him look as though he were angry, even when smiling.

"What's your name?" the man with the green cap yelled back. He had a thick Brooklyn accent. Jeff doubted anyone at the end of the line would be able to hear him.

The man stepped forward with his friend. "Don't you remember me, Kenny?" he asked the gate keeper, in an obvious attempt at familiarity. "Ryan—Ryan Kimble. We met you at that party in Soho a couple of weeks back, and you told me we'd get comped at the door."

Kenny continued to thumb through the list, effectively ignoring the one-way conversation. "I don't see your name on the list," he said.

Ryan became impatient. "What do you mean?"

Before either of them could protest any further, Kenny said, "Listen, if it's just the two of you, and if you're not with any girls, you're not gonna get in for at least another hour. Come back in an hour. I'm sorry."

"Kenny has spoken," Phil told Jeff.

"Okay, then," said Jeff. "So come on—let's go. We're wasting our time. There's no way that guy's gonna let us in. And we stand out like a couple of nerds in these suits."

"Remember what I told you—don't be so stiff."

Ten minutes passed and Jeff became more impatient with every second. The big goon at the door leaned over and whispered something in Kenny's ear. Kenny immediately stepped back into the club, behind the large metal doors. Phil instantly seized upon the opportunity. He reached into his wallet, took out four twenty-dollar bills and discreetly folded them. Then he gently scratched his forehead with them. It was subtle, but all clearly visible to the bouncer. The goliath waved Phil and Jeff forward.

"Hey, man, what's up?" he asked, and Phil shook his big bear paw, into which the eighty dollars disappeared.

"What's your name again?" asked Phil.

"I'm Kyle, but you can call me Horse. And that'll be another twenty bucks, but you can get me on the way out."

"Hey, Horse, no problem. By the way, meet my buddy Jeff."

The whole transaction took place in seconds. Horse swung the big metal door open and Jeff and Phil were inside before before Kenny returned.

Jeff gave Phil a big grin. "Oh, man—that was so smooth."

"Stick with me, kid. You ain't seen nothin' yet." They watched as two women approached a guy who looked like a smooth operator and kissed him on one cheek, and then on the other. He patted one of them on the bottom. There were several socialite types exchanging air kisses.

"Can't you smell the arrogance in this room?" asked Phil. "It's rancid."

On entering, they had passed through a glass portal entirely surrounded by water. Jeff looked up to see what appeared to be a natural spring on the other side of the glass ceiling. Rivulets from two waterfalls ran down the sides of the glass walls. It was quite a feat of architecture. They went through to the main room—a space that looked carved from a limestone cavern, complete with stalactites and stalagmites.

"So why are we here?"

"I am here, Jeffy boy, to let the good times roll."

"Are you done with the cliches? Let the good times roll—are you kidding?"

"All right, then. Try this on for size. The first thing you gotta do is check out the bathrooms. They're really funky. The doors are all glass, and when you walk in, you think you're gonna be takin' a pee and everyone's gonna be starin' at you. But the instant you close the door, the glass goes dark, like tinted windows. It's the coolest thing."

"Sounds exciting," responded Jeff.

"So get this—the last time I was here, I got a blowjob right there in the bathroom. Look for my autograph on the toilet paper dispenser."

"And I thought this was a classy place."

"It is," Phil insisted. "That's what makes it so amusing—that some society dame got me off in the loo." He laughed. "This kind of snobbery is good for business."

"What do you mean?" Jeff was baffled.

"The uppercrust and those who follow them. Bodes well for the gods of profit—and I bet it's mostly cash."

Jeff shrugged. "I guess."

"But hey—it looks promising for us, too. I tell you what, let's have some fun. You got your cell phone?"

"Yeah, I've got it. Why?"

"See those two gorgeous women over there by the bar?" Phil asked. Jeff looked. "No, not those two." Phil turned Jeff in another direction and pointed. "Those two."

"Holy shit!" Jeff responded. "Yeah. How can you miss them?"

"Stay here." With that, Phil made his way through the crowd, toward the women, and came to a stop beside them. There were mobs of people swarming all over the place—beautiful people, no doubt wearing designer labels down to their underwear. In the semi-darkness, Jeff could make out a lounge area, and there was a dance floor about twenty-five yards away. It was overflowing with humanity, most of them wearing as little clothing as possible without being arrested. Phil stood up on one of the barstools and waved to get Jeff's attention. Then, holding his right hand—in the shape of a fake phone—up to his ear he mouthed the words, "Call me."

The two women were looking at Phil, but Jeff couldn't tell whether they were startled, annoyed or perhaps amused by his antics. As Phil climbed down, Jeff pulled out his new phone, flipped it open and punched in Phil's number. He pressed the talk button and watched from across the room as Phil casually reached into his breast pocket and pulled out his phone.

"Hello?" Phil said. "Oh, yes. The lovely young lady standing next to me? Of course." Jeff was perplexed but he continued to play along. "Excuse me, Miss?" he heard Phil say to the woman. "It's for you. That guy over there—" Phil waved at Jeff, and Jeff waved back. "Well, he just called me and he said something about falling in love with you. I can't explain it."

Jeff turned red as Phil passed the phone over to her.

"Is this how you normally go about trying to meet women?" she asked. She sounded annoyed.

"Ummm . . ." Jeff wasn't sure what to say. "To be honest, this really wasn't my idea."

"Of course not." Her tone was a bit sarcastic. Apparently she wasn't amused. She passed the phone over to her friend and walked away.

"Never mind her," the other woman said into Jeff's ear. "She has a serious boyfriend, and not the best sense of humor. But I think that was original. Kind of cute."

"Well, it was actually my idea," Phil put in. Jeff could hear him in the background. "I orchestrated the entire thing."

"So what's your name?" she asked into the phone.

"I'm Jeff."

"Well, why don't you come over here, Jeff?"

Jeff folded his phone shut, placed it in his pocket and pushed through the crowd to the bar. As he arrived, he could hear Phil making his pitch. "I'm an attorney, and I work on large corporate and real estate transactions. What do you do?"

In all the smoke, haze and humanity, Jeff had to allow a moment for his eyesight to adjust. Then he walked right past Phil and his new friend without saying a word. Even in the murky light of the nightclub, he saw Red and Cassandra across the room. If they were on a date, he wouldn't intrude, but if they weren't—God, she was beautiful. The sudden, unexpected sight of her hit him like a punch to the gut. As always, she was the picture of class and elegance.

"What's his problem?" queried the woman next to Phil as Jeff took a place down the bar.

"Oh, don't mind him. He has this strange disorder. Every once in a while, he goes in and out of a trance. It's kind of freaky."

Jeff flagged one of the bartenders and sent two drinks over to Cassandra's table. Moments later, the waiter leaned over to Cassandra and pointed across the room to Jeff. Cassandra's eyes met Jeff's and she smiled and motioned for him to come over.

"Hey, buddy," Phil said, throwing his arm over Jeff's shoulder. "I got digits—you gonna congratulate me?" Jeff's eyes remained transfixed and Phil followed his gaze. "Wow—okay. I see what caught your attention!"

Ignoring Phil, Jeff made his way through the crowd, weaving in, out, around and through the barricade and bump of bodies. It was an eternity before he reached her.

"Jeff—I can't believe it. How are you?"

Before he could answer, she threw her arms around him and drew him close.

"Better now," he said, returning her embrace. She fit just under his chin.

She gave him a gentle nuzzle. "It's so good to see you. It's been too long."

"Ah—excuse me," Phil put in as he joined them. "Are you going to introduce me to this stunning woman?"

"Oh, sorry. Cassandra, Red, this is Phil, a colleague of mine at Darby."

"Good to meet you," said Cassandra, and Red shook Phil's hand before turning to Jeff.

"Congratulations again, my friend," he said. "I knew you'd get a good place."

"Thanks." Jeff replied and looked into his eyes. They were glassy, as if he was high on something. "What about you—how are you doing?"

"Oh . . . you don't want to know. I'm not the wonder boy like you and Jacob Jefferson. I think we gotta order another round of drinks to kill the pain. Cass knows what I'm having. Excuse me—I'm gonna hit the men's room in the meantime."

As soon as he was out of earshot, Jeff turned to Cassandra. "Look," he said. "I know he's your friend and all, but he's fucked up. He needs some help."

"Man, he's whacked," Phil chimed in. "I could see the bloodshot in his eyes from where I'm standing—in the dark."

"I know," Cassandra said. "The honest truth—he's getting worse. He was okay for a while, but I think Turner's anniversary is really having an impact on him."

"Turner?" queried Phil.

"Don't worry about it," Jeff said. "I'll tell you later." He turned back to Cassandra. "So—should we say something to him before he's completely out of control?"

"I talked to him about it a couple of months ago," she replied. "Look, he's gonna do what he's gonna do. He's a grown man. He makes his own choices. I'd rather hear about how you're getting on at D and B."

But he didn't want to talk about work, and he didn't want to talk about Red. He wanted to hold her in his arms again, as he had the day of Robert's funeral. "Well," he said. "I'd rather dance with you."

She smiled at him again and he hoped he saw an invitation in her eyes.

"I'd love to," she said softly.

"Yeah," Phil put in. "Why don't the two of you just, uh, go and dance and, uh, you know—I'll just hang right here by myself. Don't worry. I'll be fine. I'll just try and scare up some company, you know."

"Oh, grow up," demanded Jeff with a grin. "You'll be fine. I have the greatest degree of faith in you."

The dancing, and the conversation about movies, music, work, old memories and dreams of the yet to come, went on for hours. It was good to be among friends, Jeff thought, relaxing, free for a little while from the tension that surrounded him at Darby and Blackstone. He was in heaven, close enough to Cassandra to inhale her sweet fragrance even when he wasn't holding her body next to his on the dance floor. Red periodically emerged from his domain—the men's room—with a fair degree of regularity. As the evening wore on, he became a zombie, barely coherent. Pale and disconnected, he blended in nicely with the stark furnishings of the nightclub's interior.

"Why don't you ask someone to dance?" Jeff suggested, trying to motivate him away from the coke. "Lots of pretty girls here. Lady's man like yourself—you should be all over that."

"Nah," Red answered. "Left my dancing shoes at home. You go on. Go ahead—the two of you. You make a nice couple." He rubbed his nose and reached into his pocket, feeling around as if to make sure something was there. Then he drifted again toward the men's room.

Jeff took Cassandra's hand and led her back onto the dance floor and again they disappeared into the throbbing beat of the music and the undulating bodies. Gazing into each other's eyes, they moved to the rhythm, matching each other perfectly. It was painful for him, painful to be so close to her, desiring her as he'd never desired anyone. He wondered if he'd ever really have a chance with her. He could meet other women—that was no problem—but Cassandra was special.

"You're a good dancer," she said, breaking into his thoughts.

"What?" Jeff asked loudly, his voice rising above the music.

"I said," Cassandra repeated, "you're a good dancer. I wouldn't have guessed it."

"Thanks . . . I think. Was that a compliment?"

She laughed and he moved closer, enjoying the feel her round, firm breasts against him, and her curvaceous hips moving against his. She was so damn hot. He wanted her—badly—but some kind of invisible shield separated them, some kind of emotional shield that for some reason this alluring woman had erected. It was one he couldn't seem to penetrate. But he had to try.

Cassandra spun around on the dance floor and turned her back to him. He placed both hands gently on her waist, leaned over and kissed her neck.

Still moving to the music, she didn't react to the kiss. Was it an invitation for him to kiss her again, Jeff wondered. Or was she in shock?

Then, her back still to him, she moved closer, taking his hands and wrapping his arms around her. Her nearness was intoxicating. Gently, he kissed her neck again and when she didn't protest, he moved his lips up to her ear. Her response was warm and encouraging.

They stayed like that for a while, moving to the music, until she eased her head back, tilting it to look into his eyes. He turned her around and gazed down at her a moment before their lips finally met. Everything seemed to evaporate around them—the strobe lights, the band, the other dancers, all except one drunken fool who tripped over his own feet. He dumped an entire glass of rum and coke onto the back of Jeff's shirt.

"Shit!"

"What happened?"

"That idiot spilled his drink all over me."

Cassandra laughed. "I figured. Some of it splashed on my arm. Let's go get you some napkins."

He smiled at her. "Actually, I'd rather continue where we left off."

"We . . . got carried away. Jeff, I'm seeing someone so . . . that can't happen again."

"Sorry—I don't agree."

Lightly brushing her lips against his, she replied sweetly, "Well, then it's a good thing it's not up to you." Grabbing his hand she turned and headed for the bar, where they found Phil chatting with another woman.

As they approached, Phil winked at Jeff. "Hey, chief, how about another round?"

"Yeah, sure."

Phil ordered a Jack Daniels and Coke for Jeff, a Skyy and tonic for himself and a rum and Coke for Cassandra. Jeff took a healthy swig of his drink.

"Thanks, Phil," said Cassandra.

Phil looked Jeff dead in the eye, pretending to be serious. "Well, Jeff, I'm waiting."

"Oh—thanks, fool," said Jeff. "I mean, Phil."

Phil grinned. "I'm finally starting to rub off on you," he said.

"Not a chance," Jeff shot back. "Hey, have you seen Red?"

Phil shook he head. "Not since you guys left to go and dance—again."

"I bet I know where you can find him," said Cassandra.

"Right," said Jeff as he turned and headed toward the men's room.

He made his way through the crowd and surprisingly, there wasn't one person in line for the bathroom. Once inside, he leaned over to see a pair of feet showing underneath the distant corner stall.

"Red," Jeff said, then paused. "Red, c'mon—open the door." He tapped gently on the stall.

"That you, Jeff?"

"Yeah. Open up." Jeff heard Red fumbling with the latch, then he opened the door a crack. "You okay?"

Red was sitting on the toilet with his head in his hands. He wasn't relieving himself. His pants weren't down but his shirt and his slacks were undone. "I feel better now. Just lost my lunch."

Right above Red's head some previous visitor had scrawled, *If you want a good time, call Phyllis and her mom . . .*

Jeff tore his eyes away from the inscription and asked, "Can I get you anything? Bottle of water? A kamikaze? A screwdriver?"

"Very funny." Red started to laugh, and then stopped. He put his hands on his abdomen. There was a brief silence, and then he looked up at Jeff. There was such pain in his eyes.

"It's my fault," he said. "It's my fault, Jeff. It wouldn't have happened if it wasn't for me." His voice tore on a sob and he began to weep uncontrollably.

"Okay—so tell me about it. Here—here's some tissue. Jeff pulled some from the dispenser. Red accepted it and wiped his eyes, but the tears continued to flow. "What do you mean, Red?" Jeff asked. "What are you talking about?"

Red lifted his head and Jeff could see agonized lines etched in his face. His eyes were swollen and red from alcohol and weeping. His lower lip trembled in anticipation of the words he was about to say. "Robert Turner. It was my fault. I'm to blame." Red's head sank back into his hands as he continued to cry, his shoulders rising and falling convulsively as he gave vent to his sorrow.

Jeff was stunned. He didn't know what to make of Red's confession. "Man, you are so fucked up."

"I know."

"Okay, Red—how could it be your fault? Turner killed himself."

"I don't think so. In my gut, I know it."

Jeff was speechless. He wasn't sure if he wanted to hear any more.

"You remember that guy Keith Simon?"

"What about him?" Jeff asked.

"Keith Simon—he was at Livermore when you started. You remember, he was that rich kid? He drove around in a Porsche? They call him Candy Man Keith."

"Yeah—he was here tonight. I saw you talking to him."

"Someone tried to kill him. Tried to smash his skull by dropping a cinder block on him. They missed. Just got his hand."

"Why?"

Red looked up at him and smiled. "Because, my friend, he was dipping into the candy store, using more than he was selling. The school knows all about it—but they're keeping it quiet."

"Exactly what does the school know?" Jeff's tone was grim.

"That he's the supplier at Livermore. He's a dealer to the students, even some teachers. I get some hits from him every once in a while. I wasn't doing much back then, back when Robert—"

"As opposed to now."

"Yeah, well, I'm fucked up now. There's too much going on inside my head."

"That's not a good enough excuse."

"No, Jeff—listen to me, man! So this guy—Keith—I knew he had connections with some of the attorneys at Darby. I didn't know how he knew them, but he did. I knew how much Turner wanted to be there, so I did what I could to try and get him in. I would do anything to help the guy. I loved him like a brother. I asked Keith to use his connections to get Turner in, and he did." Tears welled up in Red's eyes again, and he began to shake.

"And then?" Jeff prompted.

"I don't know what happened. He went to work there and he just never came back. It's bullshit, that story they made up. All bullshit. You know Turner was brilliant. And you know he would never kill himself. They did it. He got mixed up in something, or maybe he found out something. I mean, his way in—through me—was a fucking drug connection."

"Wait," Jeff interrupted "You're saying that someone at D and B—"

"Yeah, man. They fucking killed him."

"I can't believe this," Jeff said slowly. "This is a fucking nightmare."

"I wish it was. I wish I could just wake up from all this. But it's not, man. It's real."

"Fix your pants. Let's get out of here." After Red pulled up his pants, Jeff took his arm and threw it over his shoulder, supporting his weight as they walked. When they emerged from the bathroom two bouncers approached.

"This dude all right?" one of them asked.

"Yeah, I got him."

Cassandra spotted them and waved. She and Phil left the bar and hurried to join them. As they headed for the exit, Cassandra draped Red's other arm over her shoulder. Jeff saw Candy Man Keith approaching.

"Hey—is he okay?" he asked.

"He'll be fine," Cassandra replied.

"I could drive him home," Keith offered.

"No," said Jeff. "We've got him."

"Well, he lives near me," Keith replied. "And I—"

"I said no." Jeff's voice was firm, no-nonsense. "You're done here, Keith."

"Who the fuck do you think you are?" Keith got up too close and personal. "Talking to me like I'm some kind of—"

Jeff cut him off. "I'm Jeff Rhodes and I'll talk to you any way I please. Now move aside. I told you—you're done here. You don't want me to say it again."

"Fine, man—Mr. Jeff Rhodes. We're cool." The candy man moved aside.

"Come on, Red," said Cassandra. "Let's go."

Outside the club, throngs of people were still clamoring to get in, even at two in the morning. The parking valet brought Cassandra's car around and she and Jeff put Red in. It was a silver-gray Pontiac Lemans, only a couple of years old.

"You want me to come with?" Jeff asked.

"No—we'll be all right," she said. "I've done this before. I'll take care of him."

"You sure?"

"Yeah. I'll put him on my couch and he'll sleep it off." Cassandra threw her arms around Jeff and hugged him close.

"Am I going to see you again?" he asked, not bothering to hide the longing in his voice.

"Definitely. Give me a call." With that, she got into her car and closed the door. Jeff looked after her a moment, watching as she drove away.

"Wow," said Phil. "Man, she is something else."

"I know," Jeff agreed. "Believe me, I know."

CHAPTER 13

The Painful Truth

"This new guy—Jeff—what's his work like?"

"It's decent enough."

"Does he know anything, Ray?" Franklin Barro's tone was serious, even a little grim, but his features remained impassive.

"I don't think he knows a goddamn thing," said Ray Alexander. "Like I told you before, I think we overreacted, bringing him in."

"You want to get rid of him?"

"If you're asking me if I think he has what it takes to pull his weight around here, I don't know. He works hard, but you and I both know that's not the issue."

"You think he has a big mouth?" Barro asked. "I mean, on the off chance that he does know something?" Ray remained silent. "Do you have an answer for anything, Ray?"

"Frank, you know you're asking me for answers about things I can't answer. The truth is I don't give a shit whether you get rid of him or you keep him. Makes no difference to me. But I don't think he knows anything, and we should keep it that way. That's my opinion."

"There's one way to find out," said Barro. "Let's put him on the Primedia account with Phil."

"You sure you want to risk that?"

Frank nodded, a slow smile creeping from his lips into his eyes. "It'll be his tell," he said. "If Robert Turner shared any information with Jeff, he'll dig into it. Jeff is bright, Ray, and he's curious—but he's not sophisticated. He won't be able to resist."

"Then what?"

"Then we'll know if we can make him a real part of our team."

Ray shrugged. "You're the boss."

"One thing is for sure. We don't need any excess baggage around here.

If it turns out Jeff is not Darby material—and he's clueless—we'll cut him loose. For now, let's put him on Primedia and pile on the work. Let's string him along—make sure he doesn't know anything. If if turns out he does, well . . . we'll figure it out from there."

The two left Barro's office for a meeting in conference room D. They didn't notice Phil at the water cooler, who quickly turned his back to them.

The motherfuckers, Phil thought. They were going to fire Jeff if he didn't quit on his own. It was a fucking shame, that's what it was. Jeff was an innocent and wouldn't see it coming, but Phil knew better than to tell tales. He couldn't get involved but he could try and watch Jeff's back, since they'd be working on the same account. But that name—Robert Turner—he'd heard it only the night before, and he'd seen it in the files somewhere. It was pulling at his brain. And why did Frank and Ray care about what Jeff might know? What was there to know? Some guy named Turner had worked at D and B the year before, and then had stopped showing up. Phil just figured he didn't make the cut. And sadly, it looked like Jeff wouldn't either.

•••

Jeff arrived in his office to find the message light blinking on his phone. He punched in his code and waited a moment, then that wonderful familiar voice said, "Jeff, give me a call—it's Cassandra. Red was rambling on and on last night. He said some pretty disturbing things. Give me a call as soon as you can."

Jeff immediately dialed the number she left.

"This is Cassandra Evans."

"Cassandra—I can't believe I got you right away."

"It's my direct line," she answered softly. "Hi, Jeff."

"Red had some disturbing things to tell me last night, too."

"About Robert," she said. It was a statement, not a question. "So what do you think?"

"You'd know better than me. I don't know what to think. I don't know what to do."

She lowered her voice when she spoke again. "Maybe we shouldn't be talking about this over the phone."

"Okay by me. When do you want to get together?"

"I'm really busy for the next few days. Let's try to hook up early next week."

"What about this weekend?" he asked. "You could stop by my place."

She hesitated a moment then, "Yeah . . . that could work. I'm having brunch with Monica and Molly on Sunday, so maybe afterward. But I can't stay long. Is that okay with you?"

"That's perfect."

"In the meantime, it might be a good idea for you to see what you can find out."

"You really think there's any truth to what Red's saying?" Jeff asked.

"You tell me," she replied. "You said it yourself, right after Robert's funeral—you didn't believe he killed himself."

•••

The transactions Jeff was working on at Darby and Blackstone were proceeding smoothly. Many of them were quite complex, structured in that fashion almost exclusively for tax purposes. Jeff found it interesting and challenging. The prospect of learning how to do deals excited him, although the due diligence that went into completing them was tedious. With more extensive exposure to various cases and more work shoved at him from a lot of different partners, it would be difficult to become expert in any one area, but the mix of work was welcome. It broke the monotony of doing only one thing. The flip side, however, was that the broad range of cases brought with it some anxiety—in spite of the fact that he was getting more comfortable at the firm every day, and more accustomed to the luxurious surroundings. And his salary—he got a thrill with each new paycheck. He would soon be able to move into a better apartment, closer to the office, if he ever had enough time to look for one. It was hard to consider giving all that up.

To think one of the partners could have had something to do with Robert's death was devastating. The notion ate daily at Jeff's gut. It was difficult to get his head around, even though he didn't believe Robert had committed suicide. Cassandra was right. They had to get answers—and then what? Could they go to the police, or would whoever-it-was have already covered his tracks? One thing was sure—if anyone at D and B was responsible, Jeff couldn't work there anymore. He didn't know how he was going to poke around for information. All he knew was he'd have to do it carefully.

Before the morning was over, Frank Barro called Jeff into his office and handed him a bulging file. "This is one of our most important accounts," Barro told him. "Primedia Aircraft Corporation. Get familiar with every aspect of it. They've got a huge transaction coming up, which means a lot of meetings and some travel. You up for that?"

"Yes sir." Jeff shifted the heavy file to his other arm. "I'll get right on it."

"Good. Phil's on it, too. You have any questions, talk to Phil."

• • •

"How can you know what they think?" asked Phil. They were standing at the coffee kiosk in front of the Darby and Blackstone building. "We never get any reviews, we never get any feedback, we rarely ever get a thank you, never mind a heart-felt 'good work' or anything like that. So how can you know?" He took a sip of his hazelnut coffee. Jeff reached into his pocket and pulled out a five-dollar bill to pay for both of them. "Thanks. I'll get you next time."

"No—you got lunch," Jeff said. "Anyway, I don't have an answer to that but I can tell you one thing. If the partners really knew what their associates thought about them, they might try to change things. Maybe a little."

"Yeah, right—they're so concerned about what we think." Phil paused for a moment and scratched his chin. "So what's your take on Franklin Barro? I mean, what do you think about him, really think about him?"

"Well, I don't want to speak too soon, but from my experience, I would agree with what I've heard. He's the T. Rex of the corporate group."

"Yeah," Phil said. He hesitated a moment before adding, "Barro's a piece of work. I'd watch my back if I were you."

Jeff nodded. "Word is he's a scumbag extraordinaire."

"Who said that?" asked Phil, breaking into a grin.

"I'm not gonna say. You have a big mouth." Jeff smiled and they headed into the lobby. He wouldn't do anything to get Adrienne in trouble. She liked him enough to get his work done expediently, and she trusted him enough to make offhand remarks about other secretaries, other associates, and occasionally even some of the partners. He wasn't about to do anything to mess that up.

"You're gonna hold out on me?"

"Yeah," Jeff responded. "If I know what's good for me."

"So what else did this person say?"

"That he's selfish and inconsiderate. I mean, I'm working on a deal right now. It's in the real estate group—one of his clients. The look and feel of the whole thing is fucked up."

"How do you mean?"

"Why don't you give me some dirt, Phil?"

"Okay, you finish your dirt and then I'll tell you a story or two."

Jeff shrugged and punched the elevator button. "Okay—well, this real estate transaction. We're representing the lender on a ten-point-eight-million-dollar loan. Small potatoes, no big deal. So this loan lands on my desk and the bank wants to close in a week and a half, and I haven't received one scrap of paper. I mean nothing, no due diligence. There's no signed commitment, nothing. All I know is the bank is giving this borrower every indication they're going to close the deal. The banks are always putting us in this kind of bullshit situation. They want us to close under a ridiculous timetable. We have to prepare loan documents and review due diligence like it's a fire drill. And if anything goes wrong, they point the finger at us."

"You sound pissed off," Phil observed. "Is that what's got you pissed off?"

"No," Jeff said. "So—we're having a conference call. I've got my lender—the bank—on the line with the borrower who, we're all aware, has come down to the bitter end. He's a Louisiana developer who's been buying up a whole string of parcels to build a shopping center. But the zoning isn't in place yet. He needs variances, and he wants the bank to give him the loan based on his good-faith assurances he'll get the proper zoning. There's no question—he's a yahoo. The bank should come straight and cut him loose. Why are they dicking him around?"

"It's what they do, Jeffy boy. Because they can, like they get some kind of twisted pleasure out of it. So what happened?"

"So the borrower wants to close. He's desperate. He's ready to do anything. He'll settle for a ridiculous interest rate just to get the money. If he doesn't get his financing in place, the whole project collapses like a house of cards, and he's already in the hole personally for a lot of money. Our searches show that he and his wife have skipped on creditors before, which I think their counsel had a stake in because he'll do just about anything to see the loan go through. I mean anything."

"Anything like what?" Phil asked.

"Anything like asking me what can he do for me. Whatever that means."

"Are you serious?"

"Oh, yeah. It was getting comical. I've got the banker on the line, and we're going through the due diligence checklist, and I am running through this long list of items the borrower still hasn't gotten in place—and the banker still doesn't want to cut him loose. He pretended this guy actually had a shot. It's pathetic. And I wasn't having it. I made it clear to my lender he should cut the guy loose, and quick."

"What did he do?" Phil asked. "The banker?"

"He hesitated. The analyst on the deal hesitated, his VP hesitated, their senior VP hesitated. Even their in-house counsel wouldn't step up and make a final decision. It was mayhem. One hand didn't know what the other was doing. And no one was doing the right thing—namely, sending a letter to this borrower to let him know the deal was dead." Jeff paused to take a breath.

"So they're trying to pin the blame on the borrower," Phil commented.

"Make it look like he's not delivering the necessary due diligence, so they can pin the collapse of the deal on him."

"Well, maybe I'm just saying bankers are pussies," Jeff replied. "What's wrong with them? Some of them are okay, but most are completely spineless. They can't make a decision without the lawyers—I mean at all—and if something goes wrong, they want to hang us."

"The suspense is killing me," Phil said. "So what happened?"

"Despite it being perfectly clear that the borrower was nowhere close to having everything in place, the bank still wouldn't cut him loose. Who knows? Maybe another bank would have been willing to do the deal. But there was no way my lender was going to do it. I could have told you right from the start the borrower wouldn't be able to deliver. But the bank would rather wait for the deal to die on its own."

"Get used to it," Phil said. "The lawyers are always caught in the middle, and everyone is always looking for someone else to blame. The name of the game is CYA—cover your ass."

"But it's horseshit. People should be more courageous. And forthright."

"Ah, Jeffy boy—now you're asking too much."

"But—"

"No buts," Phil broke in. He punched the elevator button again. "Look—I'm telling you. Just get used to it. Hey, I agree with you, and most good lawyers would agree with you as well. But you're going to frustrate yourself to death. Some lawyers are ultra-ethical, totally by the book, and a lot of them don't get anything done. Then there are the real scumbags who, regardless if something is their responsibility, try and find someone else to blame. And the business people? Despite what they think about lawyers, they depend on us for everything. That loan application should never have been started. But now it's over, you should forget about it."

"You da man, Phil."

"Anyway, you've got something more exciting to think about, now that Barro's put you on Primedia with me. Have you had time to go through the files and get up to speed?"

"He just told me this morning," Jeff said. "It'll take me a day or two."

•••

Jeff barely had time to put down his coffee and get settled in his chair when his secretary buzzed him. "Jeff, you have an urgent call, line six. Can you take it now?"

"Who is it, Adrienne?"

"Franklin Barro."

"Yeah—put him through."

Barro didn't bother with any type of preamble. "I need you in my office, Jeff. Now."

"On my way."

Jeff found Barro as he normally did—gently rocking in his high-back leather chair with his arms raised and folded behind his head. There was perspiration at his armpits, which was often the case, and somewhat of a contradiction for a man who was always impeccably dressed.

"Have a seat," he told Jeff. He continued to rock gently back and forth.

"Thanks."

"We have a construction loan that's closing in two weeks. I need the loan documents by tomorrow." Barro reached under his desk and leaned forward. He pulled a red-roped file folder from beneath it and handed it to Jeff. "It's a small loan, only five million, but it's a new client. I want you to pay extra special attention to this. Understand?"

"Sure. No problem."

"I trust you can take it and run with it."

"Absolutely," Jeff responded.

"So what do you think of those Yankees?" Barro swiveled in his chair and began typing on his computer.

"Oh—uh—their pitching is unbelievable." Jeff was surprised at the question. "I think they'll even go back to the World Series this year."

"Yeah, it looks like they have shot. Maybe the firm will be able to get some tickets."

Barro's tone suggested the tickets would be some kind of bonus for an associate who could deliver, but Jeff wasn't sure. "Well, I'll get right on it," he said, tucking the file under his arm. "Was there anything else?"

Barro turned slightly and shook his head no.

"Okay. Oh—may I have a client and matter number for my billables?"

"Adrienne will get it for you."

"Thanks," Jeff said, but Barro was already on the phone, yelling at his secretary.

"What the fuck, Pamela?" he demanded. "I want my lock changed. Don't let maintenance give you the runaround."

Jeff headed back to his office. He was going to have to turn these documents around in one night, and they would have to be perfect, or he would hear it from Barro.

Barro had an intimidating quality. He worked his associates hard—Jeff understood that—and every new associate was battling for acceptance and approval, which didn't come often. Working long hours, getting assignments at four o'clock on a Friday afternoon with a Monday morning deadline, responding to the requests of partners with a military-like degree of respect—Jeff was beginning to think it was all kind of ridiculous. After all, it was just a job, albeit a prestigious one.

"But having a life is important, too," he said aloud, remembering his dinner with Uncle Murray. The thought faded in an instant as he realized the enormity of the task ahead of him. He had worked so hard, and he had achieved his goal—a position with one of the top legal firms in New York. So he had to focus on the job for now—he would get around to having a life later—and he could learn a lot from a powerhouse like Franklin Barro.

Despite all the hard work he was throwing at Jeff, and despite the veiled intimidation, it was tough to dislike the man. He was, in effect, very charming, especially with clients. Still relatively young by partner standards Barro was, according to Adrienne, a master of manipulation. He was a bit rough around the edges, Jeff thought, but frighteningly intelligent.

Resigned, he settled in behind his desk for an all-nighter. Every associate, at least those who were honest with themselves, would get that sinking feeling when they knew they'd be up all night in order to complete an assignment. That lonely, sinking feeling.

At this very moment, he thought, throngs of people are leaving their offices and heading out to join their friends or families, ready to enjoy a home-cooked meal and relax in front of the TV before going to bed. Ninety-nine percent of the world gets to go home at five o'clock, and here I am staring at hours and hours of work still to do.

No wonder he was starting to feel lonely. It had been a long time—a really long time— since he'd had a girlfriend. Hell, since he'd even had a date. All through law school he was too busy studying, and now he was working, it seemed, all the time. And anyway, what girlfriend would understand or tolerate an absentee boyfriend? Only another lawyer. He thought of Cassandra again—beautiful, charming, witty, smart and sexy as hell.

By midnight, he had completed the loan agreement and the mortgage, but still had to complete the note and about eight other ancillary and supporting documents. He kicked back in his chair and rubbed his temples, ready for a break. Cassandra was right. He had to find out what he could about Robert Turner. He started by typing Robert's name in the search window on the D and B system. He hit enter, wondering if Robert was even in the files anymore. It would be logical, a year after his funeral, if he was not. Jeff got only half a dozen Results Found items, two of which stood out. One was Robert's human resources file, obviously from when he was hired. The other was Primedia Aircraft Corporation.

Searching through the pile on his desk, Jeff found the folders Franklin

Barro had given him earlier. There was one for every associate, including Phil, who had worked on Primedia—except for Robert—yet his name was linked with Primedia in the computer system. Perhaps, Jeff thought, it had been moved to archives. He would have to look there, and he'd have to come up with a reason Theresa Staples would believe. Human Resources and Archives were her exlusive domain. But it was late, and he was done in. It would have to wait until tomorrow.

•••

"The boss has a small job for us," Mitch said as he stepped out of the phone booth. He looked at his beeper again, then stuck it in his pocket. "Man, I gotta get a fucking cell phone."

"What's the job?" asked Vick. They started walking toward the black Lincoln.

"We gotta check out some guy's apartment—some fucking kid lawyer— and keep an eye on him for a while. It may work into something bigger down the line. All he wants for now is for us to watch him, see who he's talking to, shit like that."

•••

The next morning, after Jeff had gotten some reading done on Primedia, he went up to Human Resources and Archives. When he stepped off the elevator, the first thing he noticed was Theresa Stapples' perfume. It was one of the expensive designer brands, with a delicate floral scent that would linger a few moments, even after she'd left a room. The fragrance was light and intriguing, inspiring visions of a svelte, sophisticated fashion model. But Theresa was a sixty-something woman of substantial size who looked to be of Irish descent, with auburn hair, fair skin and blue eyes. She was tall, with broad shoulders and a massive bosom she carried with dignity. Yet her clothes were elegant and stylish and her makeup looked as if a professional artist had applied it. She was standing at her assistant's desk, holding a cup of coffee. When she heard the elevator doors open, she turned and gave Jeff a big smile.

"Well hello," she said. "What brings you up here to the back of beyond?"

"Hi, Mrs. Stapples," he replied. "I'm looking for some old files—"

"First of all," she broke in. "Nobody calls me Mrs. Stapples—for one thing, I'm not married and it sounds so wrong."

"Sorry," Jeff said. "I just assumed such an attractive woman—"

"Now, you know a good lawyer doesn't assume anything," she broke in with a chuckle. "And flattery won't get you far with me."

"Sorry. I only meant—"

She laughed. "Oh, don't worry. I'm just yanking your chain. I do it with all the new kids. What can I help you with?"

Jeff relaxed. Theresa Stapples was good at putting people at ease. "I'm looking for some old files. Mr. Barro has put me on the Primedia account and I'm playing catch up. The only one I haven't been able to locate was created by. . ." He paused, he hoped not too dramatically, reached into his pocket and pulled out a yellow Post-It. "Robert Turner," he finished. "I understand he's no longer with the firm."

"No, he's not," she answered with a slight frown. "Come on back here with me. I've got my own system for keeping track of who signed out what, and when." She led Jeff into a small office cluttered with family photos and mementos of her years with Darby and Blackstone. It looked like she'd been there for decades. She put her coffee down on top of a file cabinet and moved gracefully around her desk, then opened a drawer and pulled out a gray binder. Settling herself in her chair, she flipped it open and motioned for Jeff to have a seat across from her. After a moment, she said, "Okay—here it is." She looked up at him. "I'm afraid you're out of luck. Last person who signed it out was Franklin Barro, more than six months ago. You'll have to ask him for it."

"Okay. Thanks for your time." Jeff rose slowly and started out but turned back to her at the doorway. "Is it the usual practice to take a file out of archives and keep it for so long?"

"As a matter of fact, it is not. I've bugged Mr. Barro about it a couple of times, to no avail. If you wind up with it, be sure and let me know so I can put it in my book." She closed the gray binder.

"You got it."

•••

"She's late," said Cassandra, taking a sip of her coffee. A feeling of dread was gnawing at the pit of her stomach. She hadn't seen Monica in ages and her invitation to brunch had been a surprise.

"Typical Monica," Molly replied. "I say we go ahead and order. Who knows if she'll even come."

"She's the one who wanted to get together," Cassandra protested. "Says she has something important to tell me."

"I wonder why she wants me here. It's not like we've ever been close."

"Do you think she knows?"

Molly shrugged. "So what if she does? It's about time she finds out Alberto is a dick."

They both ordered the special, which came with a free mimosa. When the waitress returned later to give them the check, they asked for more coffee.

"Okay, this is it," Cassandra said, pouring cream and lots of sugar into hers. "If she's not here by the time I finish this, I'm leaving. She could at least show up—if whatever's on her mind is so important."

"Looks like you're about to find out," Molly responded, pointing out the window. Alberto had pulled up in his shiny new Lamborghini and double-parked in front of the restaurant. Monica got out, grim determination lining her features, and headed inside.

"So glad you could join us," Molly said, her voice touched with sarcasm as Monica took a seat across from Cassandra.

"We've already eaten," said Cassandra. "Do you want to order? We could wait."

Monica smiled. "No—this won't take long."

Cassandra glanced out the window. "Alberto's not coming in?"

Monica's smile broadened and she looked Cassandra squarely in the eye. "Sorry to disappoint you. This conversation is for just us girls. First, let me share my good news." She held up her left hand to show off her engagement ring.

After a moment, Cassandra said, "It's lovely."

"Wow—impressive." Molly's tone was full of mock admiration. "That sucker's gotta be a couple of carats."

"Four," said Monica. She turned her attention again to Cassandra. "Alberto's marrying me, Cass, and we've set a date. So even if you continue sneaking around and screwing him behind my back, you'll never be more to him than his backstreet bitch."

"Alberto's the one sneaking around," Molly said. "Cassandra has no obligation to you."

"How long have you known?" Cassandra asked.

Monica laughed. "For a while. Alberto's not good at sneaking around. But it will never go anywhere—except some occasional, sleazy motel room."

"You sure about that?" Molly asked. Cassandra frowned but Molly plunged ahead. "If Alberto's still seeing other people, I'd say a ring doesn't mean all that much to him."

"Come on, Molly—you know how it works," Monica replied, then looked at Cassandra. "I guess I shouldn't expect you to know. I mean, how could you?"

"Will you get to the fucking point?" Molly said.

"Okay, here it is," Monica replied, watching Cassandra closely. "Money marries money, Cass. Not some nobody from East Cleveland whose father is a drunk and whose mother is—God knows what."

Cassandra ignored the insult, refusing to take the bait. She looked out the window again. Alberto was staring straight ahead. It rankled her to her soul that he wouldn't even look in her direction, never mind coming in to face her. "I see you've checked up on me."

Monica laughed. "Of course. I'll bet I know more about you than anyone."

"Like what?"

"Like you worked two jobs to put yourself through college. Like you got a full ride to law school—which wouldn't have happened without the influence of that judge you clerked for—and slept with—for two summers. I also found out he contributed a living allowance and a car, rather than have you tell his wife how long you'd been enjoying his attentions. You did all right for yourself, Cass."

"You think anybody cares about that?" Molly said. "Cassandra's friends are with her no matter where she came from or how she got here."

"You've shared this information with Alberto?" asked Cassandra.

"I did—but it really doesn't matter," Monica answered. "Since he'll never take you out in public, no one cares about your unfortunate and duplicitous background."

"So why am I here?" Molly asked.

"I wasn't sure how Cass would react," Monica explained. "Considering where she came from. I've heard East Cleveland is pretty rough."

Molly studied her a moment. "I don't know how she feels, but I'd like to slap that smug look off your stupid face."

"No, it's okay," said Cassandra. She put her hand on Molly's arm to stop her. "Don't worry, Monica. I won't be seeing Alberto again."

"Sure you will," Monica replied. "If he wants to continue your sordid little affair, I have no doubt you'll go along with it—but that's okay. I don't really care, as long as you're careful and discreet. It's not unusual for a wealthy man to have a mistress, and I really don't like sex all that much. But please understand, Cass. With Alberto, that's all it will ever be. And you're welcome to it—"

"No thank you," Cassandra broke in. "Please tell him for me—he's never been my first choice. It was just something to do until someone better came along. It was never serious, not on my side anyway. So if that's all, there's somewhere I have to be." She gave Monica her best, her brightest, her most brilliant smile. "I have a date and I don't want to keep him waiting."

Cassandra picked up the check but Molly grabbed it out of her hand and put it down in front of Monica. "Tell Prince Alberto he can pay—or you can, since this was your party."

After dropping Molly off at her place, Cassandra headed to the park to meet Jeff. She saw him before he saw her and the sight of him cheered her immensely. He'd told her to meet him there but hadn't told her why. She stood next to her car and watched him for a few minutes, talking to a group of pre-teen boys outfitted with baseball bats and mitts. He looked happy, at peace with himself and the world, doing something Alberto would never have considered.

When it came time to end it with Alberto (as she'd always known it would) she'd expected to feel a terrible sense of loss. Instead, she felt relief. Maybe it was time to stop picking guys who would never commit, like Alberto and the married judge. Her shrink had told her years ago that she chose unavailable men on purpose because she didn't really want a permanent, serious relationship. She'd had to admit the truth of it, but maybe it was changing.

As she started walking toward Jeff, he looked up and spotted her. With a big grin, he waved and went to join her.

•••

The sight of her, as always, left Jeff a little breathless. Before he had time to think about it (and do something stupid), one of the older kids—Benjamin—yelled out, "Hey, coach—who's the babe?" Jeff looked around to see the entire team was following him.

Instantly, the other boys weighed in with comments like, "Good choice, coach!" and "Way to go, coach!" and a distinctive, "Woo-hoo!" Cassandra laughed.

"All right, you bums!" Jeff addressed the kids. "Grab your best manners and come say hello—and remember there's a lady present! This is my business associate—"

"Hi, I'm Cass," Cassandra broke in. "And I'm delighted to meet so many gentlemen in one place."

She had instantly settled them. A couple of them said, "Hi." Others, suddenly shy, raised a hand to wave. Jeff thought she was truly amazing.

"Okay, boys," he told them. "I want you to run that drill we practiced last time—covering first and third—until the ice cream gets here. It's winter now, but summer's coming and you gotta be ready! You remember the set-up. Get going!" The kids ran back to the baseball diamond and Jeff led Cassandra to a spot between home plate and first base.

"I didn't know you were coaching a Little League team," she said. "I'm impressed."

"No—not really," he answered. "I mean, it's not a Little League team.

Just some kids from the neighborhood. Joey—the smallest one out there—he was getting bullied by the others, so I stepped in. They just needed a little guidance."

"Well, I think that's pretty cool," she said softly. "You're a good man, Jeff."

"Nah," he replied, trying to turn aside her compliment. "It's something to do on a Sunday—when I'm not slaving away at D and B."

"Poor baby," she said, her mouth forming a seductive little pout. They watched the boys for a moment and he allowed himself the briefest fantasy, remembering how her lips had felt against his. "So," she went on. "About Robert. You find anything?"

"Not yet. There's not much information on the computer system. I went to archives to look for some relevant files, but they've been signed out for months—by guess who?"

"Tell me."

"Franklin Barro, one of the partners. I've got to get into his office and have a look."

"How?" she asked. "When will you get a chance like that?"

"I was thinking . . . tonight." She looked up at him, surprised. "No one is ever in the office after nine on a Sunday night. Everyone is resting up for the weekly grind, even the mighty Frank Barro."

"What if it's locked?"

"It won't be," Jeff said. "As of late Friday, the lock is broken. He tried to change it himself—after maintenance told him they couldn't get to it 'til Monday—and he screwed it up. So it's got to be tonight."

"What about security cameras?" Cassandra asked.

"The only ones I've seen are in the lobby, on each floor at reception directly in front of the elevator banks, and in Human Resources—I guess in case someone gets fired and freaks out."

"None in the partners' offices?"

Jeff let out a wry chuckle. "No—the partners wouldn't want closed-circuit proof of after-hours hanky-panky."

"Of which there's probably a lot," Cassandra guessed. "Okay, then. I'll be your lookout."

"I don't know," Jeff said. "I don't want to put you in that position. If the camera at reception catches you, how do I explain it? Me coming in at night—that's no big deal. I'm there almost every night."

"Simple. We'll say we stopped in after a date so you could pick up something to work on at home. I'm coming with you, Jeff. You need someone to watch your back, just in case."

He wanted to kiss her then and there but before he could figure out how to execute such a move, the Mister Softee truck coasted up to the curb blasting *Music Box Dancer.* Joey ran toward Jeff and Cassandra.

"Hey, Jeff!" he called out. "Ice cream!"

•••

The elevator stopped on the floor Jeff shared with Franklin Barro, Ray Alexander, Sean Witherspoon, half a dozen associates and a handful of secretaries. As they stepped out into the dimly lit hallway, Jeff took Cassandra's hand and led her to his office. Once inside, he closed his door and took a deep breath.

"You okay?" she asked.

"Yeah. A little tense, maybe. You think we could be wasting our time with this? I mean, could someone at a big firm like Darby and Blackstone really be involved in Robert's death? If we get caught where we don't belong, it could be over—for both of us. Are we stupid or crazy?"

"Considering that we'd be humiliated and at least one of us would be fired, I'd say . . . probably both."

Conflicting emotions washed through him as he came to the full realization of what they were about to do. "Yeah, we would. And our careers are just starting, and the money is so good. As you've probably surmised, I don't come from a privileged background like you obviously do. I love being able to have an expensive dinner out once in a while, and a few drinks with friends. I like getting driven home at dawn on a Saturday morning after an all-nighter, not to mention looking at my paycheck and knowing it will grow exponentially if I can just hang in there."

"I do get it," she said. "Someday I'll tell you all about my so-called privileged background but this is about Robert. If anyone at D and B had something to do with his death, we can't just ignore it."

"I've thought about it, a lot. You know—whether I could look the other way. Like, would my silence be worth a few trappings of wealth, which in the grand scheme of things will only amount to crumbs?"

Cassandra smiled up at him. "So you're a philosopher, too."

"No—I'm just wondering what the hell we do with the information once we get it."

"Maybe we won't find anything. Maybe this is all due to Red's drug-addled fantasy and our mutual grief after losing Robert." She reached into her purse and pulled out a small flashlight. "All I know is—I want to know."

He studied her a moment. She was everything he'd ever imagined could be possible in a woman. He was in love with her—he couldn't deny it—and he didn't know how to tell her. "Okay, then," he said. "Let's do this."

She nodded and Jeff turned out the light in his office, then opened the door and peeked out into the hall. Everything was quiet. With Jeff in the lead, they stepped into the gloom. Cassandra quietly closed the door behind them. Half way between his office and Franklin Barro's, Jeff stopped and pointed at a door.

"File room," he said. "Any point in looking in there?"

"I doubt it," Cassandra whispered. "If he's had Robert's file for months, I think he'd keep it close to him."

"Right." They kept on moving, slowly and silently toward Barro's door. Jeff pushed it open. The room was pitch dark.

Rather than turn on the overhead light, he felt around on Barro's desk for a moment , found the lamp and flicked the switch. His heart was pounding. If they got caught, he had no idea what he would say.

There was a file cabinet behind the desk but it was locked. "We need a key," he said. "Let's hope it's here somewhere and not on his key ring."

Cassandra stood near the door, listening for potential intruders while Jeff fumbled through Barro's desk drawers. In the far corner of the middle drawer, his hand brushed up against a collection of objects that rattled—the keys he hoped would open the file cabinet. After trying three, he found the right one. He turned it and pulled the top drawer. It slid open easily, without making a sound. He was happy to find all the files marked alphabetically instead of by group or division. The third drawer was labeled M, N, O, P. He closed the top drawer, pulled out the third one and quickly found Primedia; RT. Each Primedia file was labeled with the initials of the associate who had worked on it, and each file contained a copy of every paper that associate had prepared in connection with Primedia. But inside Robert's folder was only his personnel file.

"What the fuck?" Jeff exclaimed. "Look at this. What's it doing in here?" Cassandra left her post by the door and came to look over his shoulder. She switched on her little flashlight and aimed it at the file. Standing close together, they read the contents.

"This doesn't match what they told the newspapers," Cassandra said.

"No . . . it doesn't. Robert wasn't having a hard time with the job. Exactly the opposite. Look what Witherspoon had to say."

Cassandra read aloud. "'Mr.Turner has a sharp, analytical mind. I am impressed with his ability to quickly grasp and understand complex legal concepts. He is a fine young gentleman with a good work ethic. I strongly recommend he be extended an offer to join Darby and Blackstone.' So who's Sean Witherspoon?" she asked Jeff.

"Head of corporate affairs. According to Phil, he's an amazing lawyer, well respected, and an even better rainmaker. He uses his political connections to get bigger and wealthier clients. He's also a foul-mouthed philanderer, but who cares—he has a client contact list that could fill ten Rolodexes."

"Okay—what else?"

Jeff flipped the recommendation letters over and found only a couple of newspaper articles recounting Robert's death—one identical to the article he had carried, folded up in his back pocket, for months. He knew it almost word for word. He read the article again and it hit him:

The truth speaks louder than anything.

It was from the *New York Chronicle* and there was a quote from Sean Witherspoon:

The tragedy was that we would have done anything to help make this young man part of our team. But he just didn't have the skills. In the end, with his ego and ambition, it was probably too much for him to bear, so he took his own life. It's heartbreaking. I'm sorry but I have nothing more to say.

Ray Alexander, Franklin Barro, and even Gary Johnson and Art Swede were quoted in the article. They all blasted Robert's performance while lamenting his tragic departure from this earth.

"Every quote from every partner interviewed toed the party line," Jeff said.

"They all describe Robert as unreliable and not terribly bright," said Cassandra. "That contradicts the praise they heaped on him in their recommendations for hiring him. These letters raise some questions. I don't know what we can do with them, but it's a start. Let's Xerox them."

"I don't think that's an option. All the machines are turned off in the evenings," Jeff explained. "I'd have to turn on a copier and wait for it to warm up—a good ten minutes at least. Then I'd have to punch in my code, which would place me here, making copies of something in the middle of the night."

"So—you were here like a good little soldier, working late."

He shook his head. "The D and B machines save the first page of every document copied, as kind of a back-up system, and to keep people from Xeroxing fliers for a poetry reading in the Village or invitations to their kid's birthday. Phil clued me in when I first got here."

"Think you could sneak it out and take it to Kinko's?"

"And sneak it back in, right under Barro's nose?" Jeff asked. "Unlikely." He held up the file. "There's nothing here, anyway. Just the partners changing their opinions of one of their associates, which is their right to do."

"Okay," Cassandra agreed. "But at least we know we're not crazy. There's a reason they all changed their opinions, and we know it wasn't the quality of Robert's work."

"Right. So I have to keep looking," Jeff said. "Come on—let's get out of here."

He replaced Robert's folder in its hanging file, closed the drawer and locked the cabinet. Then he returned the keys to the desk, making sure everything else was as Franklin Barro had left it, right down to the last pencil.

They were half way down the hall, almost to the elevator banks, when they heard the electronic whirring of the lift coming up.

"Shit," Jeff exclaimed under his breath. He watched the indicator light above the elevator, coming closer. He grabbed Cassandra's arm and pulled her into the file room, closing the door just as the elevator arrived.

"This won't take long," Barro said, stepping out of the lift and switching on the lights. "There's a couple of files I want to grab so I can read on the train in the morning."

"Take your time," Ray replied. "I'm in no hurry to get home. The wife is on a tear for me take her to some fundraiser—a fucking gala ball, for shit's sake, where I gotta wear a tux."

Barro laughed. "You should go," he said. "Good place to get new clients."

Their footsteps echoed on the polished marble tile as they approached the file room.

From their hiding place Jeff and Cassandra could see the bright light from the hallway shining beneath the door. The footsteps came closer. Jeff held his breath, wondering how the hell they were going to get themselves out of this.

Suddenly Cassandra grabbed him and shoved him back against the file cabinets, pressing herself tightly against him while unbuttoning her blouse. As the doorknob turned, she hiked up her skirt. She had only time to say, before she covered his mouth with hers, "Trust me."

When the door opened and the light came on, Cassandra was kissing Jeff with heated passion and grinding herself against him—right where it counted.

"Oh!" she cried out, as if surprised by the intrusion. "Oh, my god!" She moved away from Jeff, closing her blouse and straightening her skirt.

Ray Alexander, clearly enjoying the sight, laughed and Barro said, "Well, well, well—what have we here?"

"Oh—uh," Jeff stammered. "We were just—I mean, I came in to get something to work on at home and—"

Barro laughed. "No need to explain, my man. It's always a thrill to screw your girl in the office—believe me, I know. But for next time, I recommend the conference table in the big room."

Jeff managed a sheepish grin. "Well, uh—thanks for understanding. We just got a little carried away."

"Aren't you going to introduce us?" Ray asked. "I mean, it's the least you can do after such an enticing display."

"Oh, right," said Jeff. "This is Cassandra Winslow. She's an attorney with Madden, Karp and Simpson."

"I thought she looked familiar," Barro said, taking the hand Cassandra offered. "I know who she is, and I know how hot she is—at practicing law." He turned his full attention on her. "As I recall, Ms. Winslow, we tried to recruit you."

"Yes, you did," she responded softly. "But then I got a better offer."

Barro gave Jeff an atta-boy slap on the arm. "Play your cards right, Jeff," he said. "Maybe you can get this lovely lady to come on board with us."

•••

In the cab, Cassandra sat close to Jeff. They had taken a taxi to Darby and Blackstone so as not to lose their parking spots in front of his place. They rode in silence for a few minutes, then Jeff said, "These fucking people. I knew they were self-centered workaholics, but scumbags?" He paused for a moment, trying to take it in. "Red's not imagining things because he's high most of the time," he said. He felt a little disoriented. "It was a cover-up."

"And you believe Barro's behind it?" asked Cassandra.

A sudden, sick realization hit him. "You think that's why they hired me? Because I was Robert's friend? Maybe Robert did put in a good word for me—he'd promised he would."

"So . . . someone at D and B believes Robert told you something? Like, he found something and told you about it?"

"I don't know—maybe. And so they invited me in like fucking vampires. They seduced me with the money, and the glory and prestige that could be mine." He pulled her even closer, taking comfort in her warmth. "You know, when I first met these people, I was dazzled—dazzled by the name and reputation of one of the biggest firms in New York, and by the possibility of making partner." His voice took on an anguished edge. "I forgot about Robert, for a while."

"Come on—don't go there," Cassandra advised. "You finally had what all of us have worked so hard for."

"I even thought Franklin Barro could be my mentor. And maybe—maybe—after a good, long working relationship, he'd be a friend, or at least an ally."

"That's probably what Robert thought."

"And they turned on him. Turned on him like a pack of wolves."

The cab pulled up in front of Jeff's brownstone. He paid the driver and as they got out, he said, "I should walk you to your car. It's late."

"Not that late," she said and her next words surprised him. "You got anything to drink?"

He smiled, hardly believing his luck. "Couple of beers in the fridge. Will that do?"

"That'll do just fine."

After feeding Yankee, he opened the beers and handed one to her. She took a sip and put it down on the kitchen counter. Then she went into his arms and kissed him, as passionately as she had in the Darby and Blackstone file room. Only this time, he could tell she wasn't pretending.

He pulled back a moment and looked into her eyes. "You sure?" he asked. She nodded, and he led her into his bedroom. They undressed each other as they walked, leaving a trail of clothing in their wake. For a moment, they stood next to his bed and he reveled in the feel of her velvet skin against his and the way she ran her hands over his body. Then she pulled him down with her. He wanted to take his time with her but she seemed eager for him—desperately eager—which was intoxicating. The first time was quick and hot and breathless, and they came together. The second time was slow, languid, erotic and sweet.

Jeff was running late. He and Cassandra had awakened well before any of his alarms went off, in time to make love again before they both left for work. Neither of them said anything about where it would go from there, but he was hopeful. Already he knew he could never get enough of her.

He made it to the office at about eight-thirty, earlier than most days but late nonetheless, and he had a considerable amount of drafting to do in order to complete the loan documents Barro had assigned him. It wasn't going to be an easy day, he knew, with the suspicions about his boss rushing around in his head, but he had to stay focused—and he had to act normal.

As he entered his office he removed his coat and hung it on the back of his desk chair, then went to the pantry to fix himself a cup of coffee. Without it, he would stumble through the day like a zombie. A nice stiff cup of Colombian, with skim milk and two packets of Sweet'n Low, he thought with anticipation. He took a sip and instantly felt better. The caffeine seemed to restore the chemical balance in his brain.

Upon returning to his office, he found a letter on his chair, with a Post-It note attached:

SEE ME RIGHT AWAY—FB

Jeff peeled off the yellow Post-It and quickly scanned the letter. It was from Cornelius Wilson, the attorney of the borrower who was not going to receive any funds from the bank. Cornelius was a nice enough fellow. He liked to call and shoot the breeze, unlike the typical, abrupt New York attorney. This good ol' southern boy from Louisiana had an easygoing demeanor and a penchant for beginning each conversation with a joke he had heard or seen on the Internet. He was pleasant enough, but somewhat of an idiot whose frequent miscalculations and sub-par drafting often led to a great degree of extra work for Jeff.

VIA FACSIMILE

Jeff Rhodes, Esq.
Darby & Blackstone

Dear Mr. Rhodes:

I am writing to address a situation which has arisen with regards to a proposed loan between your client and the principals of the developer. I am concerned that the direction this transaction has taken will result in considerable damage to the borrower and potential liability to your client. My client has been working with the bank to arrange for the loan to finance the purchase of a considerable property upon which my client intends to construct a shopping center. My client is working to obtain the necessary zoning permission to go forward with the project and has engaged in numerous discussions with the lending committee at the bank. In order to facilitate the lending process, he obtained a guarantee from prominent individuals in the real estate community to ensure performance of the obligation. In this way, the bank is guaranteed repayment in the event of default. The bank would still always maintain a first mortgage position on the property.

The bank conducted extensive due diligence with regards to the transaction. After the underwriting process was essentially completed, the loan was sent to the credit committee for approval, which was subsequently rejected.

The bank's actions have caused serious damage to my client and others who are involved with this transaction. The lengthy delays and the time and effort that have been spent in this transaction have all been in vain.

My client has relied on the bank's assurances that it was working diligently to complete the transaction and has expended significant funds in reliance on the bank's assurances that it was attempting to complete the deal.

I urge your client to reconsider the entire situation and to honor its responsibility to my client. Please feel free to contact me at your earliest convenience if you wish to consider further discussions. Otherwise, my client will enforce its rights in law or in equity and will move to recover damages due to the bank's misrepresentations.

Very truly yours,

Cornelius Wilson

A chill shuddered through Jeff. It was coming, and he was the target. Somehow, some way, if this ended up in litigation, he was going to be the fall guy, despite the fact that everyone knew the history behind this. This borrower never produced the necessary due diligence in order to close the deal. But the bank's loan officer didn't put his foot down early in the process, and thus the borrower may have been damaged and now the borrower was desperate.

That's the problem with this game, Jeff thought. It's all about covering your ass because anyone can turn on you at the drop of a dime and it sucks. Phil was right; Jeff would have to watch his back where Barro was concerned.

He dreaded going to Barro's office, but he knew he had no choice. He couldn't afford to trigger the fury of the monster.

Barro's door was closed, and rather than knock, Jeff asked Pamela, Barro's secretary, how long he would be occupied.

"I don't think he'll be long," she said, waving him to the seat beside her desk. Pamela was a great secretary—Franklin Barro wouldn't tolerate anything less—but she seemed to have a ditzy streak. Unlike most of her peers at the straight-laced, buttoned-up Darby and Blackstone office, she dressed in the most outlandish and provocative outfits she could get away with. Today she was wearing a tight, leather miniskirt. The neckline of her leopard print blouse was cut low, thus treating everyone she encountered to a fetching view of her bosom. He wondered if it was her style Barro liked, or if Barro liked her style because it was distracting to all who entered his office.

"So how's it going, Jeff?" she asked with a smile. "What have you been up to?"

"Burning the midnight oil, as usual."

"What a shame. You really should get out more." She tapped one of her long fingernails on her desk, and Jeff wondered how she got any typing done with them.

"Without a doubt," he replied easily although his gut felt twisted into a knot. "Maybe you could put in a good word for me with your boss. Might get me out of here a little earlier, especially on the weekends."

Pamela chuckled. "Oh, I know, sweetheart. Believe me, I feel for you. When I leave at the end of the day, my heart goes out to you guys. Except on payday, of course. But you know Franklin. He's such a workaholic," She glanced at her phone and flashed him another big smile. "Looks like he's off the phone now. Go ahead and peek your handsome face in there. I'm sure he'll be happy to see you."

"Thanks, Pamela." Jeff tapped lightly on Barro's door, turned the knob and cracked it open.

"Oh—hey, Jeff. Come on in."

"Good morning," Jeff said. Barro seemed to be in a good mood but Jeff didn't trust that it would last. It would likely be another day in the mine field.

"Don't sit—you won't be here that long. How we doing on those documents?"

"Great. I should have them to you after lunch."

"Well, I'll tell you what. You can put them off until tomorrow." He picked a file up off his desk and handed it to Jeff. "In the meantime, I need you to go back to your office and take a look at this. I'm having lunch with the client—you'll join me—about one-thirty, I think. It's Gene Morris from Primedia—they're purchasing more airplanes. After lunch, I have a couple of conference calls I might want you to sit in on."

"Sure—but, ah—I found the letter you left on my chair. Is there a possibility that might go to litigation?"

"Oh, never mind that bullshit. I just thought you'd find it amusing. Those guys don't have a leg to stand on. Don't worry about that. I'll take care of it."

"Anything else?"

Franklin's phone began to ring. "I gotta take this, Jeff. Arrange for a car to come and pick us up about one. On the way, I want to hear your thoughts on Primedia." He studied Jeff a moment. "I trust you've had time to go through the files I gave you."

"Yes—most of them."

Back in his office Jeff sank into his chair. It was impossible to judge Barro's mood, which could shift like quicksilver, but his own was a little elated. He had dodged two bullets that morning—the litigation issue and the fact that he didn't yet have the loan documents completed. His phone rang and his elation faded. Barro probably had something else for him to do. He picked it up. "Yeah, Adrienne?"

"There's a Nancy Kellerman on for you," she said. "She has a question about a real estate search."

"Okay, I'll take it."

"Hello, Jeff," a pleasant voice greeted him. It was somewhat husky but distinctly feminine. "Allow me to introduce myself. I'm Nancy Kellerman, with Jim Sparrow Legal Search. I understand you do real estate."

"Yes."

"So are you enjoying yourself at D and B? It's a wonderful firm."

Jeff hesitated for a moment. Why did this woman, whoever she was, concern herself with whether or not he was happy at D and B? "Well, they're certainly keeping me busy."

"Working you to the bone, are they?"

"Around the clock."

"It's an impossible lifestyle they want you to lead, if you want to call it that."

Jeff could imagine that the head honchos at D and B would put people up to calling the associates in order to find out if they actually enjoyed their jobs but he wasn't falling for it. After a moment, he said, "It's a lot of work—there's hardly any time for much of a lifestyle, as you call it."

"So, are you thinking of changing your situation?" she probed.

"Why do you ask?"

"You went to Livermore," she went on. "I'm sure you owe a pretty penny in student loans. Am I right?"

Her slight southern accent and sympathetic voice gave Jeff the impression that she wasn't a member of New York's elite Four Hundred. Although her questions were probing, her phone presence came across as endearing—almost as if she actually cared about his plight.

"Most associates owe student loans," Jeff replied. "Again, why do you ask?"

"I may have something for you," she said.

"Well, I'm pretty happy where I am." Jeff couldn't resist leading her on. "It would have to be something amazing where I could make a lot of money—maybe something in the area of entertainment, like personal counsel to a big box office superstar. Maybe I'd like to get away from real estate."

She seemed to take him seriously, and he wondered how much of their conversation she would report to Barro. "Jeff, you've really only started in your career. Are you sure you'd want to leave the area of real estate, especially when it's so hot right now?"

"Well, what do you suggest? What have you got?"

The headhunter continued, "Well, I've got positions that have opened up at Crane and Simmons, Milton and Twain, Banner and Woods, and—"

Jeff quickly jumped in. "Well, those are pretty big law firms," he teased. "But I don't think they're into entertainment. Not a rock star among 'em as far as I know."

"Would you prefer to relocate, maybe to a firm in Chicago or even California?"

What a bunch of horseshit, Jeff thought, but he said, "I'm listening."

"So, when do you want me to set you up with an interview?" she pressed on.

"Look, I appreciate your call, but I think I'm gonna stay where I am. Like you said, it's probably not such a great idea to jump around this early in my career."

"I understand, Jeff—but tell you what. I'm going to send you an information package about our firm, and my business card. If you change your mind, you know where to find me."

"Well, don't send it here. Send it to my home address."

"Not a problem."

"So do you need it—my address?"

"No, I've got it. Thanks for your time."

Jeff put down the phone. "What a load of crap," he muttered and turned his attention to the new Primedia file Barro had just given him.

It was nearing one o'clock. Jeff told Adrienne to have a car waiting for him and Mr. Barro. At five minutes to one, he buzzed Franklin. "Hey, FB. You ready to have that conference before we head off to lunch?"

"Oh, shit. I completely forgot. Lunch is cancelled. We're doing dinner instead."

Great, Jeff thought. *Thanks for telling me.* "Are we going to need a car?" he asked. He managed to keep his tone even and respectful.

"Yes, of course." Barro's voice changed. Now he sounded a bit more impatient. "So how about the docs on that small loan? Are they done yet?"

"I thought you told me to put them off until tomorrow."

"Well, now I need them right away."

Franklin hung up, leaving Jeff holding the phone, listening to the dial tone. Jeff sighed and replaced the receiver in its cradle, then swiveled around in his chair and grabbed his mouse. Clicking on a search window, he typed in the client matter number. All the necessary documents came up and he sat down to the task of drafting them.

He's crazy, Jeff thought. First he gives me twenty-four hours, and then he wants it in forty-five minutes. Franklin Barro was fuckin' loony tunes with all these false deadlines.

The phone rang again. Jeff hesitated, wondering why Adrienne wasn't picking up. It rang again, shrill and urgent. "Fuck it," he said under his breath as he grabbed it. "Jeff Rhodes."

"Hey, Jeff." It was Franklin and it sounded like he was on speaker phone. Jeff could hear other people shuffling around in the background.

"Yes, FB—what's up?"

"Jeff, how many times do I have to tell you? When you send out a fax cover sheet along with any correspondence, I want to get cc'd."

"Even on the cover sheet?"

"Especially on the cover sheet. I want to have a record of what's going out on every file—and when. Don't make me repeat myself." Surprised, Jeff didn't respond. "Well? Are we clear?"

Jeff was momentarily paralyzed. For a moment he remained speechless. Then he said, "I apologize FB. I didn't–"

"Don't apologize, just do. Oh, and another thing. When you cc me, it's Franklin A. Barro. Not FB, not Franklin Barro, and not FAB as in fabulous. Franklin A. Barro. And don't call me FB. You address me as Franklin or Mr. Barro. Got it?"

"Understood," Jeff responded, suddenly petrified. *I have to get out of here,* he thought. *I need to get away from this schizo. Why the hell does he give a shit whether I write FB or FAB? It's fucking irrelevant.* And all the while it was digging at his mind—Barro and his cronies, and the lies they'd told about Robert in that newspaper article.

Where can I go? Jeff thought. *Where can I make enough money to cover my student loan debt? Some lawyers move on to other careers, but I have no experience in anything else.*

He was no quitter, but it was all beginning to wear on him. Fear and anxiety were his constant companions. Now it was no longer the lack of sleep and the hard work that was costing him an even greater price than the potential loss of his livelihood. It was the inconsistency and unpredictability of Franklin Barro, and the worry that Robert had discovered something about the man that had cost him his life.

Jeff reached into the upper drawer of his desk and pulled out the pack of Marlboro Lights he'd bought that morning, on impulse. He'd given up smoking in college and had sworn to his mom he wouldn't pick it up again, but he felt an increasing need to release some of the tension building up in him. It wasn't just the rush he got from the nicotine—it was simply that he had one craving that could be instantly satisfied with the strike of a match, unlike everything else in his life. It's either a cigarette, he thought, or I'm going to put my fist through one of these walls—or through FAB's fabulous face.

The elevator hit the lobby and Jeff was soon stepping outdoors into the open air. He wedged himself in between the side of the building and a van parked next to the cargo elevator. Striking a match, he lit the cigarette and took a deep puff, then exhaled, his mind still racing. Yeah, he considered silently. Lawyers go on to do lots of other things—meaningful and useful things. But what?

A tear escaped from the corner of his eye and trickled down his cheek. Like a heavy raindrop, it splashed off of his right hand. Jeff flicked away the cigarette and wiped his eyes, forcing his mind back to the unexpected night with Cassandra, taking comfort in remembering how eager for him she had been. Before he could get lost in erotic recollections, he headed back to his office. He found Phil seated in his chair with his feet propped up on the desk.

"Phil, this isn't the time, man. Barro just tore my head off."

"You all right?"

"I am now, I think."

"Your face is all red. He must have really pissed you off. I'll tell you what. I dare you to go in there—and I'll back you up. I'll be right behind you. I dare you to march right into Barro's office, drop your fucking pants, bend over, and say, 'Kiss my hairy ass.'"

"Come on, Phil—not funny, not at the moment."

"No, no, I'm serious." Phil leaned back even further in Jeff's chair, reached between his legs and grabbed hold of his package. "I dare you to walk into Barro's office, whip out your schlong, and say, 'Listen, Barro, how about you blow me?' Then turn around and walk out. Then I'll smack him upside his head and I'll walk out right behind you. Then we'll be done with this place."

Without knocking, Adrienne opened the door and stuck her head inside the room. "What's wrong, Phil?" she asked. "You have an itch?" Phil blushed and they all laughed. "Jeff, I have your Mom on line one."

In her typical sweet demeanor, she told Jeff she didn't want to bother him at work. She just wanted to let him know she received the check he sent and thank him for it—but she didn't want him going without anything he needed.

"It's fine, Mom," he said. "I've got everything I need, and you earned it. It's the least I can do. I told you when I made it you wouldn't have to worry anymore."

"Then I insist—no Christmas present this year. I mean it. Will you be seeing us over the holidays?" she asked hopefully. "Everyone's coming—"

"I'll try," he broke in. "They're working me crazy hours these days but I'll do my best."

"I understand," she said. "You do what you need to do. You are the pride of this family and we want you to get to where you're meant to be going."

By five o'clock, Jeff was nearly done with his drafting. The dinner meeting would be a welcome respite from the day's aggravation. Jeff rang Barro. "Hey, Franklin, are you ready for our five o'clock?"

"Yeah, Jeff. Hey—I appreciate all the hard work you've been doing. Meet me downstairs. You okay with a steakhouse and a nice bottle of wine?"

"Sounds great."

"Good. You can cut out right after dinner."

Jeff put down the phone, put on his coat and grabbed his briefcase. The thought of Phil bending over, scratching his ass and telling Barro to go screw himself flashed through his mind. If Phil wasn't around, he would have lost his sanity a long time ago. Phil was a wise ass, but so funny, and brilliant all at the same time.

As he was about to walk out the door, Jeff noticed a piece of paper thumb-tacked to his bulletin board. It was a *New York Law Journal* article titled, *Discouraged?* and it profiled a young man who, at the age of twenty-two, had failed at his first business. At the age of twenty-three, he ran for the legislature and was defeated. At the age of twenty-four, he again failed in business. At twenty-five he was elected to the legislature. At twenty-six he lost his girlfriend. At twenty-seven he had a nervous breakdown. At twenty-nine he ran for local office and was defeated. At thirty-one, he ran again and was again defeated. At thirty-four, he ran for Congress and was defeated. At thirty-seven he was elected to Congress. At thirty-nine, he ran again for Congress and lost. At forty-six, he ran for the Senate and lost. At forty-seven he was a Vice Presidential candidate but was defeated. At forty-nine, he ran for the Senate and lost. And then, at the age of fifty-one he was elected President of the United States.

Jeff recognized Phil's handwriting at the bottom of the page where he'd written:

"Jeffy boy—this seemingly inauspicious record belongs to one of the greatest men of all time: Abraham Lincoln. It goes to show, in the end, that perseverance and toughness count for far more than anything else. Hang in there, Killer."

Jeff folded the piece of paper and placed it in his breast pocket, a slow smile spreading across his face. Then he left for dinner.

•••

They took the Brooklyn Bridge across the East River to Peter Luger's Steakhouse. Jeff had heard of the legendary restaurant, of course, but he'd never been able to afford it. There was no valet parking so the car service, vying for position with stretch limousines depositing smartly dressed socialites and businessmen, dropped them in front of the old brick structure. Franklin Barro told their driver to find a parking spot and wait for them.

Inside, the décor was simple and clean, with exposed wooden beams, brass chandeliers and big windows that gave diners an expansive view of the neighborhood. But the best thing about it, Jeff thought, was the tantalizing aroma of steak sizzling on platters the waiters carried past them. He studied the menu, hesitant to order. A Porterhouse steak was over thirty dollars, and the shrimp cocktail appetizer was fifteen and change.

"Have whatever you want, Jeff," Franklin urged happily. "Primedia's paying for it."

Jeff wondered if the exorbitant price would somehow make it taste better, and he wasn't disappointed. The steak literally (almost) melted in his mouth. *I'm such a whore,* he thought. *I could get used to this.* No one talked business until they were on coffee and dessert—the most amazing cheesecake he had ever experienced.

"Okay," said Gene motioning for the waiter to pour more coffee. "So—where are we on the nightclub closing?"

"It's a done deal," Franklin replied. "Just a couple of papers to sign and Primedia will own the club, with D and B overseeing operations in New York, including remodeling and décor. Phil will take care of it."

"That's good," said Gene. "I'm more concerned about the aircraft delivery." He looked pointedly at Barro. "We have to keep the buyers happy, and they're getting nervous."

"Just tell 'em everything's going according to schedule," Barro said.

"Well, I'm a little worried," Gene shot back. "What with the holidays almost on us. We've gotta get this done. You know what our time frame is, and it can't be changed—"

"Don't worry," Barro assured him. "I'll have Jeff run point on it."

Jeff almost choked on his last bite of cheesecake. "Me?" he asked.

Barro smiled. "Indeed."

"Okay—ah, I need you to fill me in on exactly what that involves."

"It's pretty routine," Barro said, settling back in his chair. "The aircraft will come in from the manufacturer in Tennessee, to a private airport in New Jersey, where we accept delivery. These are high-class private planes, Jeff. Luxury models. Primedia sells to private companies and to individuals all around the world. It's a big operation, but the procedure is simple."

"So I take delivery," Jeff said. "Then what?"

"These are beautiful machines," Gene put in. "But we make them even more luxurious before we send them on to the buyers. We install a better carpet and we load in a supply of top of the line pillows and blankets for the sleeping compartments, whatever the buyer wants. We try to get it turned around in one day, two at the most. Our upgrade crew will be at the airport when the plane arrives, and they'll jump right on it."

"So what am I running point on?" Jeff asked.

"Mostly the paperwork," said Barro. "It's basically a check-off list. You make sure the manufacturer delivered all the necessary goods in the standing as ordered. The upgrade crew will take it from there."

"Okay."

"Then you confirm with the FAA–it's a tax thing, see." Uncharacteristically, Barro took a moment to explain. "The documents have to be done and the transaction closed while the aircraft are either in the airspace or on the ground in the jurisdiction with the most favorable tax law. That's Tennessee, where the manufacturer is. It'll be cutting it close, with the damn holiday bullshit, but we've got to get it done. Everything has to be registered and filed with the FAA, which is in Oklahoma City, by four o'clock, end of the business day. Think you can handle it?"

"I can handle it," Jeff said.

CHAPTER 14

The Closing

Jeff jumped, startled by the alarm clock. It was four AM, and he could hear the wind howling and garbage trucks rumbling through the street below. He should get up but his bed was so warm. For a moment he hesitated, then fell back and nestled again into his fluffy pillow. His satisfaction was brief, however, cut short when his cell phone started to ring. He grabbed it off his bedside table.

"Hello?"

"Mr. Rhodes?" It was a deep male voice. "I'm calling to confirm your limousine to La Guardia Airport."

"Yes, I have a six AM flight."

"I'll be there in half an hour. Please be so kind as to wait in front of your apartment building."

"No problem."

Jeff had packed the night before, and he'd called Mrs. Bently and asked her to take care of Yankee for the next few days. He pulled off his shorts and raced to the shower, and in fifteen minutes he was shaved, dressed and ready. He slipped into a pair of khakis, pulled on his socks and shoes, slipped on a shirt and sports jacket and grabbed his overcoat. He was almost out the door when he remembered. He stopped and shook his head in disbelief.

"Can you imagine the freakin' heart attack Barro will have if I don't show up with the documents?" he asked Yankee. The cat was looking at him with condemnation, trying to make him feel guilty for leaving. He ran back into his bedroom, pulled the thick Redweld expanding folder up from beside his bed where he'd he left it—in a spot where he would trip over it so he wouldn't forget. Briefcase, Redwelds, and carry-on luggage now in hand, he went down to wait for the car.

As the black Lincoln Continental pulled up in front of his building, the electric window slid slowly down. "Mr. Rhodes?" asked the driver.

"Yes, that's me."

The driver jumped out of the car, picked up Jeff's belongings and put them in the trunk. "JFK, right?"

"No. La Guardia."

"Oh—sorry. I shoulda double-checked," responded the driver.

Jeff got in and settled into the comfortable, plush upholstery. He leaned his head back, hoping to catch another ten or fifteen minutes of sleep. It didn't work. He couldn't turn his mind off. If he couldn't sleep, he considered, he should probably review his notes—but the driver had put his briefcase in the trunk. What he really needed was a super-sized cup of coffee. There was no way he'd be able to concentrate at that time of the morning without getting some caffeine in his system.

As the darkness lifted away from the city, more and more vehicles crowded the streets. "You think we'll beat the traffic?" Jeff asked the driver.

"Oh, no problem," was the cheerful response. "We'll make it in plenty of time."

It was too late to ask him to stop at a deli so he could get coffee. They were already heading into the midtown tunnel. By the time the Lincoln emerged, the sky was gray fading to daylight, and the Long Island Expressway was still relatively empty. They raced through the toll booth and the driver informed Jeff they would arrive at the airport in about twenty minutes. Jeff's cell phone rang.

"Hello?"

"Hey, what's up, my man?"

"Phil! What the hell are you doing up?"

"Oh, man, you don't even know," Phil said with a little giggle, then he whispered, "I met this girl last night."

"Where?"

"Never mind that," Phil responded. "Anyway, let me tell you the story. She's in my bathroom right now." He paused a moment. "We were pretty much at the bar talking all night, and then I finally got up the courage to ask her if she wanted to get some breakfast with me. So she said yes. And we went to breakfast, and lo and behold, she came back to my place. And I just got L-A-I-D." Phil punctuated each letter, then added, "Yeah, baby!"

"So it was good?" asked Jeff.

"Oh, yeah. You don't even know."

"Well, what's she like?" asked Jeff.

Phil hesitated. "Umm, I'm not sure."

"What do you mean, you're not sure?"

"Well, I was so bombed when I met her, I don't even remember what she looks like. I guess I'll find out when she comes out of the bathroom."

Jeff laughed. "Phil—man, you are the most dysfunctional person I ever met."

"I love you too," Phil responded.

"Listen, I'm on my way to the airport—Barro is flying me to Chicago for some meeting with Primedia—"

"Yeah, I know. He bumped me off the trip."

"Sorry, man."

Phil laughed. "No worries. I'd rather be here, doin' what I'm doin'."

"Good. You going into the office today?"

"Fuck, yeah!" Phil exclaimed. "It's Christmas bonus time. I'm hoping for a pretty fat stocking."

"Okay—so I'll catch you later. Anyway, thanks for your words of inspiration. I appreciate the note."

"Any time, buddy. Any time. Don't let Barro bully you too much. If you need anything, I'm a phone call away."

Jeff arrived at La Guardia Airport with plenty of time to catch his flight which, according to the departure monitor, was scheduled to leave on schedule. Dreading the miniscule, prefabricated breakfast he was sure to get on the plane, he made his way to a donut shop in the terminal. He ordered coffee and an egg croissant, and picked up the *Wall Street Journal* and *The New York Times* on his way back to the gate. Barro should be showing up any minute, and he thought it wise to be waiting in plain sight.

Absorbed in an article about the disastrous NASDAQ, Jeff didn't hear the call to board his flight to Chicago's O'Hare Airport.

"You ready, Jeff?"

Startled, Jeff looked up from his paper. It was Franklin Barro. "Yes, of course."

"I've got some interesting reading for you." Franklin put a legal file folder, which looked like it weighed about twenty pounds, into his briefcase, closed it, set the combination lock and put it down on the chair next to Jeff.

"I'll get to it right away."

"Hey—I'm kidding." Franklin cracked a smile. "You gotta learn to loosen up." Jeff folded the paper, put it under his arm and started collecting his belongings as Barro continued. "Do me a favor, Jeff. Take care of my briefcase. I don't want to put it in with my luggage—which I'll need you to wait for when we land, while I take care of some phone calls." He tore his baggage claim tags off his ticket envelope and handed them to Jeff. "Oh, and I almost forgot," he added. "I got myself bumped up to first class, so we won't be sitting together. But in any event, enjoy your flight."

"Thanks," Jeff responded, trying to sound enthusiastic. Although not happy he'd be lugging Barro's briefcase around in addition to carrying his own stuff, he was glad he wouldn't have to sit next to his boss. He'd have to fight for a luggage cart or a redcap when they landed at O'Hare.

"Good, good." Franklin threw his arm around Jeff's shoulders, and then disappeared into the crowd as the flight attendant called for all first class passengers.

Jeff peered out the window. A light December snow flurry was gently dusting the runway. The gate agent called his row. Jeff tucked his boarding pass into his jacket pocket and gathered up his things and Barro's briefcase. Glancing at the boarding pass he noticed it was dated December twenty-second—three days until Christmas. He'd never gotten back to his mom to let her know if he would see her over the holidays, and he hadn't picked up any gifts for her or his brother and sister and their kids. He needed a vacation, but that wasn't likely to happen any time soon.

It took just under two hours to fly from New York to Chicago. Jeff tried to go over his notes but what with the breakfast service and some disconcerting turbulence, he found it impossible to concentrate. His frustration increased when they got to O'Hare and had to circle the airport for a while, waiting for snow to be cleared from the runway. He closed his briefcase and started to shove it under his seat before he remembered that's where he'd put Barro's.

Although the seat belt sign was still on, Jeff stood long enough to put it in the overhead compartment. When he sat back down, he wondered idly what could be so important (or secret) that his boss had to have a lock on his—and he wondered if he'd be able to figure out the combination.

Keeping his eye on the curtain separating coach from first class, he pulled Barro's briefcase from beneath the seat. Balancing it on his lap, he inspected the lock. He would need five digits to open it and he didn't know Barro's birthday or the names of his kids or pets. Maybe it was a work reference, he thought. The only thing Jeff knew about his boss was the name of his very sexy secretary—but Pamela had too many letters—so he entered Pammy.

Nothing.

He probably needed numbers in addition to letters but he didn't know Pamela's birthday either. With sudden inspiration, he entered Pam69, and heard a gratifying click.

He was in.

The flight attendant's voice came over the PA, informing passengers they would be circling O'Hare for another twenty-five minutes, and urging everyone to comply with the seat belt sign, which would remain on until landing.

Slowly, Jeff opened Barro's attaché. Lying on top of some papers were miscellaneous, unrelated items including a pack of Dentyne gum, a half-finished pack of Salem cigarettes and a comb. On the comb were a few strands of Barro's black pomaded hair and a single, fiery red strand so long it stretched across the briefcase. That had to be Pamela's. What a disgusting prick, Jeff thought. With a wife and kids at home, he was screwing his secretary—probably right on his desk.

There was nothing of any real interest—until he got to the Primedia file. Glancing at the divider curtain again, he opened it. Within the file, he found a copy of a wire transfer that had come in from a bank account in the Cayman Islands to Darby and Blackstone for Primedia. It was for an exorbitantly huge amount of money, and the Cayman account was in the name of RTC Corporation. Franklin had circled the amount and scribbled a number on the page, which seemed like a percentage of the total.

RTC. It hit Jeff like a punch in the gut.

What if RT stood for Robert Turner? But that would be impossible. Robert would have had no reason to open a bank account in the Caymans. Would he?

Jeff closed and locked Barro's briefcase. The flight attendant came over the PA again, informing passengers they were now landing, and instructing them to place loose items under their seats and put their seat backs and tray tables in the upright position.

While waiting for his and Barro's luggage at the baggage claim area, Jeff pulled out his cell phone and punched in Phil's number. With the storm, he hadn't really expected it to go through, and it didn't. He saw his boss heading toward him, his own cell phone stuck to his ear. Jeff quickly returned his phone to his pocket and waved a skycap over.

•••

Barro hailed a cab for them and ordered the driver to make a beeline for the Regency Hotel. Even before they made it out of the airport, Barro shrieked, "Goddamn traffic!"

Startled at the outburst, the driver jumped and looked in his rearview mirror. Jeff felt sorry for him. Barro's cell phone rang.

"Hello—shit!" cried Barro. "No, not you, honey," he said into the phone. "It's this damn traffic. And I just found out we might have to stay over an extra day." There was a pause in the conversation on Barro's end and he looked at Jeff and rolled his eyes. Then, "Yeah, I'll definitely make it back in time for Christmas. I know what happened two years ago and I promised. It won't happen again." Barro listened another moment, then snapped his cell phone shut. "Never a dull moment, huh, Jeff? That's marriage for you."

"Comes with the territory, I guess."

"Yeah—I gotta keep her happy or I get no peace at home. Which reminds me—I won't be in the office much until after our New Year's Eve party. You're going, right?"

"Of course," Jeff responded. "Wouldn't miss it."

"Why don't you bring that hot little number you were getting it on with in the file room?" Barro asked with a leer Jeff couldn't miss.

"Maybe I will."

Barro sat back against the seat and smiled. "Yeah—I'd like to get at least one dance with her. You got any cigarettes on you?"

Jeff reached into his jacket and pulled out a pack of Marlboro Lights. He shook one out for Barro, then popped one into his mouth before he struck the match and lit Barro's cigarette.

Barro inhaled deeply, closed his eyes and eased back into the vinyl seat. "So, we've got to jump on the nightclub closing right away. What's on your to-do list?"

Jeff fumbled through his briefcase and pulled out a tattered legal pad. It was cluttered with notes and Post-It tabs, and highlighted with four different colors. Each color had its own significance. Only Jeff knew what it all meant. The ashes on Barro's cigarette grew to about a quarter-inch. Realizing they were going to fall on his brand-new pair of leather loafers, he reached between his legs and flicked the ashes on the floor of the cab, then ground them into the carpeting with the heel of his shoe as he waited for Jeff's answer.

"First, I'm going to grab an original copy of the contract of sale," Jeff said. "I'm going to line up their paralegals, make certain all of the loan documents are in proper form. I have to review the bargain and sale deeds, the bill of sale, affidavits of title, and all the corporate resolutions. I have to make sure all of the latest comments on our last round of negotiations got into the lease agreements. I have to check in with the title officers and run through the numbers again on the closing statements."

"Okay," said Barro. "And don't forget the environmental indemnities. We still have to continue negotiations on those. You have the draft on disk, right?"

Jeff hesitated for a moment. "Yes—in my travel bag."

Barro gave a wry chuckle. "You know what?" he said. "I told Gene our computer system was down and I couldn't download them to disk. That way he'll be more apt to accept the draft in its current form as opposed to dickering over all the minutiae. It's bullshit." Barro rubbed his temples. "Okay, how about financing statements?"

"All done," responded Jeff.

"Hey!" Barro tapped on the glass divider and yelled at the driver. "Can we speed it up? We're running late for a meeting." The driver ignored him. Frustrated, he turned back to Jeff. "Holy shit! At the rate we're moving, they might as well close the deal without us."

Jeff tapped on the glass and said in a more reasonable tone, "Excuse me, sir—is there any way around this traffic?"

The driver threw his hands up in the air. "Whatamma gonna do? It looks like a big accident up ahead." He had a thick accent, possibly Greek. The drive was torturous, with Barro urging the cabbie on every few minutes and getting the same response. Finally, they made it to the hotel where, to his consternation, a message was waiting for Franklin.

"Fuck!" he exclaimed.

Jeff was embarrassed but the desk clerk seemed not to notice the profanity. "Problem?" he asked.

"I'll say there's a fucking problem," his boss replied. "The two new planes are grounded in Tennessee because of the weather. It better fucking clear up or we've got big problems."

In an effort to defuse the situation, Jeff said, "That's gotta fall under 'acts of God' that we can't control. Surely Primedia and its buyers will understand."

"Not these buyers," said Barro. "We better hope it clears up."

Jeff's room, to his amazement, was a luxurious suite. Exhausted, he sank into a chair and lit a cigarette. There was no time to unpack, to eat or even relax. He and Barro were due to meet Primedia and the aircraft purchaser's counsel in half an hour. Fortunately, their office was only a few minutes' walk from the Regency. But there was one thing that couldn't wait.

His cell phone was still getting no reception, so he used the phone in his hotel room. Phil answered right away.

"Dude! How's it going? You liking the windy city?"

"It sucks," Jeff said. "It was snowing when we arrived, so we're late getting to the hotel. Look—I need you to do me a favor."

"Name it, Jeffy boy. What do you need?"

"How long have you been working on Primedia?"

"Practically from the time I started at D and B," Phil said.

Jeff knew Barro would be banging on his door at any moment so he got right to the point. "What is RTC Corporation? What does RTC stand for?"

"Uh—I don't know. It sounds familiar but you know how much crap they throw at us. I can look into it if you like."

"Yeah," Jeff said. "Call me as soon as you find out. We're due at a meeting at Primedia, so if you can't get through on my cell, call me there. Someone will find me. And Phil—don't mention this to anyone else, okay?"

"Sure. You gonna tell me why?" Phil asked.

"Eventually. Maybe. But it's important."

Jeff hung up and took a deep drag from his cigarette, held it in for a moment, then exhaled. The smoke rose to the ceiling, thin and wispy like a ghost. He shook his head, trying to clear it, trying to make sense of his suspicions—or was it paranoia? Because it was all so unbelievable, he reasoned, it couldn't be true. An executive at a big law firm like Darby and Blackstone, a murderer? It was ridiculous. But some instinct told him there was something to it.

He took one last pull on his cigarette. As he stubbed it out, his room phone rang. It was Barro. "You ready, Jeff?"

"Meet you downstairs." Jeff gathered up his documents. It was show time.

•••

Conference Room E in the Primedia building was massive. The central table could easily seat forty or more. Every square inch of it was covered with boxes, file folders and documents. There were paralegals and secretaries scurrying back and forth.

"Franklin—glad you could make it!" Gene Morris rose from his place at the head of the table and shook hands with Barro.

"Glad to be here," Barro responded.

"Hello, sir," Jeff said, shaking the hand Gene offered. "Good to see you again."

"So, Franklin—Jeff and I have had a couple of conversations over the phone," Gene said. Then he paused. "We've got a lot of work to do, gentlemen."

"Have we started signing documents yet?" Barro asked.

"No," Gene replied affably. "I've been waiting for you. First I wanted to make certain you approve the form of all the documents."

"Thanks. I appreciate that," responded Barro. His tone was measured but Jeff was becoming acclimated to his moods. When the pressure was on, Barro was no fun to be around. He quickly motioned to Jeff. "Where are we on the real estate purchase and sale documents?"

"We're fine. Everything is done."

"Good," Barro said impatiently. "Let's get going on the airplanes, then. Sit down and get this closing underway. Or do you need an engraved invitation?"

Can I open my fucking briefcase before you jump down my throat? Jeff thought, but he replied, "Yes sir."

He took off his jacket, threw it over one of the conference room seats, opened his briefcase and began reviewing all the seller's documents. Barro and Morris left the conference room together.

Approximately an hour later, a secretary brought lunch in. Jeff scanned documents in between bites of a thick, juicy roast beef sandwich, probably the best roast beef sandwich he'd ever had. It evoked flavorful memories of Peter Luger's. It's sad, he thought. If I leave D and B, who knows when I'll be able to afford another meal like that.

Barro returned alone from his meeting with Gene. After he made sure there was no one on Gene's staff within earshot, he told Jeff, "We've negotiated some changes to the documents. We'll have to pencil them in because I told him we didn't bring anything on disk. So if anyone asks you—not that they will—you tell them our system crashed last night and we couldn't download anything."

"No problem," responded Jeff.

"I'd hoped feeding Morris that bullshit would get him to back off from some of the changes he wanted, but he's being a real prick. How are we on the documents?"

"We're looking good, with the exception of the changes we have to pencil in. How about the aircraft? Have you heard anything new?"

"The weather's cleared out, but they're still grounded in Tennessee."

"It's gonna be a long night," Jeff mumbled. Barro heard him.

"Yeah—it is. We've got half a dozen aircraft involved in this transaction, and we need to take delivery on the first two immediately. Remember—everything has to be filed with the FAA in Oklahoma City, by four."

Jeff looked at his watch. "It's one o'clock, and three days before Christmas," he protested. "Getting anyone in any government office will be virtually impossible."

"It better not be!" Barro slammed one hand down on the table. "Act of God, my ass!" he exclaimed. "You better start praying for a miracle. We need to get everything wrapped up within three hours and communicated to the FAA so they can file the documents in Oklahoma City via FedEx. We can send them for early morning, next-day delivery. They can be filed in time for everyone to get the hell out of here and fly back home for Christmas Eve."

"Even then, we'll have to spend the night with our fingers crossed in hopes everything gets filed in time," Jeff said. "Early morning on the twenty-fourth at the latest."

"Get on it," Barro ordered. "Find out why those planes are still in Tennessee, then get back over to the hotel and check us out." He reached into his pocket and pulled out a credit card. "Use this—we'll leave for the airport from here, as soon as this mess is straightened out. And hustle."

When Jeff got back from the hotel, he found Barro in one of the side conference rooms. He put his luggage down in front of him and waited patiently as Barro juggled multiple phone calls and dealt with multiple transactions simultaneously. Finally, he hung up and looked at Jeff. "Well?"

"Apparently, an FAA inspector found something wrong with the interior components of one of the aircraft. Until he has all problems registered and logged, he won't allow any of the aircraft to take off."

"You don't have any more specific information? No one specified what interior components and when the aircraft can take off?"

"Franklin, according to your guy on the ground there, all aircraft should soon have clearance. I don't think it's anything major. He said it isn't out of the ordinary."

"Okay. As soon as you know when the planes are in the requisite air space, let me know. Documents on the nightclub purchase are being signed, right?"

"Yes—that's going smoothly."

"Okay—now call those assholes in Tennessee back and see if they can give you any idea when our planes are taking off. And find me a smoke."

On his way back to the temporary desk they had assigned him, Jeff heard the Primedia operator paging him. When he picked up the phone she informed him he had a call coming in from Mr. Ginsberg at Darby and Blackstone. He looked around to make sure Barro hadn't followed him before he said, "Thanks. Put him through."

"Ho, ho, ho, Jeffy boy!"

"Phil—what did you find out?"

"Merry Christmas to you, too," Phil said brightly. His voice was a little slurred. Jeff figured the holiday partying had started early.

"Yeah, yeah—tell me. What did you find out?"

"It's weird," Phil said. "It's a name that keeps popping up ever since I met you and your friends."

"What?"

"RTC stands for Robert Turner Consolidated. And there's a bank account associated with it."

A chill shot through Jeff's body. "When was the corporation formed?" he asked. The answer was even more stunning. It was two weeks before Robert's death.

"Okay. Thanks," he told Phil.

"So what's with this guy?" Phil asked. "This Robert Turner guy?"

"You don't want to know," Jeff told him. "It's better you don't."

After he called the airport in Tennessee, Jeff went back to the conference room. "Where the hell were you?" Barro demanded.

"Sorry, Franklin—I got pulled in on a call. It doesn't look like the FAA is going to release the planes tonight. By the look of things, there's no way we're getting out of here for Christmas."

"Shit! Did you bring those cigarettes?"

"Yeah, I've got 'em right here."

"Sorry for the language." Barro apologized to one of the paralegals who was doing some filing. "Do you want a cigarette?" he asked her.

"No, I'm fine, but thank you," she said with a bright smile. "And you can go right on cursing. This deal is driving me insane too."

Barro grinned, then took a deep drag. Moments later the paralegal left the room. "Did you see the rack on that chick?" he asked Jeff.

"Yeah," Jeff said quietly, his mind racing. "Pretty impressive." A corporation formed in Robert's name, and a bank account opened—in the Caymans for fuck's sake. It could mean only one thing.

Before Barro could further extol the physical attributes of the paralegal, one of the junior associates on the other side of the transaction came in. "Excuse me—I'm looking for Franklin Barro."

"That's me."

"Franklin, I have the final revisions for the aircraft purchase agreement, and I need to deal with some issues."

For a moment, Barro stared at the associate, seemingly confused. "You need to what?"

"Gene just faxed me some final revisions—"

Barro immediately interrupted. "Don't tell me you guys are gonna start this bullshit now. You get on the phone, and you remind Gene that I brought hard copies of all the finalized agreements. They're final as far as I'm concerned."

The young associate was startled. "I understand but—well—you have them on disk, don't you?"

Deep creases formed across Barro's forehead. This happened, Jeff knew, when he was in deep thought or on the verge of erupting like a volcano. "Look," Barro went on quietly, his voice measured, "Gene was well aware, before I left New York, that we were having trouble with our system. We agreed the documents were final. I don't have them on disk, and I'm not about to start making changes fifteen minutes before we're supposed to close."

"You'd better talk to Gene," replied the associate. "We're not gonna close today. Two of the aircraft are grounded in Tennessee."

"You're telling me they're still sitting on the tarmac?"

"Gene says we can't close this deal until the aircraft are delivered to the proper jurisdiction."

"I can't believe he's pulling this shit," said Barro. "You get your ass on the phone right now, and you tell Gene that Franklin Barro is fuckin' livid. We have to close this deal today. I need those planes in New Jersey. Jeff, you get on the phone with him and see what changes they want. I will accept only minimal changes. Understood? And nothing's on disk, so you're going to have to pencil in any revisions, which, by the way, also have to be initialed. Get on it. I'm going to see if I can find a drink." His tirade complete, Franklin stalked off.

There were looks of utter astonishment from everyone in the conference room. "What does he do for an encore?" the associate asked.

"Oh, he's just getting started," Jeff responded.

The day wore on and he got all the revisions penciled in and initialed, but Franklin's tantrum had its intended effect. Jeff was amazed. Somehow the deal closed on schedule. If it hadn't been for Barro's aggressive, over-the-top style, it could have dragged on another day, or perhaps two, right through Christmas.

Once they got everything signed and delivered into the hands of the paralegals, who would make sure the documents got out to the necessary parties for distribution, Jeff and his boss grabbed their overcoats, briefcases and travel bags and headed for the limousine waiting out front. They made a mad dash for the airport and were able to get on the last flight back to New York.

CHAPTER 15

Those Scumbags

On Christmas day, Jeff went into the D and B offices. He called his mom and apologized, promising he would make it home on New Year's Day. The place was pretty much barren. None of the secretaries were at their stations, the lights in the halls were dimmed, and the phones weren't ringing. There weren't the constant distractions, like conference calls or having Barro summon him at a moment's notice to tend to a sudden whim.

A mountain of work had accumulated on Jeff's desk while he was in Chicago but it was impossible to concentrate. He organized the papers on his desk into neat piles and tossed out a lot of junk mail. Then he sat back in his chair, swiveled around and peered through the window. Gentle snowflakes floated down from the sky and nestled on his windowpane. Festive lights twinkled all over Manhattan. The city looked so beautiful, and at peace. Jeff, however, was not. In his mind a terrible battle was raging.

I have fought so hard, he thought. *I have spent my whole life trying to pull myself out of poverty, trying to make something of myself and build prestige for myself and for my family. They deserve it—my mom, especially. I can't let them down. Everyone is expecting so much of me. But what is prestige worth if I can't even look at myself in the mirror? If I can't face the truth.* It echoed in his mind: *the truth . . . the truth . . .*

"Those scumbags," he said aloud. *I know they did this. I know they screwed Turner, screwed him royally, because he knew something.*

There could be only one answer to the Turner puzzle. Red was right. Despite his problems, and despite his drug addiction, he was right about this. There was a connection between Darby and Blackstone and Robert's death. And the connection was RTC Corporation. Robert Turner Consolidated. Why would Robert have opened a corporation in the Caymans? Unless they had coerced him or tricked him . . . and what was the bank account for?

Jeff swiveled back to his desk, grabbed his cell phone and punched in

Cassandra's number. She answered on the second ring.

"Hi, Cass—it's Jeff."

"You're back from Chicago?" she asked.

"Yeah—got in last night. I'm at the office now." There was a pause, then he said, "I know why they killed Robert."

"Is it safe to talk there?" she asked.

"I think so. I'm alone—"

"But someone could come in at any minute. Why don't you come over here, to my place. Anyway, I miss you."

"I'm on my way."

He slid the mouse and turned his computer off. Cassandra missed him. Did that mean she was falling in love with him, as he already had with her?

Everything was coming to a head—his so-called career, his work at D and B, his possible relationship with the only woman he had ever truly cared for—and myriad emotions were colliding inside him. What the conclusion would be, he couldn't possibly imagine. Only one thing was clear. He had to get away from Darby and Blackstone as soon as possible. He resolved that when the holidays were over, he would resign and find a position at another firm. It wouldn't be easy, if he left D and B abruptly and without references. And he would have to decide whether or not to go to the authorities with his suspicions, none of which he could prove.

He grabbed his overcoat and headed out. On his way to the elevator, he caught a glimpse of a newspaper left on top of his secretary's computer monitor. It was opened to the Horoscope page. He picked it up and, as the lift carried him down to the lobby, he read his:

"The world needs people who are prepared to take risks, and who are not afraid; people who don't give a hoot what skeptics think. The world needs people like you. As Mars enters your birth sign this week, so your energy, enthusiasm and passion will blossom. Act on impulse. Make life an adventure. The world is yours to command, if it's ready for you."

He decided to take it as an omen—a good one.

On the street in front of the building, one of D and B's black Lincoln town cars was waiting, but he walked past it, his overcoat slung over his arm. Maybe it was a little paranoid, he thought, but he didn't want to take a chance Barro could track his movements, especially since he was going to Cassandra's apartment.

After being stuck in a high-rise office all day, he found the frigid air refreshing. When he'd walked a few blocks away, he hailed a taxi and gave the driver Cass's address. The cab sped off, dodging the remains of holiday traffic.

There was something tranquil about Manhattan on a lonely weekday evening during the holidays. It was sort of like an alien force had sucked all the energy out of the city. There were still lots of flashing lights and an occasional horn honking in the distance, yet it was calm and somehow peaceful.

The driver broke into his reverie. "You want me to put the heat on?"

"No—that's okay." Jeff reached into his coat for his pack of Marlboro Lights and then touched the automatic window button. The cold night air flooded the car. He found it exhilarating. "You mind if I smoke?"

"Be my guest," responded the driver, pulling out his own pack. "I'll have one too."

As the car neared Cassandra's block, Jeff spotted an all-night deli that was open. "Hey—you can pull over right here."

"No problem. You want me to wait for you?"

"No, I'm only a block from my destination." Jeff handed the cabbie a twenty. "Keep the change. Thanks a lot—and Merry Christmas."

The taxi sped off and Jeff entered the deli. "Come in, come in!" the clerk greeted him as if he were a long-lost friend. He had a thick East Indian accent. "Gladda see ya. Not too much people out and about. It's gonna be another long night."

"Well, don't work too hard," Jeff replied. He glanced up and saw himself in the store's closed circuit security camera feed.

"Work is good," the clerk continued. "But too much work makes life impossible."

"Anyone ever tell you you're a genius?" Jeff asked.

"Not a genius. I just work crazy hours, only I don't make the big bucks."

Jeff ordered two roast beef sandwiches and grabbed a big bag of potato chips. He smiled and paid for the food and the clerk packed his purchases in a plastic bag. "Anything else?"

"No—that'll do it," Jeff responded. "Have a good night."

He put his overcoat on and stepped back out into the cold.

•••

Cass had moved from the apartment she'd lived in all the time she was at Livermore, into a swank place on the upper east side of Manhattan. There was a doorman, who made a quick call to announce Jeff's arrival, then pointed him to the elevator.

She was waiting for him, her door open, wearing a sleek, silky bathrobe and fuzzy pink slippers. She gave him a quick kiss on the cheek, then said, "Oh—you brought food. Thank God. I'm ravenous."

After they ate, they remained at Cassandra's kitchen table, sipping on the Diet Cokes she had pulled from her refrigerator.

"So tell me," she said. "What the hell is going on?"

"Franklin Barro, the bastard. Somehow he got Robert to set up a shell corporation—Robert Turner Consolidated. They're using it to launder money."

"How? From where?"

"I don't know yet. Remember what Red told us? It's got something to do with that kid—Candy Man Keith—and drugs. Robert, being Robert, protested and it got him killed."

"You know that for sure?"

"I know about the phony corporation, and the bank account in RTC's name." He explained how he had found some paperwork in Barro's briefcase. "But I don't think we have enough to go to the police."

"If it's money laundering, that would fall under the FBI's jurisdiction."

"We still need some kind of proof," he said. "This is a nightmare. Everything I thought was true is false. Everything I thought was right is a lie. And Darby and Blackstone—it's nothing but a fucking illusion."

"So, what now?" she asked.

He thought for a moment before he replied. "We can't do anything before I get a copy of the document I found, which I can't do until after the holidays. Barro won't be in the office until after New Year's and he's got his briefcase with him. It's not much, but it might get the cops, or even the FBI, to start looking." He took a deep breath and stood up from the table. "I'd better shove off and let you get some rest."

"Stay with me tonight."

"You sure?"

She smiled up at him and nodded. "I'm very sure." She got up and moved closer to him. Standing on tiptoe, she kissed him with a sweet longing. "I don't want to lose you, Jeff. I already lost Turner." There was a pause. "I love you."

He couldn't believe what he was hearing. So many emotions welled up inside him. "I love you too," he whispered, holding her tightly. All his desires, and all his fears, came crashing down on him at the same time. "You smell delicious." The combination of her perfume and the silky feel of her hair were intoxicating.

She took his hand and led him into her bedroom. When they got there, she let out a long sigh and pulled him down onto the bed with her. He kissed her with a hunger he never thought to have for any woman, and she responded in kind—at first sweet and hesitant, then with a passion that matched his own.

They made love slowly, as if they had all the time in the world, as if that world was not filled with danger and fear and suspicion, and as if they were the only two people in it. When they were done, when they were both sated, he draped the sheet over her, gently tucking it in around the contours of her body. With sleep overtaking her, a smile formed on her full, beautiful lips.

"I love you," she said again, then fell asleep.

The next morning they awoke later than was usual for either of them. With everything that had happened, and especially the looming question of what to do with the little evidence they had, they decided to go into their respective offices and play the parts of eager young corporate attorneys. He still had to go home to shower and change his clothes.

"We'll figure it out," he said. "Let's just get through the holidays." They both had so much work to catch up on, it wouldn't be possible to get together for a few days. He told her about the annual Darby and Blackstone New Year's Eve party, and how Barro had told him to ask her to be his date.

"Is that the only reason you're asking me?" she teased, and he kissed her again.

"What do you think?"

•••

Jeff stopped at the newsstand on the corner of his block to pick up a paper. He looked down for a moment and saw a little black poodle trotting into his path. The dog's owner—a middle-aged woman, probably in her fifties—quickly yanked it out of the way. His eyes met hers for an instant, and they smiled at each other. He turned to walk away and saw a brief flash of light, as if he had smacked right into a brick wall.

"You got a fuckin' problem?" asked a deep, menacing voice.

Jeff stumbled backward and nearly dropped his briefcase. Stunned for an instant, he was speechless. The massive man blocking his way had collided with him, it seemed, intentionally. The guy was six-four or six-five, and solid muscle. He was wearing a knee-length leather coat.

"No, I don't have a problem," said Jeff. "You walked into me." At moments like these, he almost wished he wasn't an attorney. *What a fucking asshole,* he thought. *I feel like kicking his ass. I don't care how big he is.*

But there was something familiar about him, as if Jeff had seen him before—but he couldn't place where. Maybe he lived in the neighborhood.

•••

The rest of the week crawled by. Few people were in the office and some of them, like Phil, were so hung over they should have stayed home. Phil was taking full advantage of the holiday party season. Jeff went in a little later and left a little earlier every day, and he used some of his time to research possible jobs at other firms.

•••

The Darby and Blackstone Annual New Year's Eve party usually took place at the ritziest hotel in Manhattan, but this year it would be at Primedia's new acquisition, Club Primo. Gene Morris came out from Chicago, and attorneys, associates and alliances from all across the country descended on New York for the event. According to Phil, there would be lofty speeches and incredible food, and free booze would flow like the Mississippi. But the only thing lifting Jeff's spirits was the thought that he would soon be with Cassandra, and together they could figure out what to do.

He was involved in a strange, surreal scenario. If he talked, he exposed himself and Cass, and possibly his family, to danger. If he remained silent, he would forsake the memory of his good friend and indeed his own soul. His heart was heavy and his thoughts chaotic. But one thing was certain. He'd found the truth about what had happened to Robert—and he would have to do something about it.

Since they both had to work on New Year's Eve day, he and Cassandra had decided to take their dress clothes to their respective offices and get ready there, then he would grab a cab and pick her up. It was seven o'clock and he was running late, as usual. He slammed the door to his office shut, drew his blinds and started changing into his tuxedo. Then his desk phone rang.

"Are you ready?"

"No, Phil, I'm changing now."

"Well, hurry up."

"Give me five minutes. Then I'll come over to you."

"No, just come downstairs."

"Where are you?"

"Downstairs, already. Hurry up and get your ass down here."

Quickly Jeff changed into his tuxedo, rolled his suit into a ball, tossed it into his closet and grabbed his overcoat. Tonight, for the first time in months, he left the office without his briefcase in hand.

After standing in the lobby for about five minutes, he still hadn't caught sight of Phil. Then he noticed a vintage, big white Cadillac, complete with tailfins, parked in front of the building, and he saw a hand waving from the window on the driver's side. When he exited the lobby, Phil jumped out, walked around and opened the door for him

"What the hell?"

"You've never seen a classic 1959 Cadillac Eldorado before?" Phil responded with a big grin. "Completely tricked out and pristine. Get in, dude—this is a babe magnet."

"Yeah, if you're a pimp."

"Hey—don't diss my new car."

"Are you kidding me? You bought this?"

"With my Christmas bonus. The down payment, anyway. After putting up with all the D and B crap, I deserve to travel in style. Come on—we'll put in an appearance at the New Year's bash, then you and I are going partying. With these wheels, we're going to pick up women."

"Not possible. I've got a date. How much did you blow on this thing?"

"It's not a question of money," responded Phil. "It's a question of desperation."

"There's no question, Phil. You are desperate."

"Well, my friend, not exactly. But I do need some action. Get in—we'll go pick up your date."

Cassandra was waiting in her lobby, chatting with the doorman. When Jeff saw her, he actually stopped breathing for a moment. She was stunning in a white sequined, floor-length gown. It had long sleeves and a high neckline but in it, she was the sexiest, most beautiful woman he had ever seen. He held her wrap for her—some kind of soft fluffy thing with feathers, also white—and she slipped into it. Phil was waiting by the curb, holding the car door open for them. She gave him a big smile.

"Wow," she said. "Okay—I'm impressed."

"Your pumpkin awaits, Cinderella," Phil told her. "Hop in before we all turn into mice or frogs or whatever. Get in the back and pretend you're celebrities. He raised his arms and looked at the sky as if he were communicating with aliens. "Hey—I just had a brilliant idea. I constantly amaze myself. You know what we're doing tonight, Jeffy boy?"

"What?"

"We are going to Club Spit. You can come, too, Cass."

"There is no way in hell we're going to Club Spit tonight," said Jeff.

"No, I'm serious. I know one of the guys on the door. We'll definitely get in. You're going to need something to pick you up after the spectacle you're about to behold."

•••

Club Primo was decorated in a winter wonderland motif. The entire place was frosted white and ice sculptures adorned every bar. Eartha Kitt singing *Santa Baby* was playing in the background and waitresses in slinky gowns with splits up the sides were serving cocktails and hors d'oeuvres.

"Okay," said Phil. "Let's find the powers that be and say hello so they know we've come to worship at their feet. Then we'll have a couple of drinks and jump on the buffet line—and split as soon as Barro and his posse have forgotten about us."

Jeff laughed but he told Phil again, "We're not going clubbing with you." He looked down at Cassandra and she smiled up at him. "We've got better things to do tonight."

While Cassandra found them a table, Jeff went to the buffet and started piling plates with anything he thought she'd like. They had lost Phil in the crowd.

"Well if it isn't Jeff Rhodes." The voice was thick with Alabama twang. "I heard you made it to Darby and Blackstone."

Jeff turned to see Candy Man Keith behind him. "Hey, Keith," he responded. "How's it going?"

Keith was already fully inebriated, and Jeff expected his accent would get heavier with every drink. He almost tripped over his own feet as he put one arm around Jeff. He turned to the woman standing next to him and said, "Doesn't Jeff have that leading man thing going on?"

"He most certainly does." Cheryl was from D and B's Mergers and Acquisitions group, and she was well on her way to catching up to Keith in the booze department. She threw her arms around Jeff and gave him a big kiss.

Jeff figured he'd better extricate himself from the situation as soon as possible. Cheryl was nice enough—about forty-five and very successful, but a little wacky. She had made it clear every time she bumped into him that she wanted to get down his pants. He kissed her on the cheek, then said to Keith, "Good to see you, man—you ought to take it easy on those drinks."

"Don't worry about me. I'll be just fine with my buddies Jack and Daniels."

Jeff smiled at him and walked away, a plate full of amazing delicacies in each hand. As he scanned the room for Cassandra, Phil found him.

"I have a question for you, Jeffy boy," he said. "Cheryl's making it pretty clear she's into you. Don't you want to bang her?"

Jeff laughed. "There's no way I'm gonna bang Cheryl."

"Why not? She's pretty hot for an older woman."

"No—not even with your dick. Have you seen who I'm with tonight?"

"In that case, do you mind if I have a go at it—Cheryl, I mean?"

"Help yourself."

They spotted Cassandra waving to them from across the room. On their way to her, they passed Franklin Barro standing with a couple of junior partners and they paused a moment to listen. "So I'm looking at this young associate," he was telling them. "And his eyes are all glazed over, like he doesn't understand a word I'm saying, the idiot. So I tell him, 'Don't worry about the language in the foreclosure provision. Tell the jerk on the other side if he doesn't default, then there's no need to worry. It's that simple.'" His entourage laughed and Barro added, "The best part was watching him rush to make the changes, then make a mad dash for FedEx before the nine-thirty cut-off."

"He's such an asshole," said Jeff.

"You really hate that guy," said Phil. "And it's not just because he's an asshole. You're not the same since you came back from Chicago. You gonna tell me about it?"

"Maybe, but not here. Come on—Cass is waiting."

Phil and Cassandra ate with gusto while Jeff, watching Franklin Barro table hop and work the room, picked at his food. He tensed when Barro finally got to them.

"Well, Jeff, I'm glad you made it. Hey, Phil—how's it going?"

"It's a great party, Franklin," Phil said in what Jeff recognized as his best ass-kissing voice.

"I wouldn't have missed it," said Jeff.

Barro smiled at Jeff and looked at Cassandra. "And you're most welcome, my dear. Have you given some thought to jumping ship at Madden, Karp and Simpson and coming over to Darby and Blackstone with us?"

"Some," she said. "But I'm happy where I am."

"You're sticking around until the ball drops?" he asked her.

"I think so," she answered pleasantly.

"Hope you do. I'll look for you. I'd sure like a shot at stealing a New Year's kiss." He turned to Jeff again. "A word in private?"

"Of course." Jeff got up and walked with him.

When they were a few feet away from Phil and Cassandra, Barro spoke again. "I have a question for you, Jeff."

"Yes?"

Barro stood silent for a moment then, "What were you looking for in my briefcase?"

"I don't know what you mean—" Jeff protested, but Barro cut him off.

Moving closer, he said in a low, threatening tone, "Game over, you little shit. It was a setup. You were too fucking stupid to see it."

And Jeff remembered—Pamela's long, red hair stretching across Barro's briefcase. How many times had he seen it on TV cop shows, where the detective or the bad guy put a string or a hair on a door so they'd know if someone broke in.

"Okay," Jeff said. "I—I was just curious. I'm sorry. You're right—it was stupid."

"I don't know what you thought you'd find but I'm warning you. Do not fuck with me, or you will be sorry. You got that?"

"Yeah. Got it."

Barro turned and waved to Phil and Cassandra, giving them his most charming smile. Then he walked away. Jeff looked after him, his eyes sparking with contempt. He was also starting to worry. He didn't think Barro would do anything to him in a big crowd on New Year's Eve but he didn't want to stick around and find out. He went back to the table.

"Okay, that's over," he said. "Let's get the hell out of here."

"You read my mind, Jeffy boy," Phil said. "After I get Cheryl's phone number. She seems more than willing." He took off before Jeff could stop him.

"I need to make a quick trip to the ladies," Cassandra said. "I won't be long."

Jeff swigged down the rest of his champagne, intending to follow Cass and wait for her outside the restroom. That's when he saw the big, muscle-bound man, wearing a leather overcoat that made him look like the Terminator—and Jeff recognized him at last.

Quick images came crashing in on him like a tidal wave.

The driver of the black Lincoln town car, right after Robert's funeral, who accused Jeff of almost running into him.

"Hey, you little shit . . . you almost rammed into me. You better watch yourself, you know what's good for you."

And at the newspaper stand.

"You got a fuckin' problem?"

His heart racing Jeff pushed his way through the raucous party guests. He glanced back over his shoulder to the spot where he'd seen Mr. Muscle. He wasn't there anymore.

The crowd had grown and the club was filled to maximum level, with people all over the place. The dance floor was overflowing into the aisles and Jeff moved out onto it, hoping to get lost in the multitude of gyrating bodies. He looked up to the mezzanine level and there he was, but now he wasn't alone. There was another man with him.

Franklin Barro.

They were talking and Barro was looking down at the crowd and pointing. They had seen him.

Jeff pulled out his phone and punched in Cassandra's number.

"Hey, where are you?" she asked. "I thought you were going to wait—"

He cut her off quickly. "We've got to get out of here," he said. "Now. Find Phil. Tell him to get the car. I'll meet you outside."

"You okay?"

"Go now, Cass. Hurry."

He ducked into the men's room, looking around for some kind of weapon—a broom, a mop, anything! There was nothing. He quickly stepped into a stall. Although the stalls were all made of glass, the special effects mechanism kicked in and the glass went dark. He'd noticed two other stalls were dark, indicating they were in use, which would buy him some time. Desperate, he looked around.

The toilet seat was made of metal, but it was fastened to the porcelain fixture by some kind of cheap plastic. He tugged on it with all his might and heard a loud snap as the plastic hinges gave way. He had a weapon, however crude. He climbed up on the toilet and waited. The bathroom door opened and he heard heavy footsteps.

He heard one of the stall doors kicked in and the monster's voice telling the occupant to get the hell out if he knew what was good for him. He didn't have to evict the other occupant of the other stall. Jeff heard that door open and a mousy, drunken voice saying, "Going . . . going now. Don't want no trouble . . ."

Now Jeff was alone with the monster.

"I know you're in here," came the muscle-bound voice. "You don't come out before I find you, it's gonna go worse."

Jeff stood and raised the dismembered toilet seat over his head, getting ready. When his door crashed open he swung the metal seat as hard as he could, and it connected with the monster's head. The guy reeled backwards, hit the garbage can, and tumbled down on the tile with a big thud. There was blood everywhere. Carefully, Jeff reached for his cell phone.

"Phil," he said, sounding as desperate as he felt. "Is there a back way out of this place?"

"Yeah, why?"

"Never mind—just tell me where."

"There's a door next to the kitchen. It opens onto a long hallway that leads out to the back—but it's usually locked. Where are you?"

"In the men's room. I gotta get outta here quick."

"The long window over the row of sinks—it swings open and goes out onto the alley." Phil chuckled. "More than one coke dealer has evaded the law that way."

"Okay, listen—Cassandra's looking for you. Get her and the car and meet me there. And hurry. I think I just killed somebody."

"Shit, Jeff—"

"Just do it! Now!"

Hoping the monster wouldn't wake up, Jeff maneuvered around him. His forehead was swollen and still bleeding but he remained motionless. Jeff climbed on top of the radiator next to the sinks and pushed the window open, then stepped out into the night air. It was cold, but it felt good.

Only a few seconds had passed when Phil pulled the Caddy into the alley. Cass was with him. "Jeff—what happened?" she asked. "There's blood on your shirt."

He climbed into the car. "Drive, Phil—let's get out of here." He looked down at his hands, which were shaking. He slumped into the back seat, in shock after what had happened. "Just get us the fuck out of here."

Phil put the Caddy in gear and pulled around to the front of the club, dodging the line of cars with people still waiting to get in. It was past eleven, and fast approaching midnight. "Okay," he said. "Where we going?"

"I'm not sure," Jeff answered. "All I know is I can't go back to D and B—not ever. And you need to get out of there as soon as you can."

"Why? Jeff, you gotta give me something."

"You trust me, Phil?"

"Yeah, man. But tell me what the fuck is going on!"

"There's no time. Anyway, the less you know the better. All I can tell you for now is Barro's cleaning up dirty money—I don't know for who—and he was using Robert Turner to do it. That's what got Turner killed."

"Come on—you're shittin' me!" Phil exclaimed.

"No, I'm not. I just bashed his fixer's head in with a toilet seat."

"Oh, Jeff!" Cassandra reached for his hand and held on tightly.

"Yeah, I know—but I wasn't about to get hacked to death in a public bathroom." He looked out the back window to make sure they weren't followed. "There's an alley coming up, Phil," he said. "Turn in there and let us out."

"What are we doing?" Cassandra asked.

As calmly as he could, Jeff told her, "We're going to walk through, to the next street over, and grab a cab."

"You gonna be okay, man?" asked Phil.

"Yeah. I've just got to figure out what to do."

"I think you should go to the FBI," said Phil.

"Cass, too," Jeff replied. "But we've got no proof. Until we do, I think we've got to stay out of sight."

CHAPTER 16

The Chase

Jeff was tired. He was sick and tired of trying to figure out what was happening, of trying to give Franklin Barro the benefit of the doubt, of wishing all these events—these strange events—were merely a case of coincidence. Of wishing he could have a normal life, a peaceful happy life, without a constant struggle. That normal, peaceful life now seemed further away than ever. He had to find a way out of this mess, but first he had to make sure Cassandra would be okay.

"Do you have a safe place you can go for a few days?" he asked her.

"You mean now?"

"Yeah. Right now. We can't go home, either of us. That's the first place they'll look."

"I have a cousin who lives in Allentown. In Pennsylvania. You could come with me."

"Not yet," he told her. "I think it's better if we separate for now."

She started to protest. "But Jeff—"

He pulled her close and whispered in her ear. "What if they followed us? They can't come after both of us if we're going in different directions. I've got to make sure you're safe. I'll figure out what to do and then I'll call you." He reached into his pocket, pulled out a twenty-dollar bill and tapped on the Plexiglass divider. "Take us to Port Authority," he told the driver.

Jeff remained silent for the rest of the ride. He was sweating and his hands wouldn't stop shaking. For a moment, he felt sick, like he was about to vomit in the back seat of the taxi. He cracked open the window, allowing the cool, crisp air to hit his face. It cleared his head but only for a moment. He had nothing. He had absolutely nothing. He had to find a quiet place where he could figure out what to do and where to find someone who would listen to his story.

They got lucky. A bus for Allentown was scheduled to leave in ten minutes, which gave them just enough time to buy a ticket. Jeff waited for Cassandra to board, then he left the terminal by a different door than the one they'd used to enter. He looked at his watch. It was twenty minutes to midnight. Tired and dazed, he pondered his next move. For starters, he needed some coffee. Cautiously, he looked around. There was no sign of the monster who'd come after him.

He reached for his wallet, then realized he had only five dollars to his name. He had used the rest of his cash on hand to pay the cab driver and buy Cassandra's bus ticket. He didn't see an ATM machine in the terminal but there was one next to a dive restaurant across the street, which was crowded with revelers.

Keeping alert for his pursuer, he crossed over and stepped up to the ATM. He hesitated a moment before inserting his card, wondering if Franklin Barro had the resources to track him through the use of his card. Determined not to let his paranoia get the best of him, he scanned the street and sidewalk in front of the terminal one more time before he punched in his PIN and withdrew five hundred dollars.

Suddenly hungry, he went into the restaurant and made his way to a booth in the back, confident he could remain hidden in the crowd long enough to get something in his stomach. He took a deep breath, and then another, before giving his order to the bored waitress. She was well past the age of retirement and her makeup attested to years of playing in the chorus while waiting for the ever-elusive breakout Broadway role.

His food came back quickly. She placed it on the table before him and asked, "Salt and pepper?"

"Yes, and lots of ketchup."

At that moment, the ball dropped in Times Square and the crowd in the diner went nuts, hugging and kissing each other while they sang *Auld Lang Syne*. Jeff rubbed his temples, trying to dispel his tension. Easing back in his seat, he ignored the revelers and started to eat. He devoured every bit of the sandwich—egg and cheese on a roll—and even the side of coleslaw, washing it all down with a cup of coffee. He eased back in his seat again and scanned the sidewalk in front of the terminal. By now the customers in the diner had poured out onto the street.

In the distance, walking toward the terminal, he spotted a man dressed in jeans, construction boots and a baseball cap who appeared to be an ordinary working-class guy. He reminded Jeff of when, at thirteen, he'd taken the bus clear across the country to visit his cousins. Just outside of Cleveland, the bus had pulled into a truck stop and the driver announced they had thirty minutes to grab a bite or use the facilities. Jeff disembarked and went into the diner, foolishly leaving his baggage unattended while he went to the bathroom. He returned to find his lunch tray minus his Pepsi and no sign of his travel bag. Even worse, he'd left his bus ticket and his money in the bag. There he was, thirteen years old, alone in a strange town, with no money. To no avail, he begged the bus driver to let him back on. He didn't cry—even back then Jeff wouldn't allow himself to cry—but he still remembered the fear. The same fear he was feeling now, all these years later. But someone—a man wearing jeans, construction boots and a baseball cap—had overheard Jeff telling his story to a police officer. The man reached into his pocket, pulled out a hundred dollar bill and told Jeff to buy himself another ticket.

The memory of it renewed Jeff's hope and faith in humanity. He was safe for now, and so was Cass. What he needed was a place to rest and contemplate his next move. He left the waitress a generous tip and paid his bill, then he went out onto Eighth Avenue to find a cab.

The street was crowded with people wishing each other "Happy New Year," and there was no taxi in sight. Jeff leaned back on a parked car without realizing it was running. The tinted windows slid down a crack.

"Hey, baby—you looking for some sugar?"

Jeff nearly jumped out of his skin. The window slid down a little more.

"Come on, honey," a sexy, feminine voice purred at him. "Don't you want to get in here with me where it's warm?"

The window came all the way down and she looked up at him, smiling. She had red hair, brown skin and brown eyes and her full lips promised a night of pleasure. She opened the back door.

"Come on in here with me," she said. "You know you want to."

Jeff slid into the back seat. "Thanks," he said.

"Look at you—all dolled up in a tuxedo." There was another woman in the back seat. "That's Maxine. I'm Bambi."

"Nice to meet you," he responded. "I'm Jeff." His friend Bernie from the neighborhood had once told him that if you treat a working girl with respect you make a friend for life.

"You looking for a party, darlin'?" Bambi asked.

"No thanks," said Jeff. "I'm really just looking for a quiet place where I can think."

Despite the frigid temperature, the women were scantily dressed in short skirts, halter tops and knee-high boots. The engine was running and the heat was turned all the way up.

"We're both available, if you want to do a double," said Maxine.

Bambi climbed into the back seat and straddled Jeff's lap. She put her hand on his and her long red nails glided over it. "So what are you in the mood for, baby? Special tonight—only twenty-five dollars for a blow job. Or you can do both of us for forty-five."

"No, really. Nothing personal, but I have a girlfriend."

"Oh, aren't you the cutest thing," said Bambi. "What's that got to do with anything? Oh wait a minute." Her demeanor suddenly changed. "Are you a cop?"

"No—no, I'm not."

"Are you running from the cops?"

"No, not the cops." He had a sudden inspiration. "But I do need some help. I'll pay you—no problem. Two hundred dollars."

Her eyes narrowing slightly, she asked, "What do we have to do?"

"I need my car," he explained. "Only I can't go and get it myself. It's in a parking garage uptown. I'll give you and Maxine the ticket and I'll pay to get it out with a credit card, over the phone. You bring it back to me, and if you've got some place I can wait, out of sight, I'll throw in another hundred."

"Is this a joke?" she asked sharply. "You some kind of freak, I'll mace you right between those pretty eyes of yours."

She wasn't bluffing. She pulled the can out of her boot and raised it, stopping about two inches from his face.

"No—come on, I'm serious." He moved slowly, reaching for his wallet. From it he took a crisp one hundred dollar bill and laid it on the seat between them. "I'm not running from the cops but there's this guy—this really scary guy—who wants to smash my face in. I need to get out of New York and I need my car. Can you help me? A hundred now and the rest when you get back with the car."

Bambi picked up the hundred and stuffed it into her bra. "Well, we can't let anyone ruin that pretty face of yours." She turned to her friend. "You up for this Maxine?" Maxine nodded enthusiastically and slid behind the wheel. "Okay, then," Bambi continued. "You can wait at my place. It's not far from here. We'll drop you, you call the garage, and we'll make the pick-up."

•••

Bambi's place—a third-floor walkup in a brownstone near Times Square—was surprisingly neat and clean. She let Jeff in and waited while he called the parking garage and paid his bill. Maxine stayed downstairs with her car double-parked, the engine running.

"Okay, then," said Bambi when Jeff ended his call. "Back in a jif. There's coffee in the pot waiting to be made. All you gotta do is push the button. Or crash on the sofa if you like."

She left and he sat down heavily, his mind racing. Clearly, Franklin

Barro's tough guy had been watching his place. Although the monster knew about his Jeep, it was possible he didn't know where Jeff had left it in order to get through his trip to Chicago and then the holidays. He let out a big sigh. It was a chance he'd have to take. With his car, he could get through upstate New York and keep driving, on into Canada, while everyone else was recovering from New Year's Eve. He closed his eyes, just to rest them for awhile, and fell asleep instantly. An hour later, Bambi was gently shaking him awake.

"It went smoother than a baby's butt," she said. "Dude—you never said it was a Jeep. I pegged you for a BMW, but a Jeep! That's beyond cool. You sure you don't want to hang around here for a couple of days? I'd take care of you—no charge."

"That's very generous of you, Bambi. But I need to get out of the city."

"To where?" she asked.

"I'm thinking Canada. It's closer than Mexico."

"Yeah?" she said. "I've got this friend up in Canada, on the other side of the Falls. I don't have his number, but everybody in Fort Erie knows him. You ask around for Fisherman John and you'll find him. Mention my name. Maybe he can hook you up with a place to stay."

"Thanks."

"In the meantime, you should change outta that tux—and you got some blood on your shirt. You don't want to call attention to yourself. My old man left some things here when he split. You're about his size."

•••

Bambi had filled up the Jeep's gas tank before bringing it to Jeff, and he was able to make it all the way to Buffalo, only twenty miles to the American side of Niagra Falls, without refueling. By taking the Peace Bridge, he could bypass the Falls and go straight into Fort Eerie, in Ontario. But he was almost out of gas and he was hungry. The sun was high in the sky and his hope was renewed in this, the new year.

Passing a little no-tell motel called the Bella Vista, Jeff saw a Mobil station next to a truck stop diner. He quickly changed lanes and put on his turn signal, making a right into the station. His eyelids felt like they had anchors attached to them but he forced them open and climbed out of the Jeep. Not many customers there—only a Yellow Cab and a black Lincoln town car that pulled up behind him. He inserted his credit card in the slot on the gas pump. Taking the nozzle out of its holder, he took another look around. The Lincoln's passenger door opened and a man got out. He had a deep tan and a big grin on his face. Then the door on the driver's side opened and another man got out.

"Oh shit," Jeff whispered.

He was huge, a behemoth with a full beard who looked like he belonged in the WWF. His head was bandaged and he wasn't grinning. In fact, striding quickly to Jeff, he looked grim and determined. Unmindful of the taxi driver and the clerk inside the station, he grabbed Jeff by the back of the neck.

"Remember me, you little piece of shit?"

"Vaguely," Jeff said. "I think I saw you once at—"

"Shut the fuck up," the monster's sidekick cut him off, opening his jacket just enough for Jeff to see the gun tucked into his waistband. "You're coming with us."

With no time to think, Jeff's survival instinct took over. Aiming the nozzle, he sprayed fuel—regular, unleaded at a buck thirty-three a gallon—all over the sidekick's upper torso. The monster turned Jeff around and backhanded him, sending him sprawling onto the hood of the car. Jeff rolled off and landed with a thud onto the pavement. Fuel was dripping from the sidekick's chest, staining his shirt and trousers. Jeff could feel blood oozing from his right ear, his gums, lips and nose.

"Settle the fuck down, Vick," commanded the monster. "We got him."

But Vick was enraged. He stood over Jeff, screaming at him. "What the fuck's wrong with you—you crazy? Mitch—I gotta wash off, man! I could go up like a Roman candle covered with this shit!"

"Yeah, later," said Mitch the monster. "We'll stop somewhere on the way back. Let's get this dickhead into the car and go."

Alarmed, the convenience store clerk came running out. "What the hell is going on out here?" he demanded. "You got a problem here, I'll call the cops."

"Not necessary," said Mitch as he pulled Jeff up off the pavement. "We are the cops. We'll be out of your way in a minute." Again, he slammed Jeff's head on the hood of the Lincoln. "Now get in the car, asshole."

Jeff lay helpless against the car. He was disoriented and his ears were ringing. "Look," he managed. "Whatever this is, I'm sure we can work something out—"

"Shut up," Mitch ordered. To Vick, he said, "Check inside his Jeep. You see a briefcase or any kind of computer disk, grab it." Pulling Jeff off the hood of his car, he reached to the back of his trousers and slid out a gun. Jeff thought it was a nine millimeter. With it, he poked Jeff in the kidney while shoving him toward the Lincoln's back door.

This is the end, thought Jeff. They're going to kill me.

Then he saw his chance. He reached into his pocket and grabbed his lighter. All he needed was a spark. With his thumb, he spun the little wheel and threw the lighter at Vick, who was suddenly engulfed in a raging fire.

It was the most horrific sight Jeff had ever seen. Vick was thrashing and flailing his arms, trying to rip the flaming shirt from his body as his hair disintegrated from the heat. Chaos erupted as the cab driver ran for cover like a rat scurrying to find a hole. The store clerk grabbed a water hose and tried to alleviate Vick's suffering as he yelled for someone to call 9-1-1. Mitch didn't seem to notice. He shoved Jeff behind the wheel of the Lincoln. "You're driving." He aimed the gun squarely at Jeff's head as he got in on the other side. "Go now," he commanded, holding the gun against Jeff's right temple. "Drive, you son of a bitch."

Jeff started the car and peeled out onto the road, heading for the on ramp to the Interstate. "Look, man," he said. "We don't have to do this. You don't want to make it worse—"

"Shut up," Mitch interrupted. "Drive."

"Where?" Jeff asked. "What are you going to do with me?"

"Shut up—just shut the fuck up! I gotta figure this out."

"Are you going to kill me?"

"Do you know what you've done, kid?" Mitch asked impatiently. "We just needed to talk to you. You fuckin' idiot. You pussy—now I might have to erase you." He cocked the gun he was holding at Jeff's temple. "You tell me what you know—and if you told anyone else."

Cold fear inched up Jeff's spine, threatening to snake into his brain and paralyze him. He didn't know everything, but he knew more than he'd ever wanted to. He knew Mitch killed Robert, and he knew why. He would give anything, at that moment, to be as ignorant and innocent as he'd been the day he'd enrolled in law school.

"Okay, okay," Jeff said, trying to placate him.

"So what do you know?"

"About what?"

"Robert Turner, for starters."

"Did you kill him?" asked Jeff.

"Keep going," Mitch said, ignoring the question. "Get back on the highway and take the next exit to the service road." He remained silent while Jeff executed the order. Then, "What did he tell you before he died—this Robert Turner guy?"

Jeff tried to remain calm and take in his surroundings, trying to come up with a way to escape. A sign told him they were passing the Canalside Waterfront recreation area.

"He told me lots of things," said Jeff. "He was my friend. And you killed him, you bastard."

"We're coming up on the nature preserve," Mitch said. "Slow down."

Jeff felt like the bottom of his stomach lurched into outer space. *That's where he's going to do it,* he thought. He was running out of time.

Mitch pressed the gun tighter against Jeff's temple. "What did he tell you about your boss at Darby and Blackstone?"

"Nothing. Only that he liked working there and he'd put in a good word for me when I finished law school."

They passed another sign, this one for Tifft Nature Preserve. It boasted two hundred sixty-four acres of restored habitat, with several miles of trails for hiking. *And for dumping bodies,* Jeff thought.

"He never told you about any off-shore deals he was involved in?"

"No," Jeff said. "Nothing."

They drove deeper into the forest. A light drizzle began to fall, pitter-pattering on the Lincoln's hood. "Why don't I believe you?" Mitch asked. "Pull over—into that clearing next to the embankment." Slowing the car, Jeff did as he was told. "Okay—good. Park it. We're getting out."

No, Jeff thought. *I don't think so.* He had nothing to lose. He closed his eyes, took a deep breath and slammed his foot down on the gas pedal. The Lincoln rumbled down the embankment and bounced hard before it plowed into a large oak tree. An avalanche of branches, leaves, insects and bird nests came crashing down on the hood.

Jeff's air bag deployed. The passenger seat didn't have one.

CHAPTER 17

Revelation and Decision

Air and rain drops rushed through the broken windshield, stinging Jeff's blood-soaked face. He drew a long, deep breath, sucking in the crisp air, and closed his eyes, taking a few moments to appreciate the fact that he was still alive. Mitch was still sitting next to him, a big chunk of the demolished windshield protruding from his neck, his eyes wide in the horror of death.

Slowly, painfully, Jeff climbed out of the wreckage. He stood motionless for a moment, waiting for dizziness or a total blackout to hit him as shock set in. But he didn't have time for that. His head cleared a little and he looked around. In the distance, he saw some kind of silo. Maybe there was a farm nearby where he could . . . what? He couldn't ask for help, not after setting Vick on fire and killing Mitch with his own car.

It was clear to Jeff that the stakes were now far greater than they were before. He still had no proof his boss was involved in Robert's death, or that he himself had been targeted. Suddenly inspired, he walked around the car to the passenger side. Cautiously, although he knew there was no way Mitch would suddenly come to life, he reached into the monster's inside coat pocket and took out his phone and his wallet. He almost took the gun Mitch was still gripping but decided against it.

Inside the wallet was Mitch's driver's license, a thick wad of cash, and two Trojan condoms. The phone would hopefully reveal names and numbers Jeff could take to the FBI, as soon as he had time to search through it. In the meantime, he didn't see any other choice but to try and make it into Canada and find a place to hide.

He was pretty banged up. His nose had stopped bleeding but complete exhaustion was setting in and he was suddenly sleepy—maybe symptomatic of a concussion. Staying in the dense thicket along the service road, he made his way out of the nature preserve. Repeated slaps to his face from branches and twigs added to his pain but he forced himself to keep moving. The drizzle showed no sign of subsiding and it created patches of mud and some deep puddles he hoped would be enough to cover his footprints. When he got close to the silo he had seen, he stepped out of the bushes. No one else was on the road, which was not well traveled at that early morning hour.

The silo was all but falling down, sitting next to a dilapidated old house that looked abandoned. Aggravated and exhausted, Jeff removed the jacket Bambi had given him, dabbed one of the sleeves in a puddle of water and wiped his face clean.

Upon closer inspection, he saw the house resembled a property whose era had come and gone, and whose occupants had deserted long ago—except for the old Buick parked in the drive next to it. Rusted auto parts were strewn about the front yard and there were holes in the window screens. Rivulets of rain rushed down one side of the house, the result of a gaping hole in the roof gutter. In one of the windows, Jeff could see a lazy cat impassively watching his every move.

He approached the house at an angle, making sure to stay hidden behind the refuse in the yard or the shrubbery dotting the property. Carefully, he peered through another window to see an old woman sitting at the kitchen table, reading a newspaper and sipping her coffee, her gray hair pulled into a tight bun. She seemed amused by what she was reading. He slipped around the side of the house and tried the garage door. It lifted just enough for him to him to squeeze in.

The garage was even more disheveled than the front lawn. Everything looked about a hundred years old. He scanned its contents and saw a canoe.

Yeah, he thought, *I could put the canoe on my back, drop it in the nearest creek and paddle to safety.* That might be a little too conspicuous.

He could try to hotwire the Buick—Bernie had taught him how when they were in high school—but stealing the old woman's car would ensure his capture. He needed something else. He had to slip away before the old woman—or anyone else—realized he'd been there. There was a half assembled motorcycle in the corner, but that wouldn't do either.

Then Jeff found what he needed. A ball cap and a pair of overalls hung on a rack near the garage door—not exactly his size, but they weren't meant to fit snug. He knew better than to leave any clothing behind so, despite wanting desperately to get out of his wet clothes, he pulled them on over his pants. In another corner, he found a girl's bicycle, complete with a wicker basket on the handle bars and pink flowers on the seat. He dusted off the ball cap, put the bike on its side and slid it under the door.

A sense of exhilaration filled him as he made his escape. It wasn't ideal, but it was definitely not predictable.

He rode the bike for a while, until he spotted a cheap motel—one that looked like the management wouldn't ask any questions as long as guests paid in advance. He left the bicycle under a tree near the road. Maybe the old lady would come along in her old Buick and find it. Telling the clerk he'd be staying only one night, he peeled a hundred dollar bill off Mitch's stack of cash and slid it over the desk.

"You got room service?" Jeff asked, already knowing the answer.

"Nah, but there's a pizza joint that'll deliver. Number's next to the phone in the room." The clerk started to make change for the hundred, but Jeff waved it away.

"Keep it," he said.

While he was waiting for the pizza, he called Cassandra, using the motel phone. His cell was almost out of juice and he didn't have his charger so he'd have to use it only when necessary.

"Oh, thank God," she said as soon as she heard his voice. "I've been so worried. Where are you?"

"Close to the border. Checked into a motel where I'll be for a few hours. I think I can get across tomorrow. Are you okay?"

"I'm fine—are you?"

"Yeah," he said. "Anybody follow you? You see any shady characters around?"

"No," she said. "Maybe you should come back, and we get the FBI involved."

"Not yet." Mitch's phone hung heavy in Jeff's pocket. "But I've got a lead on some information I can take to them. Maybe. If it works out, I can come back and we can finish this."

Next he called his mom and explained he had to go out of town on business—suddenly and completely unexpected—but he would see her soon. She told him she understood and reminded him to get some rest and not work too hard. He could tell by her voice that she was all right, but he was relieved when she told him she was going to visit her sister in Baltimore for a few days.

The pizza arrived and suddenly ravenous, he gobbled down half of it. After spreading his clothes out to dry, he took a hot shower and collapsed in bed. He slept for the rest of the day and night. When he woke up, just before daybreak, he finished the pizza, got dressed and headed for the onramp to the highway. It didn't take long for him to hitch a ride with a trucker who would be passing through Fort Erie on his way to Toronto. Jeff volunteered little information, saying only that he was going to visit his cousin. Holding his breath, Jeff presented his driver's license at the border crossing when the Larry the trucker showed his. The guard checked them, handed them back and waved them on.

•••

Larry dropped him off in front of a coffee shop in the red light district, near the pier where several fishing boats were docked. Definitely not a Fort Erie hotspot, it was a ghost town. He thanked Larry and climbed down out of the truck. It was freezing and Bambi's friend's jacket didn't offer much protection against the chill winds coming off the river. Hurrying into the diner, he was wishing he hadn't tossed the overalls in the motel dumpster.

When he asked the cashier if she knew where he could find Fisherman John, she said, "Oh, sure. Everyone knows Cap'n John," and she told him where to find John's boat. "That's where he lives," she added. "You can't miss it. It's the biggest private fishing boat on the pier."

Chained up in front of Fisherman John's boat, was a German Shepherd. It was lying on a pile of old rugs but it snapped to attention as Jeff approached. Barking once, it tilted its head and eyed Jeff closely, then evidently concluded he was no threat. Jeff proceeded cautiously, careful not to look the dog in the eye, ignoring it as if it wasn't even there. His tactic worked and the dog settled again on its bed of rugs, curling up against the cold.

The wooden planks creaked under the weight of Jeff's footsteps. He could hear the water lapping gently against the dock posts. Dusk was setting in and more than a few lights dotted the harbor. He didn't want to startle Fisherman John, so he walked alongside the vessel and tapped lightly on one of the windows.

There was no response. He rubbed one sleeve across the window in an effort to remove the frost that had collected on it. Peering in, he could see no one inside.

Then he heard a soft click directly behind him, and he felt something poke him in the back of the neck.

"Put your hands where I can see 'em." The voice was rough, like sandpaper.

Instantly Jeff raised his arms. His assailant pushed him against the boat, which rocked in the opposite direction nearly causing him to lose his footing.

"What are you doing here?" the sandpaper voice demanded.

"Looking for Fisherman John."

"Why?"

"Bambi said we might be able to do some business."

"You know Bambi?"

"Yeah," said Jeff.

"Well, turn your ass around." John drew his pistol down and shoved it into his belt as Jeff turned to face him. "What kinda fishing you want to do? In winter there's rainbow and brown trout. Some salmon still around if you want to go out to deeper water."

"No—sorry. Not fishing. But I can pay. I'm Jeff—good to meet you." He put his hand out and John shook it.

"John—Captain John. This here's my boat. Call her the Victory."

"She's a beauty," replied Jeff.

"C'mon, aboard," John invited, climbing on and extending a hand to help Jeff. "Let's go below and get some hot coffee. You're likely to freeze to death if that's the only coat you got."

"Thanks, man."

When they were seated at the little table in John's galley with steaming cups of coffee before them, John asked, "So what's your story?"

"I need a place to stay," said Jeff. "You know, quiet, out of the way—"

"You hiding from the law?"

Jeff hesitated a moment, then he said. "It's a long story. And it's only temporary. I've got some stuff to figure out and some phone calls to make, and then I'll be on my way." And he said again, "I can pay."

Across from Jeff, the captain stroked his beard. He looked worn and world weary, like he had more than a few of his own stories to tell. Deep lines were etched in his forehead, above bushy eyebrows, and around his eyes. "There's a boarding house couple of blocks away," he said. "You got cash?" Jeff nodded. "Okay—come on. I'll walk you over."

•••

For the next few days, Jeff kept a low profile. Between a coffee shop and a little convenience store near the boarding house, he was able to stock up on food, and he'd found a Radio Depot where he bought a charger for his phone. In his room there was a small refrigerator and a hot plate, so he went out only when absolutely necessary. When Fisherman John had walked him over, he'd pointed out a thrift shop where Jeff bought a heavy, warm overcoat. Jeff gave him fifty dollars for his trouble and he wished Jeff good luck. It was a quiet neighborhood, where the only disruption to the tranquility was the shrill bell, several times a day, at the high school a block away.

His new charger didn't fit Mitch's phone, but it still had enough of a charge to allow Jeff to search through the monster's contacts. It was clear Mitch was well acquainted with two Darby and Blackstone partners— Franklin Barro and Ray Alexander. Their numbers were programmed into his phone and Jeff recognized Barro's cell. His call history showed recent communications. There were also calls to Candy Man Keith, the Livermore drug connection. Jeff didn't think Mitch and his sidekick were involved in the money laundering scheme but clearly they were Franklin Barro's muscle. He wondered if Franklin and Ray were also involved in running drugs on campus.

There was no TV or radio in Jeff's room so he had no way of getting the news. He needed to know if Mitch's body had been found, and if the other guy survived the conflagration at the gas pump, so late on his third day in the boarding house, he went out to find a computer. He still had a little of Mitch's cash—enough for another week at the boarding house, a few groceries, and a big, juicy hamburger now.

When asking for directions or information, Jeff's strategy was to approach only the elderly. In case the cops had put out a bulletin on him, he figured that with a senior's less than perfect eyesight and the beard he'd grown during his five days on the run, they'd be less likely to recognize him. One pleasant silver-haired woman told Jeff how to get to the Centennial Branch of the public library.

Jeff arrived at the loveliest little library he'd ever seen. A quaint old building, it was nestled in a garden of shrubs, evergreen, snow-frosted pines and sugar maple trees winter had stripped of their leaves. Near the front entrance a bust of some historical figure named Lord Henry greeted visitors as they walked in. At the rear of the large main room, he spotted a row of computers. As nonchalant as possible, he walked over to them and sat down at a terminal.

"Can I help you, sir?"

He jumped, then looked up to see a middle-aged woman, mousy and plain, standing next to his chair. "Oh—no thanks. I'm fine."

"We have a sixty-minute time limit on use of the computers."

"That's fine," Jeff answered pleasantly. "I won't be longer than fifteen."

"If you want to access the Internet, you have to sign in. Do you have your library card?"

"Sorry, no—I don't have one. Look—I'm visiting my cousin and he doesn't have a computer," he explained, giving her his most charming smile. "I just need to check my email. I'm waiting for word on a job I need. You think you might be able to get me online long enough for a quick look?"

She hesitated for a moment. "Well . . . I really shouldn't. But okay—fifteen minutes. Next time, you'll have to sign up for a card."

"Absolutely," he agreed. He flashed her another smile and she typed in an access number, and he was online. "Fifteen minutes," she said again and walked away.

As Jeff scrolled through emails received in the last few days, a message from Phil jumped out at him. He clicked on it. Characteristically in all caps, Phil wrote:

"YOU PSYCHO! YOU'RE ALL OVER THE NEWS. SMOOTH MOVE, LEAVING YOUR WHEELS BEHIND, ALONG WITH SECURITY CAM FOOTAGE AT GAS STATION. YOUR NY DL PHOTO'S SHOWING EVERYWHERE IN THE 5 BOROUGHS. BARRO AND ALEXANDER ARE SHREDDING FILES LIKE CRAZY BUT I GOT SOME BACKED UP ON DISC. TURN YOURSELF IN & WE'LL TAKE IT PUBLIC. I KNOW YOU'RE NOT A MURDERER. YOU'RE TOO MUCH OF A PUSSY. CASS AND I ARE HERE FOR YOU.

A deep sense of relief washed over Jeff. If the information Phil was collecting could verify a connection between Mitch and Barro, or corroborate his own story, he just might have a chance.

Jeff grabbed the mouse to respond to Phil's email, then stopped himself. It was too risky to contact Phil through D and B's server or phones but he thought it would be safe to call Phil's cell, which he would do in the privacy of his room. And it would be worth the extra charge for international calling. On his way back to the boarding house, he passed a bakery. Emanating from it was the tantalizing aroma of fresh-made croissants. Unable to resist, he bought two and wolfed them down. They seemed only to stimulate his appetite. He stopped at another little joint where he had a big, juicy cheeseburger with all the trimmings, eating it slowly and savoring every bite as he thought about turning himself in. Mitch's bankroll was almost gone, and even if he could access it safely, Jeff didn't have all that much left in his bank account. He would have to do something soon—he couldn't stay on the run indefinitely.

Back in his room, he punched in Phil's number. As soon as Phil answered, he said hurriedly, "Are you alone? Can you talk?"

"Yeah," Phil replied, surprisingly restrained. "Where the hell are you?"

"No time for that," Jeff said. "You done with the RTC download?"

"Yeah—I got all I can get. What do you want me to do with it?"

"Mail it to Cass—but not from the office. Take it directly to the post office. You can call her from there for the address. And don't go back to D and B—"

"But Jeffy boy, I've got my new ride to pay for."

"Listen to me. I've almost been killed on several occasions, and I had to kill in self-defense. But I got information that links Barro and Alexander to the men who attacked me and probably killed Robert Turner, and to drugs on the Livermore campus—and maybe even the money laundering thing. These people are serious, Phil. If they think you're involved with helping me, you're not safe."

"Got it—hang up now, bro. Barro just stepped off the elevator and he's heading my way. Probably to ask me again if I've heard from you."

Jeff hung up, more anxious than ever. He tried to relax but all he could do was pace the length of his room. What he needed to do was keep looking through Mitch's phone, but it was almost dead. Grabbing his thrift-store overcoat, he headed out to the Radio Depot to buy a charger that would fit.

Walking through the store, he tried to ignore the stereo systems blaring in the background and the rows and rows of big-screen TV sets all tuned to the same music video channel. From about fifteen feet away, he noticed someone eyeing him so he kept his head down and went over to the computer display. Stopping in front of one he put his fingers on the keyboard. From the corner of his eye could see the man approaching. Jeff clenched one fist, preparing to hurl himself at the man and make his escape. When the man was almost upon him, Jeff turned to meet him dead on. But he stopped at a row of Compaq inkjet printers.

"Is this model on sale?" he asked one of the clerks. "This floor model?"

Smiling, the clerk went to help the man. Relaxing a little, Jeff headed for the door.

Walking back to the boarding house, he considered his options. Maybe Phil was right, but it would be better if he had all the pieces of the puzzle in place. That luxury was not available. If he couldn't prove Barro's money-laundering business had led to Robert's death, and if no one believed he'd had acted in self defense he'd be arrested for killing Mitch's sidekick. Franklin Barro and Ray Alexander would continue what they were doing, and Jeff's family—and Cassandra—would be in danger.

As he passed the high school the dismissal bell sounded and students rushed out of the main entrances, filling the street. That's when he spotted them—two guys who had to be plainclothes detectives—heading resolutely toward him.

It was a small school. There wasn't much of a campus but the main building, with a soccer practice field behind it, was big—three stories high and covering most of the block. Maybe—hope against hope—he could get inside and find a place to hide. He spotted a milk crate beneath an open window and started to climb in. That's when they grabbed him.

"Hold it there, asshole."

Completely exhausted, Jeff dropped to his knees. It was finished.

"Put your hands in the air where I can see them." Jeff had no strength left to resist. He complied with the order.

"You have the right to remain silent, any statement you make may be used as evidence against you—"

"We're in Canada, Jackson," his partner interrupted. "You don't have to do the Miranda."

"Just covering all bases," Jackson shot back, "We've been tracking this guy for days. We don't want him getting off on a technicality."

Jackson cuffed Jeff's hands behind his back, causing his triceps to stretch like rubber bands. The handcuffs bit into his wrists. He caught a glimpse of the cadre of Canadian police and FBI that had assembled to take him into custody.

CHAPTER 18

Incarceration

The stench of urine permeated every square inch of the seven-by-seven foot cell in which Jeff was imprisoned. But the smell was nothing compared to the endless noise of the cell block.

"What ju in here for preety boy?" shrieked an inmate directly across from him. He tried to ignore the man, who remained persistent. "You deaf? Don't make me smack you down. I'm somebody. You betta ansa, 'cause I can get you during feedin' time. And you know you don't want to run into me in the showers. Now, what ju in here for?"

"Murder, among other infractions," Jeff said quietly.

"You kill a cop?"

"No. Two guys who were trying to kill me."

"Yeah, all right! My man, you a hard guy!"

Well at least I'm making a favorable impression on somebody, Jeff thought.

The next several days dragged by as Jeff waited. Except for a few quick questions before taking Jeff's statement, neither the cops nor the FBI interrogated him. His neighbor, fascinated by the prospect of a lawyer gone crazy, put the word out to other prisoners that no one was to bother him. Jeff was coming to believe he would actually go insane before they figured out what to do with him, but then his jailers suddenly transported him to another facility for questioning.

He was surprised when the guards removed his restraints and told him to take a seat at the table. Someone brought him coffee, a cheese Danish, and a pack of cigarettes.

"You have a visitor," the guard told him. "You can have five minutes." Moments later, Cassandra walked in. More than anything, Jeff wanted to take her in his arms and hold her close. When he got up, the guard barred his way.

"No touching," he said. "Sit back down." Then he moved a few feet away from them. It was clear he wasn't going to give them any privacy.

Cassandra smiled up at him. "You look like hell," she said.

"You don't like the beard?"

"No—I do. It makes you look distinguished."

"You look great. I want to kiss you." The guard gave him a warning look and slid one hand down to his billy club. Quickly, Jeff added, "But I'm not gonna."

Cass joined him at the table. "So what's going on?"

"I don't know. They haven't questioned me yet. Said they wanted to go through all my evidence first."

"What evidence?"

Jeff glanced briefly at the guard before he answered. "I got our assailant's cell phone—never mind how. Lots of interesting numbers on it. Are you sure it's a good idea for you to be back in the city?"

"Yeah—Phil has been keeping an eye on things—"

"Shit!" he interrupted, more harshly than he intended. "Sorry—I told him not to go back there."

"No, it's okay," Cass said. "Barro and one other guy have already been picked up. They'll make bail until their hearings, but they won't make trouble in the meantime. Anyway, I had to get back to work. Holidays are over and cases are piling up on my desk."

"Phil sent you the disk?"

"He did. He offered to drive to Allentown and bring me back when we heard you'd been arrested but I thought the bus would be less conspicuous than his Caddy." She paused a moment. "I gave the disk to the detectives a couple of days ago. Today's the first day they'd let me in to see you."

"Time's up," said the guard. "Let's go, miss."

All Cass had time to say before he ushered her to the door was, "Stay strong, Jeff. I know it's going to be okay. I miss you."

And she was gone. Half an hour later, the detectives who'd arrested Jeff came in, along with two FBI agents. Although he knew his ordeal was far from over, Jeff could tell their demeanor had changed.

The one named Jackon sat down across from Jeff. "Well, Jeffrey Rhodes, we don't know whether to keep you in here or pin a medal on you."

"What . . . what are you talking about?"

"Thanks to you—to that phone you brought in and the information on the disk your friend gave us, we got 'em all."

"I don't understand," Jeff replied. "Got who—for what?"

"The entire Primedia money laundering operation. We'd been watching those two wise guys—Mitch and Vick—for months, on a drug investigation, which led us to believe some funny business was going on with a couple of attorneys at Darby and Blackstone. The phone you brought in and the disk tied it all together for us in a neat little package."

"And you got them all?"

Jackson nodded. "Except for Gene Morris, the Primedia guy who was helping them clean up the money. He escaped to Southeast Asia, or so we believe."

"What about Robert Turner?" Jeff asked. "Were you able to tie his death to them?"

"We think so. We've opened an investigation on that."

"When will Barro go to trial?"

"Oh—you know. That's up to the courts. But it won't likely be much of one. Barro's partner, Ray Alexander, was eager to make a deal. He's turning state's evidence against Barro, but they're both going away for a very long time. According to Alexander, it started with laundering drug money for a couple of nightclubs, then Barro graduated to cleaning up bigger money for the mob. That's when he started using Primedia's new airplanes to move cash out of the country—and that's when the feds got involved."

"Will I have to testify?" Jeff asked.

"We'll see. We've got your statement."

"But what about the guy—the guy at the gas station? I killed him."

"No, you didn't. He's burned like hell and in a lot of pain, but he also wanted to make a deal. He told us how Barro sent him and Mitch to kill you. We know it was self defense."

•••

The ensuing trial was a Manhattan media circus. Although he vehemently denied any connection to the Primedia scandal and the murder of a Livermore student, Barro was facing life without parole, and the federal authorites closed and padlocked the Primedia Hotel and its infamous Club Primo.

Partners at Darby and Blackstone who had nothing to do with the operation rushed to distance themselves from the devastating publicity and bolted to other firms. Robert Turner's parents filed a civil action against D and B and the Primedia assets.

CHAPTER 19

Peace, Brother

Six months later, Jeff sat at the counter of the Silver Spoon Diner, missing Cassandra more than ever. His position as Professor of American History at the University of Montana at Billings filled his time pretty well, and the transition to his new career was seamless.

When the trial was over and sanity returned to Jeff's world, he'd decided to make the move—and to get as far away from New York as possible. The thought of going to work for another big law firm was enough to make him physically ill. His mom understood, once she knew all the facts. As always, she just wanted him to be happy.

He almost asked Cass to go with him when the teaching gig came through, but she was doing so well—and she loved her job. She was enjoying what they'd both worked so hard for. She was making her dreams come true, and he had no right to ask her to give it up.

"Hey—you hear about this New York hotel business?" The man sitting next to Jeff, two stools over, interrupted his thoughts. He was leafing through an ancient copy of People magazine and had come upon an article about the Primedia scandal.

"Actually, yes—I have," responded Jeff.

"An amazing story, isn't it?" the man said. "Wacky people out there, doing all kinds of stuff they think they can get away with."

"Yeah, amazing."

The man reached into his pocket and pulled out a pack of Marlboros. He shook one out to Jeff. "Smoke?" he asked.

"No thanks. I quit."

The man pointed at the article again. "I wonder where he ended up."

"Who?"

"That kid. The young lawyer who broke it wide open. He's got balls—

that's for certain."

"You never know. Maybe he's right here in Montana. Maybe he just needed to get away from it all."

"Well if he wanted to get away, I hope he went to Tahiti or something. Catch some rays. No question he deserves it."

"You want the usual?" the waitress asked, smiling as she popped her chewing gum. "BLT, hold the mayo?"

"You read my mind," Jeff said. "Sounds great."

Driving out to the farmhouse on the mini-ranch he had rented, Jeff tried to take comfort in the green fields, blue sky and clean air of Montana. He was lonely, but he could never have asked Cass to leave the glamour of Manhattan and live with him on a farm on a teacher's salary. No, she was destined for bigger things. He was lonely, but he had escaped the golden prison. He had gotten justice for Robert Turner, and he had stood strong. He had struggled with real-life demons and had survived. Somehow, he would survive the loneliness.

As he pulled up in front of his house, his mouth fell open in astonishment. Sitting in his driveway was a big, white, vintage Cadillac Eldorado, which Yankee was watching from his perch on the porch rail. The door of the Caddy opened and Phil got out. He was wearing cowboy boots and the biggest cowboy hat Jeff had ever seen. Then the passenger door opened, and Cass emerged from the car, looking as beautiful as ever.

"Hey, Jeffy boy!" Phil called out. "The Big Apple just wasn't any fun without you. What say we start our own law firm and show these rubes what's what? Or maybe we could be private dicks and bust crimes out here in the badlands!"

Jeff started laughing. Then suddenly, Cassandra was in his arms and they were laughing together.

The End